THE HORLA
AND OTHER STORIES

GUY DE MAUPASSANT

THE HORLA
AND OTHER STORIES

NEW YORK
PRESIDENT PUBLISHING COMPANY

TABLE OF CONTENTS

THE HORLA
AND OTHER STORIES

THE HORLA

*M*AY 8. What a lovely day! I have spent all the morning lying on the grass in front of my house, under the enormous plantain tree which covers and shades and shelters the whole of it. I like this part of the country; I am fond of living here because I am attached to it by deep roots, the profound and delicate roots which attach a man to the soil on which his ancestors were born and died, to their traditions, their usages, their food, the local expressions, the peculiar language of the peasants, the smell of the soil, the hamlets, and to the atmosphere itself.

I love the house in which I grew up. From my windows I can see the Seine, which flows by the side of my garden, on the other side of the road, almost through my grounds, the great and wide Seine, which goes to Rouen and Havre, and which is covered with boats passing to and fro.

On the left, down yonder, lies Rouen, populous Rouen with its blue roofs massing under pointed,

Gothic towers. Innumerable are they, delicate or broad, dominated by the spire of the cathedral, full of bells which sound through the blue air on fine mornings, sending their sweet and distant iron clang to me, their metallic sounds, now stronger and now weaker, according as the wind is strong or light.

What a delicious morning it was! About eleven o'clock, a long line of boats drawn by a steam-tug, as big a fly, and which scarcely puffed while emitting its thick smoke, passed my gate.

After two English schooners, whose red flags fluttered toward the sky, there came a magnificent Brazilian three-master; it was perfectly white and wonderfully clean and shining. I saluted it, I hardly know why, except that the sight of the vessel gave me great pleasure.

May 12. I have had a slight feverish attack for the last few days, and I feel ill, or rather I feel low-spirited.

Whence come those mysterious influences which change our happiness into discouragement, and our self-confidence into diffidence? One might almost say that the air, the invisible air, is full of unknowable Forces, whose mysterious presence we have to endure. I wake up in the best of spirits, with an inclination to sing in my heart. Why? I go down by the side of the water, and suddenly, after walking a short distance, I return home wretched, as if some misfortune were awaiting me there. Why? Is it a cold shiver which, passing over my skin, has upset my nerves and given me a fit of low spirits? Is it the form of the clouds, or the tints of the sky, or the colors of the surrounding objects which are so changeable, which have troubled my thoughts as they passed before my eyes? Who can tell? Everything that surrounds us, everything that we see without looking at it, everything that we touch without knowing it, everything that we handle without feeling it, everything that we meet without clearly distinguishing it, has a rapid, surprising, and inexplicable effect upon us and upon our organs, and through them on our ideas and on our being itself.

How profound that mystery of the Invisible is! We cannot fathom it with our miserable senses: our eyes are unable to perceive what is either too small or too great, too near to or too far from us; we can see neither the inhabitants of a star nor of a drop of water; our ears deceive us, for they transmit to us the vibrations of the air in sonorous notes. Our senses are fairies who work the miracle of changing that movement into noise, and by that metamorphosis give birth to music, which makes the mute agitation of nature a harmony. So with our sense of smell, which is weaker than that of a dog, and so with our sense of taste, which can scarcely distinguish the age of a wine!

Oh! if we only had other organs which could work other miracles in our favor, what a number of fresh things we might discover around us!

May 16. I am ill, decidedly! I was so well last month! I am feverish, horribly feverish, or rather I am in a state of feverish enervation, which makes my mind suffer as much as my body. I have without ceasing the horrible sensation of some danger threatening me, the apprehension of some coming misfortune or of approaching death, a presentiment which is, no doubt, an attack of some illness still unnamed, which germinates in the flesh and in the blood.

May 18. I have just come from consulting my medical man, for I can no longer get any sleep. He found that my pulse was high, my eyes dilated, my nerves highly strung, but no alarming symptoms. I must have a course of shower baths and of bromide of potassium.

May 25. No change! My state is really very peculiar. As the evening comes on, an incomprehensible feeling of disquietude seizes me, just as if night concealed some terrible menace toward me. I dine quickly, and then try to read, but I do not understand the words, and can scarcely distinguish the letters. Then I walk up and down my drawing-room, oppressed by a feeling of confused and irresistible fear, a fear of sleep and a fear of my bed.

About ten o'clock I go up to my room. As soon **as I have entered I lock and bolt the door. I am** frightened—of what? Up till the present time I have been frightened of nothing. I open my cupboards, and look under my bed; I listen—I listen—to what? How strange it is that a simple feeling of discomfort, of impeded or heightened circulation, perhaps the irritation of a nervous center, a slight congestion, a small disturbance in the imperfect and delicate functions of our living machinery, can turn the most light-hearted of men into a melancholy one, and make **a coward of the bravest?** Then, I go to bed, and I wait for sleep as a man might wait for the executioner. I wait for its coming with dread, and my heart beats and my legs tremble, while my whole body shivers beneath the warmth of the bedclothes, until the moment when I suddenly fall asleep, as a man throws himself into a pool of stagnant water in order to drown. I do not feel this perfidious sleep coming over me as I used to, but a sleep which is close to me and watching me, which is going to seize me by the head, to close my eyes and annihilate me.

I sleep—a long time—two or three hours perhaps—then a dream—no—a nightmare lays hold on me. I feel that I am in bed and asleep—I feel it and I know it—and I feel also that somebody is coming close to me, is looking at me, touching me, is getting on to my bed, is kneeling on my chest, is taking my neck between his hands and squeezing it—squeezing it with all his might in order to strangle me.

I struggle, bound by that terrible powerlessness which paralyzes us in our dreams; I try to cry out—but I cannot; I want to move—I cannot; I try, with the most violent efforts and out of breath, to turn over and throw off this being which is crushing and suffocating me—I cannot!

And then suddenly I wake up, shaken and bathed in perspiration; I light a candle and find that I am alone, and after that crisis, which occurs every night, I at length fall asleep and slumber tranquilly till morning.

June 2. My state has grown worse. What is the matter with me? The bromide does me no good, and the shower-baths have no effect whatever. Sometimes, in order to tire myself out, though I am fatigued enough already, I go for a walk in the forest of Roumare. I used to think at first that the fresh light and soft air, impregnated with the odor of herbs and leaves, would instill new life into my veins and impart fresh energy to my heart. One day I turned into a broad ride in the wood, and then I diverged toward La Bouille, through a narrow path, between two rows of exceedingly tall trees, which placed a thick, green, almost black roof between the sky and me.

A sudden shiver ran through me, not a cold shiver, but a shiver of agony, and so I hastened my steps, uneasy at being alone in the wood, frightened stupidly and without reason, at the profound solitude. Suddenly it seemed as if I were being followed, that somebody was walking at my heels, close, quite close to me, near enough to touch me.

I turned round suddenly, but I was alone. I saw nothing behind me except the straight, broad ride, empty and bordered by high trees, horribly empty; on the other side also it extended until it was lost in the distance, and looked just the same — terrible.

I closed my eyes. Why? And then I began to turn round on one heel very quickly, just like a top. I nearly fell down, and opened my eyes; the trees were dancing round me and the earth heaved; I was obliged to sit down. Then, ah! I no longer remembered how I had come! What a strange idea! What a strange, strange idea! I did not the least know. I started off to the right, and got back into the avenue which had led me into the middle of the forest.

June 3. I have had a terrible night. I shall go away for a few weeks, for no doubt a journey will set me up again.

July 2. I have come back, quite cured, and have had a most delightful trip into the bargain. I have been to Mont Saint-Michel, which I had not seen before.

What a sight, when one arrives as I did, at Avranches toward the end of the day! The town stands on a hill, and I was taken into the public garden at the extremity of the town. I uttered a cry of astonishment. An extraordinarily large bay lay extended before me, as far as my eyes could reach, between two hills which were lost to sight in the mist; and in the middle of this immense yellow bay, under a clear, golden sky, a peculiar hill rose up, somber and pointed in the midst of the sand. The sun had just disappeared, and under the still flaming sky stood out the outline of that fantastic rock, which bears on its summit a picturesque monument.

At daybreak I went to it. The tide was low, as it had been the night before, and I saw that wonderful abbey rise up before me as I approached it. After several hours' walking, I reached the enormous mass of rock which supports the little town, dominated by the great church. Having climbed the steep and narrow street, I entered the most wonderful Gothic building that has ever been erected to God on earth, large as a town, and full of low rooms which seem buried beneath vaulted roofs, and of lofty galleries supported by delicate columns.

I entered this gigantic granite jewel, which is as light in its effect as a bit of lace and is covered with towers, with slender belfries to which spiral staircases ascend. The flying buttresses raise strange heads that bristle with chimeras, with devils, with fantastic animals, with monstrous flowers, are joined togethe ·y finely carved arches, to the blue sky by day, and to the black sky by night.

When I had reached the summit, I said to the monk who accompanied me: "Father, how happy you must be here!" And he replied: "It is very windy, Monsieur"; and so we began to talk while watching the rising tide, which ran over the sand and covered it with a steel cuirass.

And then the monk told me stories, all the old stories belonging to the place—legends, nothing but legends.

One of them struck me forcibly. The country people, those belonging to the Mornet, declare that at night one can hear talking going on in the sand, and also that two goats bleat, one with a strong, the other with a weak voice. Incredulous people declare that it is nothing but the screaming of the sea birds, which occasionally resembles bleatings, and occasionally human lamentations; but belated fishermen swear that they have met an old shepherd, whose cloak-covered head they can never see, wandering on the sand, between two tides, round the little town placed so far out of the world. They declare he is guiding and walking before a he-goat with a man's face and a she-goat with a woman's face, both with white hair, who talk incessantly, quarreling in a strange language, and then suddenly cease talking in order to bleat with all their might.

"Do you believe it?" I asked the monk. "I scarcely know," he replied; and I continued: "If there are other beings besides ourselves on this earth, how comes it that we have not known it for so long a time, or why have you not seen them? How is it that I have not seen them?"

He replied: "Do we see the hundred-thousandth part of what exists? Look here; there is the wind, which is the strongest force in nature. It knocks down men, and blows down buildings, uproots trees, raises the sea into mountains of water, destroys cliffs and casts great ships on to the breakers; it kills, it whistles, it sighs, it roars. But have you ever seen it, and can you see it? Yet it exists for all that."

I was silent before this simple reasoning. That man was a philosopher, or perhaps a fool; I could not say which exactly, so I held my tongue. What he had said had often been in my own thoughts.

July 3. I have slept badly; certainly there is some feverish influence here, for my coachman is suffering in the same way as I am. When I went back home yesterday, I noticed his singular paleness, and I asked him: "What is the matter with you, Jean?"

"The matter is that I never get any rest, and my nights devour my days. Since your departure, Monsieur, there has been a spell over me."

However, the other servants are all well, but I am very frightened of having another attack, myself.

July 4. I am decidedly taken again; for my old nightmares have returned. Last night I felt somebody leaning on me who was sucking my life from between my lips with his mouth. Yes, he was sucking it out of my neck like a leech would have done. Then he got up, satiated, and I woke up, so beaten, crushed, and annihilated that I could not move. If this continues for a few days, I shall certainly go away again.

July 5. Have I lost my reason? What has happened? What I saw last night is so strange that my head wanders when I think of it!

As I do now every evening, I had locked my door; then, being thirsty, I drank half a glass of water, and I accidentally noticed that the water-bottle was full up to the cut-glass stopper.

Then I went to bed and fell into one of my terrible sleeps, from which I was aroused in about two hours by a still more terrible shock.

Picture to yourself a sleeping man who is being murdered, who wakes up with a knife in his chest, a gurgling in his throat, is covered with blood, can no longer breathe, is going to die and does not understand anything at all about it — there you have it.

Having recovered my senses, I was thirsty again, so I lighted a candle and went to the table on which my water-bottle was. I lifted it up and tilted it over my glass, but nothing came out. It was empty! It was completely empty! At first I could not understand it at all; then suddenly I was seized by such a terrible feeling that I had to sit down, or rather fall into a chair! Then I sprang up with a bound to look about me; then I sat down again, overcome by astonishment and fear, in front of the transparent crystal bottle! I looked at it with fixed eyes, trying to solve the puzzle, and my hands trembled! Somebody had drunk the water, but who? I? I without any doubt. It could surely only be I? In that case I was a somnambulist — was living, without knowing it, that double, mysterious life which makes us doubt whether there are not two beings in us — whether a strange, unknowable, and invisible being does not, during our moments of mental and physical torpor, animate the inert body, forcing it to a more willing obedience than it yields to ourselves.

Oh! Who will understand my horrible agony? Who will understand the emotion of a man sound in mind, wide-awake, full of sense, who looks in horror at the disappearance of a little water while he was asleep, through the glass of a water-bottle! And I remained sitting until it was daylight, without venturing to go to bed again.

July 6. I am going mad. Again all the contents of my water-bottle have been drunk during the night; or rather I have drunk it!

But is it I? Is it I? Who could it be? Who? Oh! God! Am I going mad? Who will save me?

July 10. I have just been through some surprising ordeals. Undoubtedly I must be mad! And yet!

On July 6, before going to bed, I put some wine, milk, water, bread, and strawberries on my table. Somebody drank — I drank — all the water and a little of the milk, but neither the wine, nor the bread, nor the strawberries were touched.

On the seventh of July I renewed the same experiment, with the same results, and on July 8 I left out the water and the milk and nothing was touched.

Lastly, on July 9 I put only water and milk on my table, taking care to wrap up the bottles in white muslin and to tie down the stoppers. Then I rubbed my lips, my beard, and my hands with pencil lead, and went to bed.

Deep slumber seized me, soon followed by a terrible awakening. I had not moved, and my sheets were not marked. I rushed to the table. The muslin round the bottles remained intact; I undid the string, trembling with fear. All the water had been drunk, and so had the milk! Ah! Great God! I must start for Paris immediately.

July 12. Paris. I must have lost my head during the last few days! I must be the plaything of my enervated imagination, unless I am really a somnambulist, or I have been brought under the power of one of those influences — hypnotic suggestion, for example — which are known to exist, but have hitherto been inexplicable. In any case, my mental state bordered on madness, and twenty-four hours of Paris sufficed to restore me to my equilibrium.

Yesterday after doing some business and paying some visits, which instilled fresh and invigorating mental air into me, I wound up my evening at the Théâtre Français. A drama by Alexander Dumas the Younger was being acted, and his brilliant and powerful play completed my cure. Certainly solitude is dangerous for active minds. We need men who can think and can talk, around us. When we are alone for a long time, we people space with phantoms.

I returned along the boulevards to my hotel in excellent spirits. Amid the jostling of the crowd I thought, not without irony, of my terrors and surmises of the previous week, because I believed, yes, I believed, that an invisible being lived beneath my roof. How weak our mind is; how quickly it is terrified and unbalanced as soon as we are confronted with a small, incomprehensible fact. Instead of dismissing the problem with: "We do not understand because we cannot find the cause," we immediately imagine terrible mysteries and supernatural powers.

July 14. *Fête* of the Republic. I walked through the streets, and the crackers and flags amused me like a child. Still, it is very foolish to make merry on a set date, by Government decree. People are like a flock of sheep, now steadily patient, now in ferocious revolt. Say to it: "Amuse yourself," and it amuses itself. Say to it: "Go and fight with your neighbor," and it goes and fights. Say to it: "Vote for the Emperor," and it votes for the Emperor; then say to it: "Vote for the Republic," and it votes for the Republic.

Those who direct it are stupid, too; but instead of obeying men they obey principles, a course which can only be foolish, ineffective, and false, for the very reason that principles are ideas which are considered as certain and unchangeable, whereas in this world one is certain of nothing, since light is an illusion and noise is deception.

July 16. I saw some things yesterday that troubled me very much.

I was dining at my cousin's, Madame Sablé, whose husband is colonel of the Seventy-sixth Chasseurs at Limoges. There were two young women there, one of whom had married a medical man, Dr. Parent, who devotes himself a great deal to nervous diseases and to the extraordinary manifestations which just now experiments in hypnotism and suggestion are producing.

He related to us at some length the enormous results obtained by English scientists and the doctors of the medical school at Nancy, and the facts which he adduced appeared to me so strange, that I declared that I was altogether incredulous.

"We are," he declared, "on the point of discovering one of the most important secrets of nature, I mean to say, one of its most important secrets on this earth, for assuredly there are some up in the stars, yonder, of a different kind of importance. Ever since man has thought, since he has been able to express and write down his thoughts, he has felt himself close to a mystery which is impenetrable to his coarse and imperfect senses, and he endeavors to supplement the feeble penetration of his organs by the efforts of his intellect. As long as that intellect remained in its elementary stage, this intercourse with invisible spirits assumed forms which were commonplace though terrifying. Thence sprang the popular belief in the supernatural, the legends of wandering spirits, of fairies, of gnomes, of ghosts, I might even say the conception of God, for our ideas of the Workman-Creator, from whatever religion they may have come down to us, are certainly the most mediocre, the stupidest, and the most unacceptable inventions that ever sprang from the frightened brain of any human creature. Nothing is truer than what Voltaire says: 'If God made man in His own image, man has certainly paid Him back again.'

"But for rather more than a century, men seem to have had a presentiment of something new. Mesmer and some others have put us on an unexpected track, and within the last two or three years especially, we have arrived at results really surprising."

My cousin, who is also very incredulous, smiled, and Dr. Parent said to her: "Would you like me to try and send you to sleep, Madame?"

"Yes, certainly."

She sat down in an easy-chair, and he began to look at her fixedly, as if to fascinate her. I suddenly felt myself somewhat discomposed; my heart beat rapidly and I had a choking feeling in my throat. I saw that Madame Sablé's eyes were growing heavy, her mouth twitched, and her bosom heaved, and at the end of ten minutes she was asleep.

"Go behind her," the doctor said to me; so I took a seat behind her. He put a visiting-card into her hands, and said to her: "This is a looking-glass; what do you see in it?"

She replied: "I see my cousin."

"What is he doing?"

"He is twisting his mustache."

"And now?"

"He is taking a photograph out of his pocket."

"Whose photograph is it?"

"His own."

That was true, for the photograph had been given me that same evening at the hotel.

"What is his attitude in this portrait?"

"He is standing up with his hat in his hand."

She saw these things in that card, in that piece of white pasteboard, as if she had seen them in a looking-glass.

The young women were frightened, and exclaimed: "That is quite enough! Quite, quite enough!"

But the doctor said to her authoritatively: "You will get up at eight o'clock to-morrow morning; then you will go and call on your cousin at his hotel and ask him to lend you the five thousand francs which your husband asks of you, and which he will ask for when he sets out on his coming journey."

Then he woke her up.

On returning to my hotel, I thought over this curious *séance* and I was assailed by doubts, not as to my cousin's absolute and undoubted good faith, for I had known her as well as if she had been my own sister ever since she was a child, but as to a possible trick on the doctor's part. Had not he, perhaps, kept a glass hidden in his hand, which he showed to the young woman in her sleep at the same time as he did the card? Professional conjurers do things which are just as singular.

However, I went to bed, and this morning, at about half past eight, I was awakened by my footman, who said to me: "Madame Sablé has asked to see you immediately, Monsieur." I dressed hastily and went to her.

She sat down in some agitation, with her eyes on the floor, and without raising her veil said to me: "My dear cousin, I am going to ask a great favor of you."

"What is it, cousin?"

"I do not like to tell you, and yet I must. I am in absolute want of five thousand francs."

"What, you?"

"Yes, I, or rather my husband, who has asked me to procure them for him."

I was so stupefied that I hesitated to answer. I asked myself whether she had not really been making fun of me with Dr. Parent, if it were not merely a very well-acted farce which had been got up beforehand. On looking at her attentively, however, my doubts disappeared. She was trembling with grief, so painful was this step to her, and I was sure that her throat was full of sobs.

I knew that she was very rich and so I continued: "What! Has not your husband five thousand francs at his disposal? Come, think. Are you sure that he commissioned you to ask me for them?"

She hesitated for a few seconds, as if she were making a great effort to search her memory, and then she replied: "Yes—yes, I am quite sure of it."

"He has written to you?"

She hesitated again and reflected, and I guessed the torture of her thoughts. She did not know. She only knew that she was to borrow five thousand francs of me for her husband. So she told a lie.

"Yes, he has written to me."

"When, pray? You did not mention it to me yesterday."

"I received his letter this morning."

"Can you show it to me?"

"No; no—no—it contained private matters, things too personal to ourselves. I burned it."

"So your husband runs into debt?"

She hesitated again, and then murmured: "I do not know."

Thereupon I said bluntly: "I have not five thousand francs at my disposal at this moment, my dear cousin."

She uttered a cry, as if she were in pain and said: "Oh! oh! I beseech you, I beseech you to get them for me."

She got excited and clasped her hands as if she were praying to me! I heard her voice change its tone; she wept and sobbed, harassed and dominated by the irresistible order that she had received.

2   G. de M.—2

"Oh! oh! I beg you to—if you knew what I am suffering—I want them to-day."

I had pity on her: "You shall have them by and by, I swear to you."

"Oh! thank you! thank you! How kind you are."

I continued: "Do you remember what took place at your house last night?"

"Yes."

"Do you remember that Dr. Parent sent you to sleep?"

"Yes."

"Oh! Very well then; he ordered you to come to me this morning to borrow five thousand francs, and at this moment you are obeying that suggestion."

She considered for a few moments, and then replied: "But as it is my husband who wants them—"

For a whole hour I tried to convince her, but could not succeed, and when she had gone I went to the doctor. He was just going out, and he listened to me with a smile, and said: "Do you believe now?"

"Yes, I cannot help it."

"Let us go to your cousin's."

She was already resting on a couch, overcome with fatigue. The doctor felt her pulse, looked at her for some time with one hand raised toward her eyes, which she closed by degrees under the irresistible power of this magnetic influence. When she was asleep, he said:

"Your husband does not require the five thousand

francs any longer! You must, therefore, forget that
you asked your cousin to lend them to you, and, if
he speaks to you about it, you will not understand
him."

Then he woke her up, and I took out a pocket-
book and said: "Here is what you asked me for
this morning, my dear cousin." But she was so surprised, that I did not venture to persist; nevertheless,
I tried to recall the circumstance to her, but she
denied it vigorously, thought that I was making fun
of her, and in the end, very nearly lost her temper.

There! I have just come back, and I have not been
able to eat any lunch, for this experiment has altogether upset me.

July 19. Many people to whom I have told the
adventure have laughed at me. I no longer know
what to think. The wise man says: Perhaps?

July 21. I dined at Bougival, and then I spent
the evening at a boatmen's ball. Decidedly everything depends on place and surroundings. It would
be the height of folly to believe in the supernatural
on the *Ile de la Grenouillière.** But on the top of
Mont Saint-Michel or in India, we are terribly under
the influence of our surroundings. I shall return home
next week.

July 30. I came back to my own house yesterday. Everything is going on well.

August 2. Nothing fresh; it is splendid weather,
and I spend my days in watching the Seine flow
past.

---

* Frog-island.

August 4. Quarrels among my servants. They declare that the glasses are broken in the cupboards at night. The footman accuses the cook, she accuses the needlewoman, and the latter accuses the other two. Who is the culprit? It would take a clever person to tell.

August 6. This time, I am not mad. I have seen —I have seen—I have seen!—I can doubt no longer —*I have seen it!*

I was walking at two o'clock among my rose-trees, in the full sunlight—in the walk bordered by autumn roses which are beginning to fall. As I stopped to look at a Géant de Bataille, which had three splendid blooms, I distinctly saw the stalk of one of the roses bend close to me, as if an invisible hand had bent it, and then break, as if that hand had picked it! Then the flower raised itself, following the curve which a hand would have described in carrying it toward a mouth, and remained suspended in the transparent air, alone and motionless, a terrible red spot, three yards from my eyes. In desperation I rushed at it to take it! I found nothing; it had disappeared. Then I was seized with furious rage against myself, for it is not wholesome for a reasonable and serious man to have such hallucinations.

But was it a hallucination? I turned to look for the stalk, and I found it immediately under the bush, freshly broken, between the two other roses which remained on the branch. I returned home, then, with a much disturbed mind; for I am certain now, certain as I am of the alternation of day and night, that there exists close to me an invisible being who lives on milk and on water, who can touch objects,

take them and change their places; who is, consequently, endowed with a material nature, although
imperceptible to sense, and who lives as I do, under
my roof—

August 7. I slept tranquilly. He drank the water
out of my decanter, but did not disturb my sleep.

I ask myself whether I am mad. As I was walking just now in the sun by the riverside, doubts as
to my own sanity arose in me; not vague doubts
such as I have had hitherto, but precise and absolute
doubts. I have seen mad people, and I have known
some who were quite intelligent, lucid, even clear-
sighted in every concern of life, except on one point.
They could speak clearly, readily, profoundly on everything; till their thoughts were caught in the breakers
of their delusions and went to pieces there, were
dispersed and swamped in that furious and terrible
sea of fogs and squalls which is called *madness.*

I certainly should think that I was mad, absolutely mad, if I were not conscious that I knew my
state, if I could not fathom it and analyze it with the
most complete lucidity. I should, in fact, be a reasonable man laboring under a hallucination. Some
unknown disturbance must have been excited in my
brain, one of those disturbances which physiologists
of the present day try to note and to fix precisely,
and that disturbance must have caused a profound
gulf in my mind and in the order and logic of my
ideas. Similar phenomena occur in dreams, and lead
us through the most unlikely phantasmagoria, without
causing us any surprise, because our verifying
apparatus and our sense of control have gone to
sleep, while our imaginative faculty wakes and works.

Was it not possible that one of the imperceptible keys of the cerebral finger-board had been paralyzed in me? Some men lose the recollection of proper names, or of verbs, or of numbers, or merely of dates, in consequence of an accident. The localization of all the avenues of thought has been accomplished nowadays; what, then, would there be surprising in the fact that my faculty of controlling the unreality of certain hallucinations should be destroyed for the time being?

I thought of all this as I walked by the side of the water. The sun was shining brightly on the river and made earth delightful, while it filled me with love for life, for the swallows, whose swift agility is always delightful in my eyes, for the plants by the riverside, whose rustling is a pleasure to my ears.

By degrees, however, an inexplicable feeling of discomfort seized me. It seemed to me as if some unknown force were numbing and stopping me, were preventing me from going further and were calling me back. I felt that painful wish to return which comes on you when you have left a beloved invalid at home, and are seized by a presentiment that he is worse.

I, therefore, returned despite of myself, feeling certain that I should find some bad news awaiting me, a letter or a telegram. There was nothing, however, and I was surprised and uneasy, more so than if I had had another fantastic vision.

August 8. I spent a terrible evening, yesterday. He does not show himself any more, but I feel that He is near me, watching me, looking at me, penetrating me, dominating me, and more terrible to me when He hides himself thus than if He were to manifest his constant and invisible presence by supernatural phenomena. However, I slept.

August 9. Nothing, but I am afraid.

August 10. Nothing; but what will happen to-morrow?

August 11. Still nothing. I cannot stop at home with this fear hanging over me and these thoughts in my mind; I shall go away.

August 12. Ten o'clock at night. All day long I have been trying to get away, and have not been able. I contemplated a simple and easy act of liberty, a carriage ride to Rouen—and I have not been able to do it. What is the reason?

August 13. When one is attacked by certain maladies, the springs of our physical being seem broken, our energies destroyed, our muscles relaxed, our bones to be as soft as our flesh, and our blood as liquid as water. I am experiencing the same in my moral being, in a strange and distressing manner. I have no longer any strength, any courage, any self-control, nor even any power to set my own will in motion. I have no power left to *will* anything, but some one does it for me and I obey.

August 14. I am lost! Somebody possesses my soul and governs it! Somebody orders all my acts, all my movements, all my thoughts. I am no longer master of myself, nothing except an enslaved and terrified spectator of the things which I do. I wish to go out; I cannot. *He* does not wish to; and so I remain, trembling and distracted in the armchair in which he keeps me sitting. I merely wish to get up and to rouse myself, so as to think that I am still master of myself: I cannot! I am riveted to my chair, and my chair adheres to the floor in such a manner that no force of mine can move us.

Then suddenly, I must, I *must* go to the foot of my garden to pick some strawberries and eat them —and I go there. I pick the strawberries and I eat them! Oh! my God! my God! Is there a God? If there be one, deliver me! save me! succor me! Pardon! Pity! Mercy! Save me! Oh! what sufferings! what torture! what horror!

August 15. Certainly this is the way in which my poor cousin was possessed and swayed, when she came to borrow five thousand francs of me. She was under the power of a strange will which had entered into her, like another soul, a parasitic and ruling soul. Is the world coming to an end?

But who is he, this invisible being that rules me, this unknowable being, this rover of a supernatural race?

Invisible beings exist, then! How is it, then, that since the beginning of the world they have never manifested themselves in such a manner as they do to me? I have never read anything that resembles what goes on in my house. Oh! If I could only leave it, if I could only go away and flee, and never return, I should be saved; but I cannot.

August 16. I managed to escape to-day for two hours, like a prisoner who finds the door of his dungeon accidentally open. I suddenly felt that I was free and that He was far away, and so I gave orders to put the horses in as quickly as possible, and I drove to Rouen. Oh! how delightful to be able to say to my coachman: "Go to Rouen!"

I made him pull up before the library, and I
begged them to lend me Dr. Herrmann Herestauss's
treatise on the unknown inhabitants of the ancient
and modern world.

Then, as I was getting into my carriage, I intended
to say: "To the railway station!" but instead of
this I shouted — I did not speak, but I shouted — in
such a loud voice that all the passers-by turned
round: "Home!" and I fell back on to the cushion
of my carriage, overcome by mental agony. He had
found me out and regained possession of me.

August 17. Oh! What a night! what a night!
And yet it seems to me that I ought to rejoice. I
read until one o'clock in the morning! Herestauss,
Doctor of Philosophy and Theogony, wrote the history and the manifestation of all those invisible beings
which hover around man, or of whom he dreams.
He describes their origin, their domains, their power;
but none of them resembles the one which haunts
me. One might say that man, ever since he has
thought, has had a foreboding and a fear of a new
being, stronger than himself, his successor in this
world, and that, feeling him near, and not being able
to foretell the nature of the unseen one, he has, in
his terror, created the whole race of hidden beings,
vague phantoms born of fear.

Having, therefore, read until one o'clock in the
morning, I went and sat down at the open window,
in order to cool my forehead and my thoughts in the
calm night air. It was very pleasant and warm!
How I should have enjoyed such a night formerly!

There was no moon, but the stars darted out their
rays in the dark heavens. Who inhabits those worlds?

What forms, what living beings, what animals are there yonder? Do those who are thinkers in those distant worlds know more than we do? What can they do more than we? What do they see which we do not? Will not one of them, some day or other, traversing space, appear on our earth to conquer it, just as formerly the Norsemen crossed the sea in order to subjugate nations feebler than themselves?

We are so weak, so powerless, so ignorant, so small—we who live on this particle of mud which revolves in liquid air.

I fell asleep, dreaming thus in the cool night air, and then, having slept for about three quarters of an hour, I opened my eyes without moving, awakened by an indescribably confused and strange sensation. At first I saw nothing, and then suddenly it appeared to me as if a page of the book, which had remained open on my table, turned over of its own accord. Not a breath of air had come in at my window, and I was surprised and waited. In about four minutes, I saw, I saw—yes I saw with my own eyes—another page lift itself up and fall down on the others, as if a finger had turned it over. My armchair was empty, appeared empty, but I knew that He was there, He, and sitting in my place, and that He was reading. With a furious bound, the bound of an enraged wild beast that wishes to disembowel its tamer, I crossed my room to seize him, to strangle him, to kill him! But before I could reach it, my chair fell over as if somebody had run away from me. My table rocked, my lamp fell and went out, and my window closed as if some thief had been surprised and had fled out into the night, shutting it behind him.

So He had run away; He had been afraid; He, afraid of me!

So to-morrow, or later — some day or other, I should be able to hold him in my clutches and crush him against the ground! Do not dogs occasionally bite and strangle their masters?

August 18. I have been thinking the whole day long. Oh! yes, I will obey Him, follow His impulses, fulfill all His wishes, show myself humble, submissive, a coward. He is the stronger; but an hour will come.

August 19. I know, I know, I know all! I have just read the following in the "Revue du Monde Scientifique": "A curious piece of news comes to us from Rio de Janeiro. Madness, an epidemic of madness, which may be compared to that contagious madness which attacked the people of Europe in the Middle Ages, is at this moment raging in the Province of San-Paulo. The frightened inhabitants are leaving their houses, deserting their villages, abandoning their land, saying that they are pursued, possessed, governed like human cattle by invisible, though tangible beings, by a species of vampire, which feeds on their life while they are asleep, and which, besides, drinks water and milk without appearing to touch any other nourishment.

"Professor Don Pedro Henriques, accompanied by several medical savants, has gone to the Province of San-Paulo, in order to study the origin and the manifestations of this surprising madness on the spot, and to propose such measures to the Emperor as may appear to him to be most fitted to restore the mad population to reason."

Ah'! Ah! I remember now that fine Brazilian three-master which passed in front of my windows as it was going up the Seine, on the eighth of last May! I thought it looked so pretty, so white and bright! That Being was on board of her, coming from there, where its race sprang from. And it saw me! It saw my house, which was also white, and He sprang from the ship on to the land. Oh! Good heavens!

Now I know, I can divine. The reign of man is over, and He has come. He whom disquieted priests exorcised, whom sorcerers evoked on dark nights, without seeing him appear, He to whom the imaginations of the transient masters of the world lent all the monstrous or graceful forms of gnomes, spirits, genii, fairies, and familiar spirits. After the coarse conceptions of primitive fear, men more enlightened gave him a truer form. Mesmer divined him, and ten years ago physicians accurately discovered the nature of his power, even before He exercised it himself. They played with that weapon of their new Lord, the sway of a mysterious will over the human soul, which had become enslaved. They called it mesmerism, hypnotism, suggestion, I know not what? I have seen them diverting themselves like rash children with this horrible power! Woe to us! Woe to man! He has come, the—the—what does He call himself—the—I fancy that he is shouting out his name to me and I do not hear him—the—yes—He is shouting it out—I am listening—I cannot—repeat—it—Horla—I have heard—the Horla—it is He—the Horla—He has come!—

Ah! the vulture has eaten the pigeon, the wolf

has eaten the lamb; the lion has devoured the sharp-horned buffalo; man has killed the lion with an arrow, with a spear, with gunpowder; but the Horla will make of man what man has made of the horse and of the ox: his chattel, his slave, and his food, by the mere power of his will. Woe to us!

But, nevertheless, sometimes the animal rebels and kills the man who has subjugated it. I should also like—I shall be able to—but I must know Him, touch Him, see Him! Learned men say that eyes of animals, as they differ from ours, do not distinguish as ours do. And my eye cannot distinguish this newcomer who is oppressing me.

Why? Oh! Now I remember the words of the monk at Mont Saint-Michel: "Can we see the hundred-thousandth part of what exists? Listen; there is the wind which is the strongest force in nature; it knocks men down, blows down buildings, uproots trees, raises the sea into mountains of water, destroys cliffs, and casts great ships on to the breakers; it kills, it whistles, it sighs, it roars,—have you ever seen it, and can you see it? It exists for all that, however!"

And I went on thinking: my eyes are so weak, so imperfect, that they do not even distinguish hard bodies, if they are as transparent as glass! If a glass without quicksilver behind it were to bar my way, I should run into it, just like a bird which has flown into a room breaks its head against the windowpanes. A thousand things, moreover, deceive a man and lead him astray. How then is it surprising that he cannot perceive a new body which is penetrated and pervaded by the light?

A new being! Why not? It was assuredly bound
to come! Why should we be the last? We do not
distinguish it, like all the others created before us?
The reason is, that its nature is more delicate, its
body finer and more finished than ours. Our make-
up is so weak, so awkwardly conceived; our body is
encumbered with organs that are always tired, always
being strained like locks that are too complicated;
it lives like a plant and like an animal nourishing
itself with difficulty on air, herbs, and flesh; it is a
brute machine which is a prey to maladies, to mal-
formations, to decay; it is broken-winded, badly
regulated, simple and eccentric, ingeniously yet
badly made, a coarse and yet a delicate mechanism,
in brief, the outline of a being which might become
intelligent and great.

There are only a few — so few — stages of devel-
opment in this world, from the oyster up to man.
Why should there not be one more, when once that
period is accomplished which separates the successive
products one from the other?

Why not one more? Why not, also, other trees
with immense, splendid flowers, perfuming whole
regions? Why not other elements beside fire, air,
earth, and water? There are four, only four, nursing
fathers of various beings! What a pity! Why should
not there be forty, four hundred, four thousand!
How poor everything is, how mean and wretched —
grudgingly given, poorly invented, clumsily made!
Ah! the elephant and the hippopotamus, what power!
And the camel, what suppleness!

But the butterfly, you will say, a flying flower!
I dream of one that should be as large as a hundred

worlds, with wings whose shape, beauty, colors, and motion I cannot even express. But I see it—it flutters from star to star, refreshing them and perfuming them with the light and harmonious breath of its flight! And the people up there gaze at it as it passes in an ecstasy of delight!

What is the matter with me? It is He, the Horla who haunts me, and who makes me think of these foolish things! He is within me, He is becoming my soul; I shall kill him!

August 20. I shall kill Him. I have seen Him! Yesterday I sat down at my table and pretended to write very assiduously. I knew quite well that He would come prowling round me, quite close to me, so close that I might perhaps be able to touch him, to seize him. And then—then I should have the strength of desperation; I should have my hands, my knees, my chest, my forehead, my teeth to strangle him, to crush him, to bite him, to tear him to pieces. And I watched for him with all my overexcited nerves.

I had lighted my two lamps and the eight wax candles on my mantelpiece, as if, by this light I should discover Him.

My bed, my old oak bed with its columns, was opposite to me; on my right was the fireplace; on my left the door, which was carefully closed, after I had left it open for some time, in order to attract Him; behind me was a very high wardrobe with a looking-glass in it, which served me to dress by every day, and in which I was in the habit of inspecting myself from head to foot every time I passed it.

So I pretended to be writing in order to deceive Him, for He also was watching me, and suddenly I felt, I was certain, that He was reading over my shoulder, that He was there, almost touching my ear.

I got up so quickly, with my hands extended, that I almost fell. Horror! It was as bright as at midday, but I did not see myself in the glass! It was empty, clear, profound, full of light! But my figure was not reflected in it—and I, I was opposite to it! I saw the large, clear glass from top to bottom, and I looked at it with unsteady eyes. I did not dare advance; I did not venture to make a movement; feeling certain, nevertheless, that He was there, but that He would escape me again, He whose imperceptible body had absorbed my reflection.

How frightened I was! And then suddenly I began to see myself through a mist in the depths of the looking-glass, in a mist as it were, or through a veil of water; and it seemed to me as if this water were flowing slowly from left to right, and making my figure clearer every moment. It was like the end of an eclipse. Whatever hid me did not appear to possess any clearly defined outlines, but was a sort of opaque transparency, which gradually grew clearer.

At last I was able to distinguish myself completely, as I do every day when I look at myself.

I had seen Him! And the horror of it remained with me, and makes me shudder even now.

August 21. How could I kill Him, since I could not get hold of Him? Poison? But He would see me mix it with the water; and then, would our poisons have any effect on His impalpable body? No—no—no doubt about the matter. Then?—then?

August 22. I sent for a blacksmith from Rouen and ordered iron shutters of him for my room, such as some private hotels in Paris have on the ground floor, for fear of thieves, and he is going to make me a similar door as well. I have made myself out a coward, but I do not care about that!

September 10. Rouen, Hotel Continental. It is done; it is done—but is He dead? My mind is thoroughly upset by what I have seen.

Well then, yesterday, the locksmith having put on the iron shutters and door, I left everything open until midnight, although it was getting cold.

Suddenly I felt that He was there, and joy, mad joy took possession of me. I got up softly, and I walked to the right and left for some time, so that He might not guess anything; then I took off my boots and put on my slippers carelessly; then I fastened the iron shutters and going back to the door quickly I double-locked it with a padlock, putting the key into my pocket.

Suddenly I noticed that He was moving restlessly round me, that in his turn He was frightened and was ordering me to let Him out. I nearly yielded, though I did not quite, but putting my back to the door, I half opened it, just enough to allow me to go out backward, and as I am very tall, my head touched the lintel. I was sure that He had not been able to escape, and I shut Him up quite alone, quite alone. What happiness! I had Him fast. Then I ran downstairs into the drawing-room which was under my bedroom. I took the two lamps and poured all the oil on to the carpet, the furniture, everywhere; then

2 G. de M.—3

I set fire to it and made my escape, after having carefully double-locked the door.

I went and hid myself at the bottom of the garden, in a clump of laurel bushes. How long it was! how long it was! Everything was dark, silent, motionless, not a breath of air and not a star, but heavy banks of clouds which one could not see, but which weighed, oh! so heavily on my soul.

I looked at my house and waited. How long it was! I already began to think that the fire had gone out of its own accord, or that He had extinguished it, when one of the lower windows gave way under the violence of the flames, and a long, soft, caressing sheet of red flame mounted up the white wall, and kissed it as high as the roof. The light fell on to the trees, the branches, and the leaves, and a shiver of fear pervaded them also! The birds awoke; a dog began to howl, and it seemed to me as if the day were breaking! Almost immediately two other windows flew into fragments, and I saw that the whole of the lower part of my house was nothing but a terrible furnace. But a cry, a horrible, shrill, heart-rending cry, a woman's cry, sounded through the night, and two garret windows were opened! I had forgotten the servants! I saw the terror-struck faces, and the frantic waving of their arms!

Then, overwhelmed with horror, I ran off to the village, shouting: "Help! help! fire! fire!" Meeting some people who were already coming on to the scene, I went back with them to see!

By this time the house was nothing but a horrible and magnificent funeral pile, a monstrous pyre which lit up the whole country, a pyre where men were burning, and where He was burning also, He, He, my prisoner, that new Being, the new Master, the Horla!

Suddenly the whole roof fell in between the walls, and a volcano of flames darted up to the sky. Through all the windows which opened on to that furnace, I saw the flames darting, and I reflected that He was there, in that kiln, dead.

Dead? Perhaps? His body? Was not his body, which was transparent, indestructible by such means as would kill ours?

If He were not dead? Perhaps time alone has power over that Invisible and Redoubtable Being. Why this transparent, unrecognizable body, this body belonging to a spirit, if it also had to fear ills, infirmities, and premature destruction?

Premature destruction? All human terror springs from that! After man the Horla. After him who can die every day, at any hour, at any moment, by any accident, He came, He who was only to die at his own proper hour and minute, because He had touched the limits of his existence!

No — no — there is no doubt about it — He is not dead. Then — then — I suppose I must kill *myself!*

MISS HARRIET

THERE were seven of us in a four-in-hand, four women and three men, one of whom was on the box seat beside the coachman. We were following, at a foot pace, the broad highway which serpentines along the coast.

Setting out from Etretat at break of day, in order to visit the ruins of Tancarville, we were still asleep, chilled by the fresh air of the morning. The women, especially, who were but little accustomed to these early excursions, let their eyelids fall and rise every moment, nodding their heads or yawning, quite insensible to the glory of the dawn.

It was autumn. On both sides of the road the bare fields stretched out, yellowed by the corn and wheat stubble which covered the soil like a bristling growth of beard. The spongy earth seemed to smoke. Larks were singing high up in the air, while other birds piped in the bushes.

At length the sun rose in front of us, a bright red on the plane of the horizon; and as it ascended, growing clearer from minute to minute, the country seemed to awake, to smile, to shake and stretch itself, like a young girl who is leaving her bed in her white airy chemise. The Count d'Etraille, who was seated on the box, cried:

"Look! look! a hare!" and he pointed toward the left, indicating a piece of hedge. The leveret threaded its way along, almost concealed by the field, only its large ears visible. Then it swerved across a deep rut, stopped, again pursued its easy course, changed its direction, stopped anew, disturbed, spying out every danger, and undecided as to the route it should take. Suddenly it began to run, with great bounds from its hind legs, disappearing finally in a large patch of beet-root. All the men had woke up to watch the course of the beast.

René Lemanoir then exclaimed:

"We are not at all gallant this morning," and looking at his neighbor, the little Baroness of Sérennes, who was struggling with drowsiness, he said to her in a subdued voice: "You are thinking of your husband, Baroness. Reassure yourself; he will not return before Saturday, so you have still four days."

She responded to him with a sleepy smile:

"How rude you are." Then, shaking off her torpor, she added: "Now, let somebody say something that will make us all laugh. You, Monsieur Chenal, who have the reputation of possessing a larger fortune than the Duke of Richelieu, tell us a love story in which you have been mixed up, anything you like."

Léon Chenal, an old painter, who had once been very handsome, very strong, who was very proud of his physique and very amiable, took his long white beard in his hand and smiled; then, after a few moments' reflection, he became suddenly grave.

"Ladies, it will not be an amusing tale; for I am going to relate to you the most lamentable love affair of my life, and I sincerely hope that none of my friends has ever passed through a similar experience.

I.

"At that time I was twenty-five years old, and was making daubs along the coast of Normandy. I call 'making daubs' that wandering about, with a bag on one's back, from mountain to mountain, under the pretext of studying and of sketching nature. I know nothing more enjoyable than that happy-go-lucky wandering life, in which you are perfectly free, without shackles of any kind, without care, without pre-occupation, without thought even of to-morrow. You go in any direction you please, without any guide save your fancy, without any counselor save your eyes. You pull up, because a running brook seduces you, or because you are attracted, in front of an inn, by the smell of potatoes frying. Sometimes it is the perfume of clematis which decides you in your choice, or the naïve glance of the servant at an inn. Do not despise me for my affection for these rustics. These girls have soul as well as feeling, not to mention firm cheeks and fresh lips; while their hearty and willing kisses have the flavor of wild fruit. Love always has

its price, come whence it may. A heart that beats
when you make your appearance, an eye that weeps
when you go away, these are things so rare, so
sweet, so precious, that they must never be despised.

"I have had rendezvous in ditches in which cattle
repose, and in barns among the straw, still steaming
from the heat of the day. I have recollections of
canvas spread on rude and creaky benches, and of
hearty, fresh, free kisses, more delicate, free from
affectation, and sincere than the subtle attractions of
charming and distinguished women.

"But what you love most amid all these varied
adventures are the country, the woods, the risings of
the sun, the twilight, the light of the moon. For
the painter these are honeymoon trips with Nature.
You are alone with her in that long and tranquil
rendezvous. You go to bed in the fields amid marguerites and wild poppies, and, with eyes wide open,
you watch the going down of the sun, and descry in
the distance the little village, with its pointed clock-
tower, which sounds the hour of midnight.

"You sit down by the side of a spring which
gushes out from the foot of an oak, amid a covering
of fragile herbs, growing and redolent of life. You
go down on your knees, bend forward, and drink
the cold and pellucid water, wetting your mustache
and nose; you drink it with a physical pleasure, as
though you were kissing the spring, lip to lip. Sometimes, when you encounter a deep hole, along the
course of these tiny brooks, you plunge into it, quite
naked, and on your skin, from head to foot, like an
icy and delicious caress, you feel the lovely and
gentle quivering of the current.

"You are gay on the hills, melancholy on the verge of pools, exalted when the sun is crowned in an ocean of blood-red shadows, and when it casts on the rivers its red reflection. And at night, under the moon, as it passes across the vault of heaven, you think of things, singular things, which would never have occurred to your mind under the brilliant light of day.

"So, in wandering through the same country we are in this year, I came to the little village of Benouville, on the Falaise, between Yport and Etretat. I came from Fécamp, following the coast, a high coast, perpendicular as a wall, with projecting and rugged rocks falling sheer down into the sea. I had walked since the morning on the close clipped grass, as smooth and as yielding as a carpet. Singing lustily, I walked with long strides, looking sometimes at the slow and lazy flight of a gull, with its short, white wings, sailing in the blue heavens, sometimes at the green sea, or at the brown sails of a fishing bark. In short, I had passed a happy day, a day of listlessness and of liberty.

"I was shown a little farmhouse, where travelers were put up, a kind of inn, kept by a peasant, which stood in the center of a Norman court, surrounded by a double row of beeches.

"Quitting the Falaise, I gained the hamlet, which was hemmed in by great trees, and I presented myself at the house of Mother Lecacheur.

"She was an old, wrinkled, and austere rustic, who always seemed to yield to the pressure of new customs with a kind of contempt.

"It was the month of May: the spreading apple-trees covered the court with a whirling shower of blossoms which rained unceasingly both upon people and upon the grass.

"I said:

"'Well, Madame Lecacheur, have you a room for me?'

"Astonished to find that I knew her name, she answered:

"'That depends; everything is let; but, all the same, there will be no harm in looking.'

"In five minutes we were in perfect accord, and I deposited my bag upon the bare floor of a rustic room, furnished with a bed, two chairs, a table, and a washstand. The room opened into the large and smoky kitchen, where the lodgers took their meals with the people of the farm and with the farmer himself, who was a widower.

"I washed my hands, after which I went out. The old woman was fricasseeing a chicken for dinner in a large fireplace, in which hung the stew-pot, black with smoke.

"'You have travelers, then, at the present time?' said I to her.

"She answered in an offended tone of voice:

"'I have a lady, an English lady, who has attained to years of maturity. She is occupying my other room.'

"By means of an extra five sous a day, I obtained the privilege of dining out in the court when the weather was fine.

"My cover was then placed in front of the door, and I commenced to gnaw with hunger the lean members of the Normandy chicken, to drink the clear cider, and to munch the hunk of white bread, which, though four days old, was excellent.

"Suddenly, the wooden barrier which opened on to the highway was opened, and a strange person directed her steps toward the house. She was very slender, very tall, enveloped in a Scotch shawl with red borders. You would have believed that she had no arms, if you had not seen a long hand appear just above the hips, holding a white tourist umbrella. The face of a mummy, surrounded with sausage rolls of plaited gray hair, which bounded at every step she took, made me think, I know not why, of a sour herring adorned with curling papers. Lowering her eyes, she passed quickly in front of me, and entered the house.

"This singular apparition made me curious. She undoubtedly was my neighbor, the aged English lady of whom our hostess had spoken.

"I did not see her again that day. The next day, when I had begun to paint at the end of that beautiful valley, which you know extends as far as Etretat, lifting my eyes suddenly, I perceived something singularly attired standing on the crest of the declivity; it looked like a pole decked out with flags. It was she. On seeing me, she suddenly disappeared. I re-entered the house at midday for lunch, and took my seat at the common table, so as to make the acquaintance of this old and original creature. But she did not respond to my polite advances, was insensible even to my little attentions. I poured water out for her with great alacrity, I passed her the dishes with great eagerness. A slight, almost imperceptible movement of the head, and an English word, murmured so low that I did not understand it, were her only acknowledgments.

"I ceased occupying myself with her, although she had disturbed my thoughts. At the end of three days, I knew as much about her as did Madame Lecacheur herself.

"She was called Miss Harriet. Seeking out a secluded village in which to pass the summer, she had been attracted to Benouville, some six months before, and did not seem disposed to quit it. She never spoke at table, ate rapidly, reading all the while a small book, treating of some Protestant propaganda. She gave a copy of it to everybody. The curé himself had received no less than four copies, at the hands of an urchin to whom she had paid two sous' commission. She said sometimes to our hostess, abruptly, without preparing her in the least for the declaration:

"'I love the Saviour more than all; I worship him in all creation; I adore him in all nature; I carry him always in my heart.'

"And she would immediately present the old woman with one of her brochures which were destined to convert the universe.

"In the village she was not liked. In fact, the schoolmaster had declared that she was an atheist, and that a sort of reproach attached to her. The curé, who had been consulted by Madame Lecacheur, responded:

"'She is a heretic, but God does not wish the death of the sinner, and I believe her to be a person of pure morals.'

"These words, 'atheist,' 'heretic,' words which no one can precisely define, threw doubts into some minds. It was asserted, however, that this English-woman was rich, and that she had passed her life in traveling through every country in the world, because her family had thrown her off. Why had her family thrown her off? Because of her natural impiety?

"She was, in fact, one of those people of exalted principles, one of those opinionated puritans of whom England produces so many, one of those good and insupportable old women who haunt the *tables d'hôte* of every hotel in Europe, who spoil Italy, poison Switzerland, render the charming cities of the Mediterranean uninhabitable, carry everywhere their fantastic manias, their petrified vestal manners, their indescribable toilettes, and a certain odor of india-rubber, which makes one believe that at night they slip themselves into a case of that material. When I meet one of these people in a hotel, I act like birds which see a manikin in a field.

"This woman, however, appeared so singular that she did not displease me.

"Madame Lecacheur, hostile by instinct to everything that was not rustic, felt in her narrow soul a kind of hatred for the ecstatic extravagances of the old girl. She had found a phrase by which to describe her, I know not how, but a phrase assuredly contemptuous, which had sprung to her lips, invented probably by some confused and mysterious travail of soul. She said: 'That woman is a demoniac.' This phrase, as uttered by that austere and sentimental creature, seemed to me irresistibly comic. I, myself, never called her now anything else but 'the demoniac.' feeling a singular pleasure in pronouncing this word on seeing her.

"I would ask Mother Lecacheur: 'Well, what is our demoniac about to-day?' To which my rustic friend would respond, with an air of having been scandalized:

"'What do you think, sir? She has picked up a toad which has had its leg battered, and carried it to her room, and has put it in her washstand, and dressed it up like a man. If that is not profanation, I should like to know what is!'

"On another occasion, when walking along the Falaise, she had bought a large fish which had just been caught, simply to throw it back into the sea again. The sailor, from whom she had bought it, though paid handsomely, was greatly provoked at this act — more exasperated, indeed, than if she had put her hand into his pocket and taken his money. For a whole month he could not speak of the circumstance without getting into a fury and denouncing it as an outrage. Oh yes! She was indeed a demoniac, this Miss Harriet, and Mother Lecacheur must have had an inspiration of genius in thus christening her.

"The stable-boy, who was called Sapeur, because he had served in Africa in his youth, entertained other aversions. He said, with a roguish air: 'She is an old hag who has lived her days.' If the poor woman had but known!

"Little kind-hearted Céleste did not wait upon her willingly, but I was never able to understand why. Probably her only reason was that she was a stranger, of another race, of a different tongue, and of another religion. She was in good truth a demoniac!

"She passed her time wandering about the country, adoring and searching for God in nature. I found her one evening on her knees in a cluster of bushes. Having discovered something red through the leaves, I brushed aside the branches, and Miss Harriet at once rose to her feet, confused at having been found thus, looking at me with eyes as terrible as those of a wild cat surprised in open day.

"Sometimes, when I was working among the rocks, I would suddenly descry her on the banks of the Falaise standing like a semaphore signal. She gazed passionately at the vast sea, glittering in the sunlight, and the boundless sky empurpled with fire. Sometimes I would distinguish her at the bottom of a valley, walking quickly, with her elastic English step; and I would go toward her, attracted by I know not what, simply to see her illuminated visage, her dried-up features, which seemed to glow with an ineffable, inward, and profound happiness.

"Often I would encounter her in the corner of a field sitting on the grass, under the shadow of an apple-tree, with her little Bible lying open on her knee, while she looked meditatively into the distance.

"I could no longer tear myself away from that quiet country neighborhood, bound to it as I was by a thousand links of love for its soft and sweeping landscapes. At this farm I was out of the world, far removed from everything, but in close proximity to the soil, the good, healthy, beautiful green soil. And, must I avow it, there was something besides curiosity which retained me at the residence of Mother Lecacheur. I wished to become acquainted a little with this strange Miss Harriet, and to learn what passes in the solitary souls of those wandering old, English dames.

II.

"We became acquainted in a rather singular manner. I had just finished a study which appeared to me to display genius and power; as it must have, since it was sold for ten thousand francs, fifteen years later. It was as simple, however, as that two and two make four, and had nothing to do with academic rules. The whole of the right side of my canvas represented a rock, an enormous rock, covered with sea-wrack, brown, yellow, and red, across which the sun poured like a stream of oil. The light, without which one could see the stars concealed in the background, fell upon the stone, and gilded it as if with fire. That was all. A first stupid attempt at dealing with light, with burning rays, with the sublime.

"On the left was the sea, not the blue sea, the slate-colored sea, but a sea of jade, as greenish, milky, and thick as the overcast sky.

"I was so pleased with my work that I danced from sheer delight as I carried it back to the inn. I wished that the whole world could have seen it at one and the same moment. I can remember that I showed it to a cow, which was browsing by the wayside, exclaiming, at the same time: 'Look at that, my old beauty; you will not often see its like again.'

"When I had reached the front of the house, I immediately called out to Mother Lecacheur, shouting with all my might:

"'Ohé! Ohé! my mistress, come here and look at this.'

"The rustic advanced and looked at my work with stupid eyes, which distinguished nothing, and did not even recognize whether the picture was the representation of an ox or a house.

"Miss Harriet came into the house, and passed in rear of me just at the moment when, holding out my canvas at arm's length, I was exhibiting it to the female innkeeper. The 'demoniac' could not help but see it, for I took care to exhibit the thing in such a way that it could not escape her notice. She stopped abruptly and stood motionless, stupefied. It was her rock which was depicted, the one which she usually climbed to dream away her time undisturbed.

"She uttered a British 'Oh,' which was at once so accentuated and so flattering, that I turned round to her, smiling, and said:

"'This is my last work, Mademoiselle.'

"She murmured ecstatically, comically, and tenderly:

"'Oh! Monsieur, you must understand what it is to have a palpitation.'

"I colored up, of course, and was more excited by that compliment than if it had come from a queen. I was seduced, conquered, vanquished. I could have embraced her—upon my honor.

"I took my seat at the table beside her, as I had always done. For the first time, she spoke, drawling out in a loud voice:

"'Oh! I love nature so much.'

"I offered her some bread, some water, some wine. She now accepted these with the vacant smile of a mummy. I then began to converse with her about the scenery.

"After the meal, we rose from the table together and walked leisurely across the court; then, attracted by the fiery glow which the setting sun cast over the surface of the sea, I opened the outside gate which faced in the direction of the Falaise, and we walked on side by side, as satisfied as any two persons could be who have just learned to understand and penetrate each other's motives and feelings.

"It was a misty, relaxing evening, one of those enjoyable evenings which impart happiness to mind and body alike. All is joy, all is charm. The luscious and balmy air, loaded with the perfumes of herbs, with the perfumes of grass-wrack, with the odor of the wild flowers, caresses the soul with a penetrating sweetness. We were going to the brink of the abyss which overlooked the vast sea and rolled past us at the distance of less than a hundred meters.

"We drank with open mouth and expanded chest, that fresh breeze from the ocean which glides slowly over the skin, salted as it is by long contact with the waves.

"Wrapped up in her square shawl, inspired by the balmy air and with teeth firmly set, the Englishwoman gazed fixedly at the great sun-ball, as it descended toward the sea. Soon its rim touched the waters, just in rear of a ship which had appeared on the horizon, until, by degrees, it was swallowed up by the ocean. We watched it plunge, diminish, and finally disappear.

"Miss Harriet contemplated with passionate regard the last glimmer of the flaming orb of day.

"She muttered: 'Oh! I love—I love—' I saw a tear start in her eye. She continued: 'I wish I were a little bird, so that I could mount up into the firmament.'

"She remained standing as I had often before seen her, perched on the river bank, her face as red as her flaming shawl. I should have liked to have sketched her in my album. It would have been an ecstatic caricature. I turned my face away from her so as to be able to laugh.

"I then spoke to her of painting, as I would have done to a fellow-artist, using the technical terms common among the devotees of the profession. She listened attentively to me, eagerly seeking to divine the sense of the obscure words, so as to penetrate my thoughts. From time to time, she would exclaim: 'Oh! I understand, I understand. This is very interesting.' We returned home.

"The next day, on seeing me, she approached me eagerly, holding out her hand; and we became firm friends immediately.

"She was a brave creature, with an elastic sort of a soul, which became enthusiastic at a bound. She lacked equilibrium, like all women who are spinsters at the age of fifty. She seemed to be pickled in vinegary innocence, though her heart still retained something of youth and of girlish effervescence. She loved both nature and animals with a fervent ardor, a love like old wine, mellow through age, with a sensual love that she had never bestowed on men.

"One thing is certain: a mare roaming in a meadow with a foal at its side, a bird's nest full of young ones, squeaking, with their open mouths and enormous heads, made her quiver with the most violent emotion.

"Poor solitary beings! Sad wanderers from *table d'hôte* to *table d'hôte*, poor beings, ridiculous and lamentable, I love you ever since I became acquainted with Miss Harriet!

"I soon discovered that she had something she would like to tell me, but dared not, and I was amused at her timidity. When I started out in the morning with my box on my back, she would accompany me as far as the end of the village, silent, but evidently struggling inwardly to find words with which to begin a conversation. Then she would leave me abruptly, and, with jaunty step, walk away quickly.

"One day, however, she plucked up courage:

"'I would like to see how you paint pictures? Will you show me? I have been very curious.'

"And she colored up as though she had given utterance to words extremely audacious.

"I conducted her to the bottom of the Petit-Val, where I had commenced a large picture.

"She remained standing near me, following all my gestures with concentrated attention. Then, suddenly, fearing, perhaps, that she was disturbing me, she said to me: 'Thank you,' and walked away.

"But in a short time she became more familiar, and accompanied me every day, her countenance exhibiting visible pleasure. She carried her folding stool under her arm, would not consent to my carrying it, and she sat always by my side. She would remain there for hours immovable and mute, following with her eye the point of my brush in its every movement. When I would obtain, by a large splatch of color spread on with a knife, a striking and unexpected effect, she would, in spite of herself, give vent to a half-suppressed 'Oh!' of astonishment, of joy, of admiration. She had the most tender respect for my canvases, an almost religious respect for that human reproduction of a part of nature's work divine. My studies appeared to her to be pictures of sanctity, and sometimes she spoke to me of God, with the idea of converting me.

"Oh! He was a queer good-natured being, this God of hers. He was a sort of village philosopher without any great resources, and without great power; for she always figured him to herself as a being quivering over injustices committed under his eyes, and helpless to prevent them.

"She was, however, on excellent terms with him, affecting even to be the confidant of his secrets and of his whims. She said:

"'God wills, or God does not will,' just like a sergeant announcing to a recruit: 'The colonel has commanded.'

"At the bottom of her heart she deplored my ignorance of the intentions of the Eternal, which she strove, nay, felt herself compelled, to impart to me.

"Almost every day, I found in my pockets, in my hat when I lifted it from the ground, in my box of colors, in my polished shoes, standing in the mornings in front of my door, those little pious brochures, which she, no doubt, received directly from Paradise.

"I treated her as one would an old friend, with unaffected cordiality. But I soon perceived that she had changed somewhat in her manner; but, for a while, I paid little attention to it.

"When I walked about, whether to the bottom of the valley, or through some country lanes, I would see her suddenly appear, as though she were returning from a rapid walk. She would then sit down abruptly, out of breath, as though she had been running or overcome by some profound emotion. Her face would be red, that English red which is denied to the people of all other countries; then, without any reason, she would grow pale, become the color of the ground, and seem ready to faint away. Gradually, however, I would see her regain her ordinary color, whereupon she would begin to speak.

"Then, without warning, she would break off in the middle of a sentence, spring up from her seat, and march off so rapidly and so strangely, that it would, sometimes, put me to my wits' end to try and discover whether I had done or said anything to displease or offend her.

"I finally came to the conclusion that this arose from her early habits and training, somewhat modified, no doubt, in honor of me, since the first days of our acquaintanceship.

"When she returned to the farm, after walking for hours on the wind-beaten coast, her long curled hair would be shaken out and hanging loose, as though it had broken away from its bearings. It was seldom that this gave her any concern; though sometimes she looked as though she had been dining *sans cérémonie;* her locks having become disheveled by the breezes.

"She would then go up to her room in order to adjust what I called her glass lamps. When I would say to her, in familiar gallantry, which, however, always offended her:

"'You are as beautiful as a planet to-day, Miss Harriet,' a little blood would immediately mount into her cheeks, the blood of a young maiden, the blood of sweet fifteen.

"Then she would become abruptly savage and cease coming to watch me paint. But I always thought:

"'This is only a fit of temper she is passing through.'

"But it did not always pass away. When I spoke to her sometimes, she would answer me, either with an air of affected indifference, or in sullen anger; and she became by turns rude, impatient, and nervous. For a time I never saw her except at meals, and we spoke but little. I concluded, at length, that I must have offended her in something: and, accordingly, I said to her one evening:

"'Miss Harriet, why is it that you do not act toward me as formerly? What have I done to displease you? You are causing me much pain!'

"She responded, in an angry tone, in a manner altogether *sui generis:*

"'I am always with you the same as formerly. It is not true, not true,' and she ran upstairs and shut herself up in her room.

"At times she would look upon me with strange eyes. Since that time I have often said to myself that those condemned to death must look thus when informed that their last day has come. In her eye there lurked a species of folly, a folly at once mysterious and violent — even more, a fever, an exasperated desire, impatient, at once incapable of being realized and unrealizable!

"Nay, it seemed to me that there was also going on within her a combat, in which her heart struggled against an unknown force that she wished to overcome — perhaps, even, something else. But what could I know? What could I know?

III.

"This was indeed a singular revelation.

"For some time I had commenced to work, as soon as daylight appeared, on a picture, the subject of which was as follows:

"A deep ravine, steep banks dominated by two declivities, lined with brambles and long rows of trees, hidden, drowned in milky vapor, clad in that misty robe which sometimes floats over valleys at break of day. At the extreme end of that thick and transparent fog, you see coming, or rather already come, a human couple, a stripling and a maiden embraced, interlaced, she, with head leaning on him, he, inclined toward her, and lip to lip.

"A ray of the sun, glistening through the branches, has traversed the fog of dawn and illuminated it with a rosy reflection, just behind the rustic lovers, whose vague shadows are reflected on it in clear silver. It was well done, yes, indeed, well done.

"I was working on the declivity which led to the Val-d'Etretat. This particular morning, I had, by chance, the sort of floating vapor which was necessary for my purpose. Suddenly, an object appeared in front of me, a kind of phantom; it was Miss Harriet. On seeing me, she took to flight. But I called after her saying: 'Come here, come here, Mademoiselle, I have a nice little picture for you.'

"She came forward, though with seeming reluctance. I handed her my sketch. She said nothing, but stood for a long time motionless, looking at it. Suddenly she burst into tears. She wept spasmodically, like men who have been struggling hard against shedding tears, but who can do so no longer, and abandon themselves to grief, though unwillingly. I got up, trembling, moved myself by the sight of a sorrow I did not comprehend, and I took her by the hand with a gesture of brusque affection, a true French impulse which impels one quicker than one thinks.

"She let her hands rest in mine for a few seconds, and I felt them quiver, as if her whole nervous system was twisting and turning. Then she withdrew her hands abruptly, or, rather, tore them out of mine.

"I recognized that shiver as soon as I had felt it; I was deceived in nothing. Ah! the love shudder of a woman, whether she is fifteen or fifty years of age, whether she is one of the people or one of the *monde*, goes so straight to my heart that I never had any difficulty in understanding it!

"Her whole frail being trembled, vibrated, yielded. I knew it. She walked away before I had time to say a word, leaving me as surprised as if I had witnessed a miracle, and as troubled as if I had committed a crime.

"I did not go in to breakfast. I took a walk on the banks of the Falaise, feeling that I could just as soon weep as laugh, looking on the adventure as both comic and deplorable, and my position as ridiculous, fain to believe that I had lost my head.

"I asked myself what I ought to do. I debated whether I ought not to take my leave of the place and almost immediately my resolution was formed.

"Somewhat sad and perplexed, I wandered about until dinner time, and entered the farmhouse just when the soup had been served up.

"I sat down at the table, as usual. Miss Harriet was there, munching away solemnly, without speaking to anyone, without even lifting her eyes. She wore, however, her usual expression, both of countenance and manner.

"I waited, patiently, till the meal had been finished. Then, turning toward the landlady, I said: 'Madame Lecacheur, it will not be long now before I shall have to take my leave of you.'

"The good woman, at once surprised and troubled, replied in a quivering voice: 'My dear sir, what is it I have just heard you say? Are you going to leave us, after I have become so much accustomed to you?'

"I looked at Miss Harriet from the corner of my eye. Her countenance did not change in the least; but the under-servant came toward me with eyes wide open. She was a fat girl, of about eighteen years of age, rosy, fresh, strong as a horse, yet possessing a rare attribute in one in her position—she was very neat and clean. I had kissed her at odd times, in out of the way corners, in the manner of a mountain guide, nothing more.

"The dinner being over, I went to smoke my pipe under the apple-trees, walking up and down at my ease, from one end of the court to the other. All the reflections which I had made during the day, the strange discovery of the morning, that grotesque and passionate attachment for me, the recollections which that revelation had suddenly called up, recollections at once charming and perplexing, perhaps, also, that look which the servant had cast on me at the announcement of my departure—all these things, mixed up and combined, put me now in an excited bodily state, with the tickling sensation of kisses on my lips, and in my veins something which urged me on to commit some folly.

"Night having come on, casting its dark shadows under the trees, I descried Céleste, who had gone to shut the hen-coops, at the other end of the inclosure. I darted toward her, running so noiselessly that she heard nothing, and as she got up from closing the small traps by which the chickens went in and out, I clasped her in my arms and rained on her coarse, fat face a shower of kisses. She made a struggle, laughing all the same, as she was accustomed to do in such circumstances. What made me suddenly loose my grip of her? Why did I at once experience a shock? What was it that I heard behind me?

"It was Miss Harriet who had come upon us, who had seen us, and who stood in front of us, as motionless as a specter. Then she disappeared in the darkness.

"I was ashamed, embarrassed, more annoyed at having been surprised by her than if she had caught me committing some criminal act.

"I slept badly that night; I was worried and haunted by sad thoughts. I seemed to hear loud weeping; but in this I was no doubt deceived. Moreover, I thought several times that I heard some one walking up and down in the house, and that some one opened my door from the outside.

"Toward morning, I was overcome by fatigue, and sleep seized on me. I got up late and did not go downstairs until breakfast time, being still in a bewildered state, not knowing what kind of face to put on.

"No one had seen Miss Harriet. We waited for her at table, but she did not appear. At length, Mother Lecacheur went to her room. The Englishwoman had gone out. She must have set out at break of day, as she was wont to do, in order to see the sun rise.

"Nobody seemed astonished at this and we began to eat in silence.

"The weather was hot, very hot, one of those still sultry days when not a leaf stirs. The table had been placed out of doors, under an apple-tree; and from time to time Sapeur had gone to the cellar to draw a jug of cider, everybody was so thirsty. Céleste brought the dishes from the kitchen, a ragout of mutton with potatoes, a cold rabbit, and a salad. Afterward she placed before us a dish of strawberries, the first of the season.

"As I wanted to wash and freshen these, I begged the servant to go and bring a pitcher of cold water.

"In about five minutes she returned, declaring that the well was dry. She had lowered the pitcher to the full extent of the cord, and had touched the bottom, but on drawing the pitcher up again, it was empty. Mother Lecacheur, anxious to examine the thing for herself, went and looked down the hole. She returned announcing that one could see clearly something in the well, something altogether unusual. But this, no doubt, was pottles of straw, which, out of spite, had been cast down it by a neighbor.

"I wished also to look down the well, hoping to clear up the mystery, and perched myself close to its brink. I perceived, indistinctly, a white object. What could it be? I then conceived the idea of lowering a lantern at the end of a cord. When I did so, the yellow flame danced on the layers of stone and gradually became clearer. All four of us were leaning over the opening, Sapeur and Céleste having now joined us. The lantern rested on a black and white, indistinct mass, singular, incomprehensible. Sapeur exclaimed:

"'It is a horse. I see the hoofs. It must have escaped from the meadow, during the night, and fallen in headlong.'

"But, suddenly, a cold shiver attacked my spine, I first recognized a foot, then a clothed limb; the body was entire, but the other limb had disappeared under the water.

"I groaned and trembled so violently that the light of the lamp danced hither and thither over the object, discovering a slipper.

"'It is a woman! who — who — can it be? It is Miss Harriet.'

"Sapeur alone did not manifest horror. He had witnessed many such scenes in Africa.

"Mother Lecacheur and Céleste began to scream and to shriek, and ran away.

"But it was necessary to recover the corpse of the dead. I attached the boy securely by the loins to the end of the pulley-rope; then I lowered him slowly, and watched him disappear in the darkness. In the one hand he had a lantern, and held on to the rope with the other. Soon I recognized his voice, which seemed to come from the center of the earth, crying:

"'Stop.'

"I then saw him fish something out of the water. It was the other limb. He bound the two feet together, and shouted anew:

"'Haul up.'

"I commenced to wind him up, but I felt my arms strain, my muscles twitch, and was in terror lest I should let the boy fall to the bottom. When his head appeared over the brink, I asked:

"'What is it?' as though I only expected that he would tell me what he had discovered at the bottom.

"We both got on to the stone slab at the edge of the well, and, face to face, hoisted the body.

"Mother Lecacheur and Céleste watched us from a distance, concealed behind the wall of the house. When they saw, issuing from the well, the black slippers and white stockings of the drowned person, they disappeared.

"Sapeur seized the ankles of the poor chaste woman, and we drew it up, inclined, as it was, in the most immodest posture. The head was in a shocking state, bruised and black; and the long, gray hair, hanging down, was tangled and disordered.

"'In the name of all that is holy, how lean she is!' exclaimed Sapeur, in a contemptuous tone.

"We carried her into the room, and as the women did not put in an appearance, I, with the assistance of the lad, dressed the corpse for burial.

"I washed her disfigured face. By the touch of my hand an eye was slightly opened; it seemed to scan me with that pale stare, with that cold, that terrible look which corpses have, a look which seems to come from the beyond. I plaited up, as well as I could, her disheveled hair, and I adjusted on her forehead a novel and singularly formed lock. Then I took off her dripping wet garments, baring, not without a feeling of shame, as though I had been guilty of some profanation, her shoulders and her chest, and her long arms, slim as the twigs of branches.

"I next went to fetch some flowers, corn poppies, blue beetles, marguerites, and fresh and perfumed herbs, with which to strew her funeral couch.

"Being the only person near her, it was necessary for me to perform the usual ceremonies. In a letter found in her pocket, written at the last moment, she asked that her body be buried in the village in which she had passed the last days of her life. A frightful thought then oppressed my heart. Was it not on my account that she wished to be laid at rest in this place?

"Toward the evening, all the female gossips of the locality came to view the remains of the defunct; but I would not allow a single person to enter; I wanted to be alone; and I watched by the corpse the whole night.

"By the flickering light of the candles, I looked at the body of this miserable woman, wholly unknown, who had died so lamentably and so far away from home. Had she left no friends, no relatives behind her? What had her infancy been? What had been her life? Whence had she come thither, all alone, a wanderer, like a dog driven from home? What secrets of suffering and of despair were sealed up in that disagreeable body, in that spent and withered body, that impenetrable hiding place of a mystery which had driven her far away from affection and from love?

"How many unhappy beings there are! I felt that upon that human creature weighed the eternal injustice of implacable nature! Life was over with her, without her ever having experienced, perhaps, that which sustains the most miserable of us all—to wit, the hope of being once loved! Otherwise, why should she thus have concealed herself, have fled from the face of others? Why did she love everything so tenderly and so passionately, everything living that was not a man?

"I recognized, also, that she believed in a God, and that she hoped for compensation from him for the miseries she had endured. She had now begun to decompose, and to become, in turn, a plant. She who had blossomed in the sun was now to be eaten up by the cattle, carried away in herbs, and in the flesh of beasts, again to become human flesh. But that which is called the soul had been extinguished at the bottom of the dark well. She suffered no longer. She had changed her life for that of others yet to be born.

"Hours passed away in this silent and sinister communion with the dead. A pale light at length announced the dawn of a new day, and a bright ray glistened on the bed, shedding a dash of fire on the bedclothes and on her hands. This was the hour she had so much loved, when the waking birds began to sing in the trees.

"I opened the window to its fullest extent, I drew back the curtains, so that the whole heavens might look in upon us. Then bending toward the glassy corpse, I took in my hands the mutilated head, and slowly, without terror or disgust, imprinted a long, long kiss upon those lips which had never before received the salute of love."

*   *   *   *   *   *   *

Léon Chenal remained silent. The women wept. We heard on the box seat Count d'Etraille blow his nose, from time to time. The coachman alone had gone to sleep. The horses, which felt no longer the sting of the whip, had slackened their pace and dragged softly along. And the four-in-hand, hardly moving at all, became suddenly torpid, as if laden with sorrow.

THE HOLE

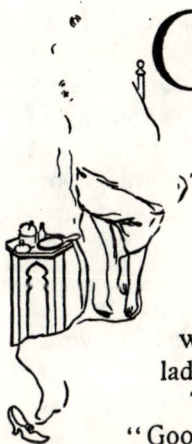

CUTS AND WOUNDS WHICH CAUSED DEATH. That was the heading of the charge which brought Leopold Renard, upholsterer, before the Assize Court.

Round him were the principal witnesses, Madame Flamèche, widow of the victim, Louis Ladureau, cabinetmaker, and Jean Durdent, plumber.

Near the criminal was his wife, dressed in black, a little ugly woman, who looked like a monkey dressed as a lady.

This is how Renard described the drama:

"Good heavens, it is a misfortune of which I am the first and last victim, and with which my will has nothing to do. The facts are their own commentary, Monsieur le Président. I am an honest man, a hard-working man, an upholsterer in the same street for the last sixteen years, known, liked, respected, and esteemed by all, as my neighbors have testified, even the porter, who is not *folâtre* every day. I am fond of work, I am fond of saving, I like honest men, and respectable pleasures. That is what has ruined me, so much the worse for me; but as my will had nothing to do with it, I continue to respect myself.

"Every Sunday for the last five years, my wife and I have spent the day at Passy. We get fresh air, not to say that we are fond of fishing — as fond of it as we are of small onions. Mélie inspired me with that passion, the jade; she is more enthusiastic than I am, the scold, and all the mischief in this business is her fault, as you will see immediately.

"I am strong and mild-tempered, without a pennyworth of malice in me. But she! oh! la! la! she looks insignificant, she is short and thin, but she does more mischief than a weasel. I do not deny that she has some good qualities; she has some, and those very important to a man in business. But her character! Just ask about it in the neighborhood; even the porter's wife, who has just sent me about my business — she will tell you something about it.

"Every day she used to find fault with my mild temper: 'I would not put up with this! I would not put up with that.' If I had listened to her, Monsieur le Président, I should have had at least three bouts of fisticuffs a month."

Madame Renard interrupted him: "And for good reasons too; they laugh best who laugh last."

He turned toward her frankly: "Oh! very well, I can blame you, since you were the cause of it."

Then, facing the President again he said:

"I will continue. We used to go to Passy every Saturday evening, so as to be able to begin fishing at daybreak the next morning. It is a habit which has become second nature with us, as the saying is. Three years ago this summer I discovered a place, oh! such a spot! There, in the shade, were eight feet of water at least and perhaps ten, a hole with a *retour* under the bank, a regular retreat for fish and a paradise for any fisherman. I might look upon that hole as my property, Monsieur le Président, as I was its Christopher Columbus. Everybody in the neighborhood knew it, without making any opposition. They used to say: 'That is Renard's place'; and nobody would have gone to it, not even Monsieur Plumsay, who is renowned, be it said without any offense, for appropriating other people's places.

"Well, I went as usual to that place, of which I felt as certain as if I had owned it. I had scarcely got there on Saturday, when I got into 'Delila,' with my wife. 'Delila' is my Norwegian boat, which I had built by Fourmaise, and which is light and safe. Well, as I said, we got into the boat and we were going to bait, and for baiting there is nobody to be compared with me, and they all know it. You want to know with what I bait? I cannot answer that question; it has nothing to do with the accident; I cannot answer, that is my secret. There are more than three hundred people who have asked me; I have been offered glasses of brandy and liquors, fried fish, matelots,* to make me tell! But just go and try whether the chub will come. Ah! they have patted my stomach to get at my secret, my recipe. Only my wife knows, and she will not tell it, any more than I shall! Is not that so, Mélie?"

---

* A preparation of several kinds of fish, with a sharp sauce.

The President of the Court interrupted him:

"Just get to the facts as soon as you can."

The accused continued: "I am getting to them; I am getting to them. Well, on Saturday, July 8, we left by the five twenty-five train, and before dinner we went to ground-bait as usual. The weather promised to keep fine, and I said to Mélie: 'All right for to-morrow!' And she replied: 'It looks like it.' We never talk more than that together.

"And then we returned to dinner. I was happy and thirsty, and that was the cause of everything. I said to Mélie: 'Look here Mélie, it is fine weather, so suppose I drink a bottle of *Casque à mèche*. That is a little white wine which we have christened so, because if you drink too much of it it prevents you from sleeping and is the opposite of a nightcap. Do you understand me?

"She replied: 'You can do as you please, but you will be ill again, and will not be able to get up to-morrow.' That was true, sensible, prudent, and clear-sighted, I must confess. Nevertheless, I could not withstand it, and I drank my bottle. It all comes from that.

"Well, I could not sleep. By Jove! It kept me awake till two o'clock in the morning, and then I went to sleep so soundly that I should not have heard the angel shouting at the Last Judgment.

"In short, my wife woke me at six o'clock and I jumped out of bed, hastily put on my trousers and jersey, washed my face and jumped on board 'Delila.' But it was too late, for when I arrived at my hole it was already taken! Such a thing had never happened to me in three years, and it made me feel as if I were being robbed under my own eyes. I said to myself, 'Confound it all! confound it!' And then my wife began to nag at me. 'Eh! What about your *Casque à mèche!* Get along, you drunkard! Are you satisfied, you great fool?' I could say nothing, because it was all quite true, and so I landed all the same near the spot and tried to profit by what was left. Perhaps after all the fellow might catch nothing, and go away.

"He was a little thin man, in white linen coat and waistcoat, and with a large straw hat, and his wife, a fat woman who was doing embroidery, was behind him.

"When she saw us take up our position close to their place, she murmured: 'I suppose there are no other places on the river!' And my wife, who was furious, replied: 'People who know how to behave make inquiries about the habits of the neighborhood before occupying reserved spots.'

"As I did not want a fuss, I said to her: 'Hold your tongue, Mélie. Let them go on, let them go on; we shall see.'

"Well, we had fastened 'Delila' under the willow-trees, and had landed and were fishing side by side Mélie and I, close to the two others; but here, Monsieur, I must enter into details.

"We had only been there about five minutes when our male neighbor's float began to go down two or three times, and then he pulled out a chub as thick as my thigh, rather less, perhaps, but nearly as big! My heart beat, and the perspiration stood on my forehead, and Mélie said to me: 'Well, you sot, did you see that?'

"Just then, Monsieur Bru, the grocer of Poissy, who was fond of gudgeon fishing, passed in a boat, and called out to me: 'So somebody has taken your usual place, Monsieur Renard?' And I replied: 'Yes, Monsieur Bru, there are some people in this world who do not know the usages of common politeness.'

"The little man in linen pretended not to hear, nor his fat lump of a wife, either."

Here the President interrupted him a second time: "Take care, you are insulting the widow, Madame Flamèche, who is present."

Renard made his excuses: "I beg your pardon, I beg your pardon, my anger carried me away. Well, not a quarter of an hour had passed when the little man caught another chub and another almost immediately, and another five minutes later.

"The tears were in my eyes, and then I knew that Madame Renard was boiling with rage, for she kept on nagging at me: 'Oh! how horrid! Don't you see that he is robbing you of your fish? Do you think that you will catch anything? Not even a frog, nothing whatever. Why, my hands are burning, just to think of it.'

"But I said to myself: 'Let us wait until twelve o'clock. Then this poaching fellow will go to lunch, and I shall get my place again.' As for me, Monsieur le Président, I lunch on the spot every Sunday; we bring our provisions in 'Delila.' But there! At twelve o'clock, the wretch produced a fowl out of a newspaper, and while he was eating, actually he caught another chub!

"Mélie and I had a morsel also, just a mouthful, a mere nothing, for our heart was not in it.

"Then I took up my newspaper, to aid my digestion. Every Sunday I read the 'Gil Blas' in the shade like that, by the side of the water. It is Columbine's day, you know, Columbine who writes the articles in the 'Gil Blas.' I generally put Madame Renard into a passion by pretending to know this Columbine. It is not true, for I do not know her, and have never seen her, but that does not matter; she writes very well, and then she says things straight out for a woman. She suits me, and there are not many of her sort.

"Well, I began to tease my wife, but she got angry immediately, and very angry, and so I held my tongue. At that moment our two witnesses, who are present here, Monsieur Ladureau and Monsieur Durdent, appeared on the other side of the river. We knew each other by sight. The little man began to fish again, and he caught so many that I trembled with vexation, and his wife said: 'It is an uncommonly good spot, and we will come here always, Desiré.' As for me, a cold shiver ran down my back, and Madame Renard kept repeating: 'You are not a man; you have the blood of a chicken in your veins'; and suddenly I said to her: 'Look here, I would rather go away, or I shall only be doing something foolish.'

"And she whispered to me as if she had put a red-hot iron under my nose: 'You are not a man. Now you are going to run away, and surrender your place! Off you go, Bazaine!'

"Well, I felt that, but yet I did not move, while the other fellow pulled out a bream, Oh! I never saw such a large one before, never! And then my

wife began to talk aloud, as if she were thinking,
and you can see her trickery. She said: 'That is
what one might call stolen fish, seeing that we baited
the place ourselves. At any rate, they ought to give
us back the money we have spent on bait.'

"Then the fat woman in the cotton dress said in
turn: 'Do you mean to call us thieves, Madame?'
And they began to explain, and then they came to
words. Oh! Lord! those creatures know some good
ones. They shouted so loud, that our two witnesses,
who were on the other bank, began to call out by
way of a joke: 'Less noise over there; you will prevent your husbands from fishing.'

"The fact is that neither of us moved any more
than if we had been two tree-stumps. We remained
there, with our noses over the water, as if we had
heard nothing, but by Jove, we heard all the same.
'You are a mere liar.'

"'You are nothing better than a street-walker.'

"'You are only a trollop.'

"'You are a regular strumpet.'

"And so on, and so on; a sailor could not have
said more.

"Suddenly I heard a noise behind me, and turned
round. It was the other one, the fat woman who
had fallen on to my wife with her parasol. *Whack!*
whack! Mélie got two of them, but she was furious,
and she hits hard when she is in a rage, so she
caught the fat woman by the hair and then, *thump,*
thump. Slaps in the face rained down like ripe
plums. I should have let them go on — women
among themselves, men among themselves — it does
not do to mix the blows, but the little man in the

linen jacket jumped up like a devil and was going to
rush at my wife. Ah! no, no, not that, my friend!
I caught the gentleman with the end of my fist,
crash, crash, one on the nose, the other in the
stomach. He threw up his arms and legs and fell on
his back into the river, just into the hole.

"I should have fished him out most certainly,
Monsieur le Président, if I had had the time. But unfortunately the fat woman got the better of it, and she
was drubbing Mélie terribly. I know that I ought not
to have assisted her while the man was drinking his
fill, but I never thought that he would drown, and
said to myself: 'Bah, it will cool him.'

"I therefore ran up to the women to separate
them, and all I received was scratches and bites.
Good Lord, what creatures! Well, it took me five
minutes, and perhaps ten, to separate those two vira-
goes. When I turned round, there was nothing to
be seen, and the water was as smooth as a lake.
The others yonder kept shouting: 'Fish him out!'
It was all very well to say that, but I cannot swim
and still less dive!

"At last the man from the dam came, and two
gentlemen with boat-hooks, but it had taken over a
quarter of an hour. He was found at the bottom of
the hole in eight feet of water, as I have said, but he
was dead, the poor little man in his linen suit! There
are the facts, such as I have sworn to. I am innocent, on my honor."

The witnesses having deposed to the same effect,
the accused was acquitted.

LOVE

THREE PAGES FROM A SPORTSMAN'S BOOK

I HAVE just read among the general news in one of the papers a drama of passion. He killed her and then he killed himself, so he must have loved her. What matters He or She? Their love alone matters to me; and it does not interest me because it moves me or astonishes me, or because it softens me or makes me think, but because it recalls to my mind a remembrance of my youth, a strange recollection of a hunting adventure where Love appeared to me, as the Cross appeared to the early Christians, in the midst of the heavens.

I was born with all the instincts and the senses of primitive man, tempered by the arguments and the restraints of a civilized being. I am passionately fond of shooting, yet the sight of the wounded animal, of the blood on its feathers and on my hands, affects my heart so as almost to make it stop.

That year the cold weather set in suddenly toward the end of autumn, and I was invited by one

of my cousins, Karl de Rauville, to go with him and
shoot ducks on the marshes, at daybreak.

My cousin was a jolly fellow of forty, with red
hair, very stout and bearded, a country gentleman,
an amiable semi-brute, of a happy disposition and
endowed with that Gallic wit which makes even
mediocrity agreeable. He lived in a house, half farmhouse, half château, situated in a broad valley through
which a river ran. The hills right and left were covered with woods, old manorial woods where magnificent trees still remained, and where the rarest
feathered game in that part of France was to be
found. Eagles were shot there occasionally, and birds of
passage, such as rarely venture into our over-populated
part of the country, invariably lighted amid these giant
oaks, as if they knew or recognized some little corner
of a primeval forest which had remained there to serve
them as a shelter during their short nocturnal halt.

In the valley there were large meadows watered
by trenches and separated by hedges; then, further
on, the river, which up to that point had been kept
between banks, expanded into a vast marsh. That
marsh was the best shooting ground I ever saw. It
was my cousin's chief care, and he kept it as a
preserve. Through the rushes that covered it, and
made it rustling and rough, narrow passages had been
cut, through which the flat-bottomed boats, impelled
and steered by poles, passed along silently over dead
water, brushing up against the reeds and making the
swift fish take refuge in the weeds, and the wild fowl,
with their pointed, black heads, dive suddenly.

I am passionately fond of the water: of the sea,
though it is too vast, too full of movement, impossi-

ble to hold; of the rivers which are so beautiful, but which pass on, and flee away; and above all of the marshes, where the whole unknown existence of aquatic animals palpitates. The marsh is an entire world in itself on the world of earth—a different world, which has its own life, its settled inhabitants and its passing travelers, its voices, its noises, and above all its mystery. Nothing is more impressive, nothing more disquieting, more terrifying occasionally, than a fen. Why should a vague terror hang over these low plains covered with water? Is it the low rustling of the rushes, the strange will-o'-the-wisp lights, the silence which prevails on calm nights, the still mists which hang over the surface like a shroud; or is it the almost inaudible splashing, so slight and so gentle, yet sometimes more terrifying than the cannons of men or the thunders of the skies, which make these marshes resemble countries one has dreamed of, terrible countries holding an unknown and dangerous secret?

No, something else belongs to it—another mystery, profounder and graver, floats amid these thick mists, perhaps the mystery of the creation itself! For was it not in stagnant and muddy water, amid the heavy humidity of moist land under the heat of the sun, that the first germ of life pulsated and expanded to the day?

I arrived at my cousin's in the evening. It was freezing hard enough to split the stones.

During dinner, in the large room whose sideboards, walls, and ceiling were covered with stuffed birds, with wings extended or perched on branches to which they were nailed,—hawks, herons, owls, nightjars, buzzards, tiercels, vultures, falcons,—my cousin who, dressed in a sealskin jacket, himself resembled some strange animal from a cold country, told me what preparations he had made for that same night.

We were to start at half past three in the morning, so as to arrive at the place which he had chosen for our watching-place at about half past four. On that spot a hut had been built of lumps of ice, so as to shelter us somewhat from the trying wind which precedes daybreak, a wind so cold as to tear the flesh like a saw, cut it like the blade of a knife, prick it like a poisoned sting, twist it like a pair of pincers, and burn it like fire.

My cousin rubbed his hands: "I have never known such a frost," he said; "it is already twelve degrees below zero at six o'clock in the evening."

I threw myself on to my bed immediately after we had finished our meal, and went to sleep by the light of a bright fire burning in the grate.

At three o'clock he woke me. In my turn, I put on a sheepskin, and found my cousin Karl covered with a bearskin. After having each swallowed two cups of scalding coffee, followed by glasses of liqueur brandy, we started, accompanied by a gamekeeper and our dogs, Plongeon and Pierrot.

From the first moment that I got outside, I felt chilled to the very marrow. It was one of those nights on which the earth seems dead with cold. The frozen air becomes resisting and palpable, such pain does it cause; no breath of wind moves it, it is fixed and motionless; it bites you, pierces through you, dries you, kills the trees, the plants, the insects, the small birds themselves, who fall from the branches on to the hard ground, and become stiff themselves under the grip of the cold.

The moon, which was in her last quarter and was inclining all to one side, seemed fainting in the midst of space, so weak that she was unable to wane, forced to stay up yonder, seized and paralyzed by the severity of the weather. She shed a cold, mournful light over the world, that dying and wan light which she gives us every month, at the end of her period.

Karl and I walked side by side, our backs bent, our hands in our pockets and our guns under our arms. Our boots, which were wrapped in wool so that we might be able to walk without slipping on the frozen river, made no sound, and I looked at the white vapor which our dogs' breath made.

We were soon on the edge of the marsh, and entered one of the lanes of dry rushes which ran through the low forest.

Our elbows, which touched the long, ribbonlike leaves, left a slight noise behind us, and I was seized, as I had never been before, by the powerful and singular emotion which marshes cause in me. This one was dead, dead from cold, since we were walking on it, in the middle of its population of dried rushes.

Suddenly, at the turn of one of the lanes, I perceived the ice-hut which had been constructed to shelter us. I went in, and as we had nearly an hour to wait before the wandering birds would awake, I rolled myself up in my rug in order to try and get warm. Then, lying on my back, I began to look at

the misshapen moon, which had four horns through
the vaguely transparent walls of this polar house.
But the frost of the frozen marshes, the cold of these
walls, the cold from the firmament penetrated me so
terribly that I began to cough. My cousin Karl became uneasy.

"No matter if we do not kill much to-day," he
said: "I do not want you to catch cold; we will light
a fire." And he told the gamekeeper to cut some
rushes.

We made a pile in the middle of our hut which
had a hole in the middle of the roof to let out the
smoke, and when the red flames rose up to the clear,
crystal blocks they began to melt, gently, impercep-
tibly, as if they were sweating. Karl, who had remained outside, called out to me: "Come and look
here!" I went out of the hut and remained struck
with astonishment. Our hut, in the shape of a cone,
looked like an enormous diamond with a heart of fire,
which had been suddenly planted there in the midst
of the frozen water of the marsh. And inside, we
saw two fantastic forms, those of our dogs, who were
warming themselves at the fire.

But a peculiar cry, a lost, a wandering cry, passed
over our heads, and the light from our hearth showed
us the wild birds. Nothing moves one so much as
the first clamor of a life which one does not see,
which passes through the somber air so quickly and
so far off, just before the first streak of a winter's day
appears on the horizon. It seems to me, at this glacial
hour of dawn, as if that passing cry which is carried
away by the wings of a bird is the sigh of a soul
from the world!

"Put out the fire," said Karl, "it is getting day-light."

The sky was, in fact, beginning to grow pale, and the flights of ducks made long, rapid streaks which were soon obliterated on the sky.

A stream of light burst out into the night; Karl had fired, and the two dogs ran forward.

And then, nearly every minute, now he, now I, aimed rapidly as soon as the shadow of a flying flock appeared above the rushes. And Pierrot and Plongeon, out of breath but happy, retrieved the bleeding birds, whose eyes still, occasionally, looked at us.

The sun had risen, and it was a bright day with a blue sky, and we were thinking of taking our departure, when two birds with extended necks and outstretched wings, glided rapidly over our heads. I fired, and one of them fell almost at my feet. It was a teal, with a silver breast, and then, in the blue space above me, I heard a voice, the voice of a bird. It was a short, repeated, heart-rending lament; and the bird, the little animal that had been spared began to turn round in the blue sky, over our heads, looking at its dead companion which I was holding in my hand.

Karl was on his knees, his gun to his shoulder watching it eagerly, until it should be within shot. "You have killed the duck," he said, "and the drake will not fly away."

He certainly did not fly away; he circled over our heads continually, and continued his cries. Never have any groans of suffering pained me so much as that desolate appeal, as that lamentable reproach of this poor bird which was lost in space.

Occasionally he took flight under the menace of the gun which followed his movements, and seemed ready to continue his flight alone, but as he could not make up his mind to this, he returned to find his mate.

"Leave her on the ground," Karl said to me, "he will come within shot by and by." And he did indeed come near us, careless of danger, infatuated by his animal love, by his affection for his mate, which I had just killed.

Karl fired, and it was as if somebody had cut the string which held the bird suspended. I saw something black descend, and I heard the noise of a fall among the rushes. And Pierrot brought it to me.

I put them — they were already cold — into the same game-bag, and I returned to Paris the same evening.

THE INN

LIKE all the little wooden inns in the higher Alps, tiny auberges situated in the bare and rocky gorges which intersect the white summits of the mountains, the inn of Schwarenbach is a refuge for travelers who are crossing the Gemmi.

It is open six months in the year, and is inhabited by the family of Jean Hauser. As soon as the snow begins to fall, and fills the valley so as to make the road down to Loëche impassable, the father, with mother, daughter, and the three sons depart, leaving the house in charge of the old guide, Gaspard Hari, with the young guide, Ulrich Kunsi, and Sam, the great mountain dog.

The two men and the dog remain till spring in their snowy prison, with nothing before their eyes except immense, white slopes of the Balmhorn, surrounded by light, glistening summits, and shut up, blocked up, and buried by the snow which rises around them, enveloping and almost burying the little house up to the eaves.

It was the day on which the Hauser family were going to return to Loëche, as winter was approaching, and the descent was becoming dangerous. Three mules started first, laden with baggage and led by the three sons. Then the mother, Jeanne Hauser, and her daughter Louise mounted a fourth mule, and set off in their turn. The father followed them, accompanied by the two men in charge, who were to escort the family as far as the brow of the descent. First of all they skirted the small lake, now frozen over, at the foot of the mass of rocks which stretched in front of the inn; then they followed the valley, which was dominated on all sides by snow-covered peaks.

A ray of sunlight glinted into that little white, glistening, frozen desert, illuminating it with a cold and dazzling flame. No living thing appeared among this ocean of hills; there was no stir in that immeasurable solitude, no noise disturbed the profound silence.

By degrees the young guide, Ulrich Kunsi, a tall, long-legged Swiss, left daddy Hauser and old Gaspard behind, in order to catch up· with the mule which carried the two women. The younger one looked at him as he approached, as if she would call him with her sad eyes. She was a young, light-haired peasant girl, whose milk-white cheeks and pale hair seemed to have lost their color by long dwelling amid the ice. When Ulrich had caught up with the animal which carried the women, he put his hand on the crupper, and relaxed his speed. Mother Hauser began to talk to him, and enumerated with minutest detail all that he would have to attend to during the winter. It was the first winter he would spend up there, while old Hari had already spent fourteen winters amid the snow, at the inn of Schwarenbach.

Ulrich Kunsi listened, without appearing to understand, and looked incessantly at the girl. From time to time he replied: "Yes, Madame Hauser"; but his thoughts seemed far away, and his calm features remained unmoved.

They reached Lake Daube, whose broad, frozen surface reached to the bottom of the valley. On the right, the Daubenhorn showed its black mass, rising up in a peak above the enormous moraines of the Lömmeon glacier, which soared above the Wildstrubel. As they approached the neck of the Gemmi, where the descent to Loëche begins, the immense horizon of the Alps of the Valais, from which the broad, deep valley of the Rhône separated them, came in view.

In the distance, there was a group of white, unequal, flat or pointed mountain summits, which glistened in the sun; the Mischabel with its twin peaks, the huge group of the Weisshorn, the heavy Brunegghorn, the lofty and formidable pyramid of Mont Cervin, slayer of men, and the Dent Blanche, that terrible coquette.

Then beneath them, as at the bottom of a terrible abyss, they saw Loëche, its houses looking like grains of sand which had been thrown into that enormous crevice which finishes and closes the Gemmi, and which opens, down below, on to the Rhône.

The mule stopped at the edge of the path, which turns and twists continually, zigzagging fantastically and strangely along the steep side of the mountain, as far as the almost invisible little village at its feet. The women jumped into the snow, and the two old men joined them.

"Well," father Hauser said, "good-bye, and keep up your spirits till next year, my friends," and old Hari replied: "Till next year."

They embraced each other, and then Madame Hauser in her turn, offered her cheek, and the girl did the same. When Ulrich Kunsi's turn came, he whispered in Louise's ear:

"Do not forget those up yonder," and she replied: "No," in such a low voice, that he guessed what she had said, without hearing it.

"Well, adieu," Jean Hauser repeated, "and don't fall ill." Then, going before the two women, he commenced the descent, and soon all three disappeared at the first turn in the road, while the two men returned to the inn at Schwarenbach.

They walked slowly side by side, without speaking. The parting was over, and they would be alone together for four or five months. Then Gaspard Hari began to relate his life last winter. He had remained with Michael Canol, who was too old now to stand it; for an accident might happen during that long solitude. They had not been dull, however; the only thing was to be resigned to it from the first, and in the end one would find plenty of distraction, games and other means of whiling away the time.

Ulrich Kunsi listened to him with his eyes on the ground, for in thought he was with those who were descending to the village. They soon came in sight of the inn, which was scarcely visible, so small did it look, a mere black speck at the foot of that enormous billow of snow. When they opened the door, Sam, the great curly dog, began to romp round them.

"Come, my boy," old Gaspard said, "we have no women now, so we must get our own dinner ready. Go and peel the potatoes." And they both sat down on wooden stools, and began to put the bread into the soup.

The next morning seemed very long to Kunsi. Old Hari smoked and smoked beside the hearth, while the young man looked out of the window at the snow-covered mountain opposite the house. In the afternoon he went out, and going over the previous day's ground again, he looked for the traces of the mule that had carried the two women; then when he had reached the neck of the Gemmi, he laid himself down on his stomach, and looked at Loëche.

The village, in its rocky pit, was not yet buried under the snow, although the white masses came quite close to it, balked, however, of their prey by the pine woods which protected the hamlet. From his vantage point the low houses looked like paving-stones in a large meadow. Hauser's little daughter was there now in one of those gray-colored houses. In which? Ulrich Kunsi was too far away to be able to make them out separately. How he would have liked to go down while he was yet able!

But the sun had disappeared behind the lofty crest of the Wildstrubel, and the young man returned to the chalet. Daddy Hari was smoking, and, when he saw his mate come in, proposed a game of cards to him. They sat down opposite each other for a long time and played the simple game called *brisque;* then they had supper and went to bed.

The following days were like the first, bright and cold, without any more snow. Old Gaspard spent his afternoons in watching the eagles and other rare birds which ventured on to those frozen heights, while Ulrich journeyed regularly to the neck of the Gemmi to look at the village. In the evening they played at cards, dice, or dominoes, and lost and won trifling sums, just to create an interest in the game.

One morning Hari, who was up first, called his companion. A moving cloud of white spray, deep and light, was falling on them noiselessly, and burying them by degrees under a dark, thick coverlet of foam. This lasted four days and four nights. It was necessary to free the door and the windows, to dig out a passage, and to cut steps to get over this frozen powder, which a twelve-hours' frost had made as hard as the granite of the moraines.

They lived like prisoners, not venturing outside their abode. They had divided their duties and performed them regularly. Ulrich Kunsi undertook the scouring, washing, and everything that belonged to cleanliness. He also chopped up the wood, while Gaspard Hari did the cooking and attended to the fire. Their regular and monotonous work was relieved by long games at cards or dice, but they never quarreled, and were always calm and placid. They were never even impatient or ill-humored, nor did they ever use hard words, for they had laid in a stock of patience for this wintering on the top of the mountain.

Sometimes old Gaspard took his rifle and went after chamois, and occasionally killed one. Then there was a feast in the inn at Schwarenbach, and they reveled in fresh meat. One morning he went out as usual. The thermometer outside marked eighteen degrees of frost, and as the sun had not yet risen, the hunter hoped to surprise the animals at the approaches to the Wildstrubel. Ulrich, being alone, remained in bed until ten o'clock. He was of a sleepy nature, but would not have dared to give way like that to his inclination in the presence of the old guide, who was ever an early riser. He breakfasted leisurely with Sam, who also spent his days and nights in sleeping in front of the fire; then he felt low-spirited and even frightened at the solitude, and was seized by a longing for his daily game of cards, as one is by the domination of an invincible habit. So he went out to meet his companion, who was to return at four o'clock.

The snow had leveled the whole deep valley, filled up the crevasses, obliterated all signs of the two lakes and covered the rocks, so that between the high summits there was nothing but an immense, white, regular, dazzling, and frozen surface. For three weeks, Ulrich had not been to the edge of the precipice, from which he had looked down on to the village, and he wanted to go there before climbing the slopes which led to the Wildstrubel. Loëche was now covered by the snow, and the houses could scarcely be distinguished, hidden as they were by that white cloak.

Turning to the right, Ulrich reached the Lämmern glacier. He strode along with a mountaineer's long swinging pace, striking the snow, which was as hard as a rock, with his iron-shod stick, and with piercing eyes looking for the little black, moving speck in the distance, on that enormous, white expanse.

When he reached the end of the glacier he stopped, and asked himself whether the old man had taken that road, and then he began to walk along the moraines with rapid and uneasy steps. The day was declining; the snow was assuming a rosy tint, and a dry, frozen wind blew in rough gusts over its crystal surface. Ulrich uttered a long, shrill, vibrating call. His voice sped through the deathlike silence in which the mountains were sleeping; it reached into the distance, over the profound and motionless waves of glacial foam, like the cry of a bird over the waves of the sea; then it died away and nothing answered him.

He started off again. The sun had sunk behind the mountain tops, which still were purpled with the reflection from the heavens; but the depths of the valley were becoming gray, and suddenly the young man felt frightened. It seemed to him as if the silence, the cold, the solitude, the wintry death of these mountains were taking possession of him, were stopping and freezing his blood, making his limbs grow stiff, and turning him into a motionless and frozen object; and he began to run rapidly toward the dwelling. The old man, he thought, would have returned during his absence. He had probably taken another road; and would, no doubt, be sitting before the fire, with a dead chamois at his feet.

He soon came in sight of the inn, but no smoke rose from it. Ulrich ran faster. Opening the door he met Sam who ran up to him to greet him, but Gaspard Hari had not returned. Kunsi, in his alarm, turned round suddenly, as if he had expected to find his comrade hidden in a corner. Then he relighted the fire and made the soup; hoping every moment to see the old man come in. From time to time he went out to see if Gaspard were not in sight. It was night now, that wan night of the mountain, a livid night, with the crescent moon, yellow and dim, just disappearing behind the mountain tops, and shining faintly on the edge of the horizon.

Then the young man went in and sat down to warm his hands and feet, while he pictured to himself every possible sort of accident. Gaspard might have broken a leg, have fallen into a crevasse, have taken a false step and dislocated his ankle. Perhaps he was lying on the snow, overcome and stiff with the cold, in agony of mind, lost and perhaps shouting for help, calling with all his might, in the silence of the night.

But where? The mountain was so vast, so rugged, so dangerous in places, especially at that time of the year, that it would have required ten or twenty guides walking for a week in all directions, to find a man in that immense space. Ulrich Kunsi, however, made up his mind to set out with Sam, if Gaspard did not return by one in the morning; and he made his preparations.

He put provisions for two days into a bag, took his steel climbing-irons, tied a long, thin, strong rope round his waist and looked to see that his iron-shod stick and his ax, which served to cut steps in the ice, were in order. Then he waited. The fire was burning on the hearth, the great dog was snoring in front of it, and the clock was ticking in its case of resounding wood, as regularly as a heart beating.

He waited, his ears on the alert for distant sounds, and shivered when the wind blew against the roof and the walls. It struck twelve, and he trembled. Then, as he felt frightened and shivery, he put some water on the fire, so that he might have hot coffee before starting. When the clock struck one he got up, woke Sam, opened the door and went off in the direction of the Wildstrubel. For five hours he ascended, scaling the rocks by means of his climbing-irons, cutting into the ice, advancing continually, and occasionally hauling up the dog, who remained below at the foot of some slope that was too steep for him, by means of the rope. About six o'clock he reached one of the summits to which old Gaspard often came after chamois, and he waited till it should be daylight.

The sky was growing pale overhead, and suddenly a strange light, springing, nobody could tell whence, suddenly illuminated the immense ocean of pale mountain peaks, which stretched for many leagues around him. It seemed as if this vague brightness arose from the snow itself, in order to spread itself into space. By degrees the highest and most distant summits assumed a delicate, fleshlike rose color, and the red sun appeared behind the ponderous giants of the Bernese Alps.

Ulrich Kunsi set off again, walking like a hunter, stooping and looking for any traces, and saying to his dog: "Seek old fellow, seek!"

He was descending the mountain now, scanning the depths closely, and from time to time shouting, uttering a loud, prolonged familiar cry which soon died away in that silent vastness. Then, he put his ear to the ground, to listen. He thought he could distinguish a voice, and so he began to run and shout again. But he heard nothing more and sat down, worn out and in despair. Toward midday he breakfasted and gave Sam, who was as tired as himself, something to eat also; then he recommenced his search.

When evening came he was still walking, having traveled more than thirty miles over the mountains. As he was too far away to return home, and too tired to drag himself along any further, he dug a hole in the snow and crouched in it with his dog, under a blanket which he had brought with him. The man and the dog lay side by side, warming themselves one against the other, but frozen to the marrow, nevertheless. Ulrich scarcely slept, his mind haunted by visions and his limbs shaking with cold.

Day was breaking when he got up. His legs were as stiff as iron bars, and his spirits so low that he was ready to weep, while his heart was beating so that he almost fell with excitement whenever he thought he heard a noise.

Suddenly he imagined that he *also* was going to die of cold in the midst of this vast solitude. The terror of such a death roused his energies and gave him renewed vigor. He was descending toward the inn, falling down and getting up again, and followed at a distance by Sam, who was limping on three legs. They did not reach Schwarenbach until four o'clock in the afternoon. The house was empty, and the young man made a fire, had something to eat, and

went to sleep, so worn-out that he did not think of
anything more.

He slept for a long time, for a very long time, the
unconquerable sleep of exhaustion. But suddenly a
voice, a cry, a name: "Ulrich," aroused him from
his profound slumber, and made him sit up in bed.
Had he been dreaming? Was it one of those strange
appeals which cross the dreams of disquieted minds?
No, he heard it still, that reverberating cry,—which
had entered at his ears and remained in his brain,—
thrilling him to the tips of his sinewy fingers. Certainly, somebody had cried out, and called: "Ulrich!"
There was somebody there, near the house, there
could be no doubt of that, and he opened the door
and shouted: "Is it you, Gaspard?" with all the
strength of his lungs. But there was no reply, no
murmur, no groan, nothing. It was quite dark, and
the snow looked wan.

The wind had risen, that icy wind which cracks
the rocks, and leaves nothing alive on those deserted
heights. It came in sudden gusts, more parching and
more deadly than the burning wind of the desert,
and again Ulrich shouted: "Gaspard! Gaspard! Gaspard!" Then he waited again. Everything was
silent on the mountain! Then he shook with terror,
and with a bound he was inside the inn. He shut
and bolted the door, and then fell into a chair,
trembling all over, for he felt certain that his comrade
had called him at the moment of dissolution.

He was certain of that, as certain as one is of conscious life or of taste when eating. Old Gaspard Hari
had been dying for two days and three nights somewhere, in some hole, in one of those deep, untrodden

ravines whose whiteness is more sinister than subter-
ranean darkness. He had been dying for two days
and three nights and he had just then died, thinking
of his comrade. His soul, almost before it was released, had taken its flight to the inn where Ulrich
was sleeping, and it had called him by that terrible
and mysterious power which the spirits of the dead
possess. That voiceless soul had cried to the worn-
out soul of the sleeper; it had uttered its last fare-
well, or its reproach, or its curse on the man who
had not searched carefully enough.

And Ulrich felt that it was there, quite close to
him, behind the wall, behind the door which he had
just fastened. It was wandering about, like a night
bird which skims a lighted window with his wings,
and the terrified young man was ready to scream
with horror. He wanted to run away, but did not
dare go out; he did not dare, and would never dare
in the future, for that phantom would remain there
day and night, round the inn, as long as the old
man's body was not recovered and deposited in the
consecrated earth of a churchyard.

Daylight came, and Kunsi recovered· some of his
courage with the return of the bright sun. He prepared his meal, gave his dog some food, and then
remained motionless on a chair, tortured at heart as
he thought of the old man lying on the snow. Then,
as soon as night once more covered the mountains,
new terrors assailed him. He now walked up and
down the dark kitchen, which was scarcely lighted
by the flame of one candle. He walked from one
end of it to the other with great strides, listening,
listening to hear the terrible cry of the preceding night

again break the dreary silence outside. He felt himself alone, unhappy man, as no man had ever been
alone before ! Alone in this immense desert of snow,
alone five thousand feet above the inhabited earth,
above human habitations, above that stirring, noisy,
palpitating life, alone under an icy sky ! A mad
longing impelled him to run away, no matter where,
to get down to Loëche by flinging himself over the
precipice; but he did not even dare to open the door,
as he felt sure that the other, the *dead*, man would
bar his road, so that he might not be obliged to
remain up there alone.

Toward midnight, tired with walking, worn-out
by grief and fear, he fell into a doze in his chair, for
he was afraid of his bed, as one is of a haunted
spot. But suddenly the strident cry of the preceding
evening pierced his ears, so shrill that Ulrich stretched
out his arms to repulse the ghost, and he fell on to
his back with his chair.

Sam, who was awakened by the noise, began to
howl as frightened dogs do, and trotted all about the
house trying to find out where the danger came
from. When he got to the door, he sniffed beneath
it, smelling vigorously, with his coat bristling and
his tail stiff while he growled angrily. Kunsi, who
was terrified, jumped up, and holding his chair by
one leg, cried: "Don't come in, don't come in,
or I shall kill you." And the dog, excited by this
threat, barked angrily at that invisible enemy who
defied his master's voice. By degrees, however, he
quieted dcwn, came back and stretched himself in
front of the fire. But he was uneasy, and kept his
head up, and growled between his teeth.

Ulrich, in turn, recovered his senses, but as he felt faint with terror, he went and got a bottle of brandy out of the sideboard, and drank off several glasses, one after another, at a gulp. His ideas became vague, his courage revived, and a feverish glow ran through his veins.

He ate scarcely anything the next day, and limited himself to alcohol; so he lived for several days, like a drunken brute. As soon as he thought of Gaspard Hari he began to drink again, and went on drinking until he fell on to the floor, overcome by intoxication. And there he remained on his face, dead drunk, his limbs benumbed, and snoring with his face to the ground. But scarcely had he digested the maddening and burning liquor, than the same cry, "Ulrich," woke him like a bullet piercing his brain, and he got up, still staggering, stretching out his hands to save himself from falling, and calling to Sam to help him. And the dog, who appeared to be going mad like his master, rushed to the door, scratched it with his claws, and gnawed it with his long white teeth, while the young man, his neck thrown back, and his head in the air, drank the brandy in gulps, as if it were cold water, so that it might by and by send his thoughts, his frantic terror, and his memory, to sleep again.

In three weeks he had consumed all his stock of ardent spirits. But his continual drunkenness only lulled his terror, which awoke more furiously than ever, as soon as it was impossible for him to calm it by drinking. His fixed idea, which had been intensified by a month of drunkenness, and which was continually increasing in his absolute solitude, penetrated him like a gimlet. He now walked about his house like a wild beast in its cage, putting his ear to the door to listen if the other were there, and defying him through the wall. Then as soon as he dozed, overcome by fatigue, he heard the voice which made him leap to his feet.

At last one night, as cowards do when driven to extremity, he sprang to the door and opened it, to see who was calling him, and to force him to keep quiet. But such a gust of cold wind blew into his face that it chilled him to the bone. He closed and bolted the door again immediately, without noticing that Sam had rushed out. Then, as he was shivering with cold, he threw some wood on the fire, and sat down in front of it to warm himself. But suddenly he started, for somebody was scratching at the wall, and crying. In desperation he called out: "Go away!" but was answered by another long, sorrowful wail.

Then all his remaining senses forsook him, from sheer fright. He repeated: "Go away!" and turned round to find some corner in which to hide, while the other person went round the house still crying, and rubbing against the wall. Ulrich went to the oak sideboard, which was full of plates and dishes and of provisions, and lifting it up with superhuman strength, he dragged it to the door, so as to form a barricade. Then piling up all the rest of the furniture, the mattresses, paillasses, and chairs, he stopped up the windows as men do when assailed by an enemy.

But the person outside now uttered long, plaintive, mournful groans, to which the young man replied by similar groans, and thus days and nights passed without their ceasing to howl at each other. The one was continually walking round the house and scraped the walls with his nails so vigorously that it seemed as if he wished to destroy them, while the other, inside, followed all his movements, stooping down, and holding his ear to the walls, and replying to all his appeals with terrible cries. One evening, however, Ulrich heard nothing more, and he sat down, so overcome by fatigue that he went to sleep immediately, and awoke in the morning without a thought, without any recollection of what had happened, just as if his head had been emptied during his heavy sleep. But he felt hungry, and he ate.

The winter was over, and the Gemmi pass was practicable again, so the Hauser family started off to return to their inn. As soon as they had reached the top of the ascent, the women mounted their mule, and spoke about the two men who they would meet again shortly. They were, indeed, rather surprised that neither of them had come down a few days before, as soon as the road became passable, in order to tell them all about their long winter sojourn. At last, however, they saw the inn, still covered with snow, like a quilt. The door and the windows were closed, but a little smoke was coming out of the chimney, which reassured old Hauser; on going up to the door, however, he saw the skeleton of an animal which had been torn to pieces by the eagles, a large skeleton lying on its side.

They all looked closely at it, and the mother said: "That must be Sam." Then she shouted: "Hi !

Gaspard!" A cry from the interior of the house
answered her, so sharp a cry that one might have
thought some animal uttered it. Old Hauser repeated:
"Hi! Gaspard!" and they heard another cry, similar to the first.

Then the three men, the father and the two sons,
tried to open the door, but it resisted their efforts.
From the empty cow-stall they took a beam to serve
as a battering-ram, and hurled it against the door
with all their might. The wood gave way, and the
boards flew into splinters; then the house was shaken
by a loud voice, and inside, behind the sideboard
which was overturned, they saw a man standing
upright, his hair falling on to his shoulders and a
beard descending to his breast, with shining eyes
and nothing but rags to cover him. They did not
recognize him, but Louise Hauser exclaimed: "It is
Ulrich, mother." And her mother declared that it
was Ulrich, although his hair was white.

He allowed them to go up to him, and to touch
him, but he did not reply to any of their questions,
and they were obliged to take him to Loëche, where
the doctors found that he was mad. Nobody ever
knew what had become of his companion.

Little Louise Hauser nearly died that summer of
decline, which the medical men attributed to the cold
air of the mountains.

A FAMILY

I WAS going to see my friend Simon Radevin once more, for I had not seen him for fifteen years. Formerly he was my most intimate friend, and I used to spend long, quiet, and happy evenings with him. He was one of those men to whom one tells the most intimate affairs of the heart, and in whom one finds, when quietly talking, rare, clever, ingenious, and refined thoughts — thoughts which stimulate and capture the mind.

For years we had scarcely been separated: we had lived, traveled, thought, and dreamed together; had liked the same things with the same liking, admired the same books, comprehended the same works, shivered with the same sensations, and very often laughed at the same individuals, whom we understood completely. by merely exchanging a glance.

Then he married — quite unexpectedly married a little girl from the provinces, who had come to Paris in search of a husband. How ever could that little, thin, insipidly fair girl, with her weak hands, her light, vacant eyes, and her clear, silly voice, who was exactly like a hundred thousand marriageable dolls, have picked up that intelligent, clever young fellow? Can anyone understand these things? No doubt he had hoped for happiness, simple, quiet, and long-enduring happiness, in the arms of a good, tender, and faithful woman; he had seen all that in the transparent looks of that schoolgirl with light hair.

He had not dreamed of the fact that an active, living, and vibrating man grows tired as soon as he has comprehended the stupid reality of a common-place life, unless indeed, he becomes so brutalized as to be callous to externals.

What would he be like when I met him again? Still lively, witty, light-hearted, and enthusiastic, or in a state of mental torpor through provincial life? A man can change a great deal in the course of fifteen years!

The train stopped at a small station, and as I got out of the carriage, a stout, a very stout man with red cheeks and a big stomach rushed up to me with open arms, exclaiming: "George!"

I embraced him, but I had not recognized him, and then I said, in astonishment: "By Jove! You have not grown thin!"

And he replied with a laugh: "What did you expect? Good living, a good table, and good nights! Eating and sleeping, that is my existence!"

I looked at him closely, trying to find the features I held so dear in that broad face. His eyes alone had not altered, but I no longer saw the same looks in them, and I said to myself: "If looks be the reflection of the mind, the thoughts in that head are not what they used to be—those thoughts which I knew so well."

Yet his eyes were bright, full of pleasure and friendship, but they had not that clear, intelligent expression which tells better than do words the value of the mind. Suddenly he said to me:

"Here are my two eldest children." A girl of fourteen, who was almost a woman, and a boy of thirteen, in the dress of a pupil from a lycée, came forward in a hesitating and awkward manner, and I said in a low voice: "Are they yours?"

"Of course they are," he replied laughing.

"How many have you?"

"Five! There are three more indoors."

He said that in a proud, self-satisfied, almost triumphant manner, and I felt profound pity, mingled with a feeling of vague contempt for this vainglorious and simple reproducer of his species, who spent his nights in his country house in uxorious pleasures.

I got into a carriage, which he drove himself, and we set off through the town, a dull, sleepy, gloomy town where nothing was moving in the streets save a few dogs and two or three maidservants. Here and there a shopkeeper standing at his door took off his hat, and Simon returned the salute and told me the man's name—no doubt to show me that he knew all the inhabitants personally. The thought struck me that he was thinking of becoming a candidate for the Chamber of Deputies, that dream of all who have buried themselves in the provinces.

We were soon out of the town; the carriage

turned into a garden which had some pretensions to a park, and stopped in front of a turreted house, which tried to pass for a château.

"That is my den," Simon said, so that he might be complimented on it, and I replied that it was delightful.

A lady appeared on the steps, dressed up for a visitor, her hair done for a visitor, and with phrases ready prepared for a visitor. She was no longer the light-haired, insipid girl I had seen in church fifteen years previously, but a stout lady in curls and flounces, one of those ladies of uncertain age, without intellect, without any of those things which constitute a woman. In short she was a mother, a stout, commonplace mother, a human layer and brood mare, a machine of flesh which procreates, without mental care save for her children and her housekeeping book.

She welcomed me, and I went into the hall, where three children, ranged according to their height, were ranked for review, like firemen before a mayor. "Ah! ah! so there are the others?" said I. And Simon, who was radiant with pleasure, named them: "Jean, Sophie, and Gontran."

The door of the drawing-room was open. I went in, and in the depths of an easy-chair I saw something trembling, a man, an old, paralyzed man. Madame Radevin came forward and said: "This is my grandfather, Monsieur; he is eighty-seven." And then she shouted into the shaking old man's ears: "This is a friend of Simon's, grandpapa."

The old gentleman tried to say "Good day" to me, and he muttered: "Oua, oua, oua," and waved his hand.

I took a seat saying: "You are very kind, Monsieur."

Simon had just come in, and he said with a laugh: "So! You have made grandpapa's acquaintance. He is priceless, is that old man. He is the delight of the children, and he is so greedy that he almost kills himself at every meal. You have no idea what he would eat if he were allowed to do as he pleased. But you will see, you will see. He looks all the sweets over as if they were so many girls. You have never seen anything funnier; you will see it presently."

I was then shown to my room to change my dress for dinner, and hearing a great clatter behind me on the stairs, I turned round and saw that all the children were following me behind their father — to do me honor, no doubt.

My windows looked out on to a plain, a bare, interminable plain, an ocean of grass, of wheat, and of oats, without a clump of trees or any rising ground, a striking and melancholy picture of the life which they must be leading in that house.

A bell rang; it was for dinner, and so I went downstairs. Madame Radevin took my arm in a ceremonious manner, and we went into the dining-room. A footman wheeled in the old man's arm-chair, who gave a greedy and curious look at the dessert, as with difficulty he turned his shaking head from one dish to the other.

Simon rubbed his hands, saying: "You will be amused." All the children understood that I was going to be indulged with the sight of their greedy grandfather and they began to laugh accordingly, while their mother merely smiled and shrugged her shoulders. Simon, making a speaking trumpet of his hands, shouted at the old man: "This evening there is sweet rice-cream," and the wrinkled face of the grandfather brightened, he trembled violently all over, showing that he had understood and was very pleased. The dinner began.

"Just look!" Simon whispered. The grandfather did not like the soup, and refused to eat it; but he was made to, on account of his health. The footman forced the spoon into his mouth, while the old man blew energetically, so as not to swallow the soup, which was thus scattered like a stream of water on to the table and over his neighbors. The children shook with delight at the spectacle, while their father, who was also amused, said: "Isn't the old man funny?"

During the whole meal they were all taken up solely with him. With his eyes he devoured the dishes which were put on the table, and with trembling hands tried to seize them and pull them to him. They put them almost within his reach to see his useless efforts, his trembling clutches at them, the piteous appeal of his whole nature, of his eyes, of his mouth, and of his nose as he smelled them. He slobbered on to his table napkin with eagerness, while uttering inarticulate grunts, and the whole family was highly amused at this horrible and grotesque scene.

Then they put a tiny morsel on to his plate, which he ate with feverish gluttony, in order to get something more as soon as possible. When the rice-cream was brought in, he nearly had a fit, and groaned with greediness. Gontran called out to

him: "You have eaten too much already; you will
have no more." And they pretended not to give him
any. Then he began to cry—cry and tremble more
violently than ever, while all the children laughed.
At last, however, they gave him his helping, a very
small piece. As he ate the first mouthful of the pud-
ding, he made a comical and greedy noise in his throat,
and a movement with his neck like ducks do, when
they swallow too large a morsel, and then, when he
had done, he began to stamp his feet, so as to get
more.

I was seized with pity for this pitiable and ridiculous Tantalus, and interposed on his behalf: "Please,
will you not give him a little more rice?"

But Simon replied: "Oh! no my dear fellow, if
he were to eat too much, it might harm him at his
age."

I held my tongue, and thought over these words.
Oh! ethics! Oh! logic! Oh! wisdom! At his age!
So they deprived him of his only remaining pleasure
out of regard for his health! His health! What
would he do with it, inert and trembling wreck that
he was? They were taking care of his life, so they
said. His life? How many days? Ten, twenty, fifty,
or a hundred? Why? For his own sake? Or to
preserve for some time longer, the spectacle of his
impotent greediness in the family.

There was nothing left for him to do in this life,
nothing whatever. He had one single wish left, one
sole pleasure; why not grant him that last solace
constantly, until he died?

After playing cards for a long time, I went up to
my room and to bed; I was low-spirited and sad,

sad, sad! I sat at my window, but I heard nothing
but the beautiful warbling of a bird in a tree, somewhere in the distance. No doubt the bird was singing thus in a low voice during the night, to lull his
mate, who was sleeping on her eggs.

And I thought of my poor friend's five children,
and to myself pictured him snoring by the side of
his ugly wife.

BELLFLOWER *

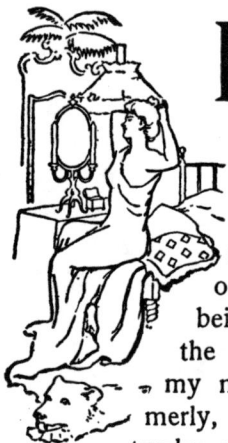

How strange are those old recollections which haunt us, without
our being able to get rid of them!
This one is so very old that I
cannot understand how it has clung
so vividly and tenaciously to my
memory. Since then I have seen so
many sinister things, either affecting
or terrible, that I am astonished at not
being able to pass a single day without
the face of Mother Bellflower recurring to
my mind's eye, just as I knew her formerly, long, long ago, when I was ten or
twelve years old.

She was an old seamstress who came to my
parents' house once a week, every Thursday, to mend
the linen. My parents lived in one of those country
houses called châteaux, which are merely old houses
with pointed roofs, to which are attached three or
four adjacent farms.

---

* Clochette.

The village, a large village, almost a small market town, was a few hundred yards off, and nestled round the church, a red brick church, which had become black with age.

Well, every Thursday Mother Bellflower came between half past six and seven in the morning, and went immediately into the linen-room and began to work. She was a tall, thin, bearded or rather hairy woman, for she had a beard all over her face, a surprising, an unexpected beard, growing in improbable tufts, in curly bunches which looked as if they had been sown by a madman over that great face, the face of a gendarme in petticoats. She had them on her nose, under her nose, round her nose, on her chin, on her cheeks; and her eyebrows, which were extraordinarily thick and long, and quite gray, bushy and bristling, looked exactly like a pair of mustaches stuck on there by mistake.

She limped, but not like lame people generally do, but like a ship pitching. When she planted her great, bony, vibrant body on her sound leg, she seemed to be preparing to mount some enormous wave, and then suddenly she dipped as if to disappear in an abyss, and buried herself in the ground. Her walk reminded one of a ship in a storm, and her head, which was always covered with an enormous white cap, whose ribbons fluttered down her back, seemed to traverse the horizon from North to South and from South to North, at each limp.

I adored Mother Bellflower. As soon as I was up I used to go into the linen-room, where I found her installed at work, with a foot-warmer under her feet. As soon as I arrived, she made me take the foot-warmer and sit upon it, so that I might not catch cold in that large, chilly room under the roof.

"That draws the blood from your head," she would say to me.

She told me stories, while mending the linen with her long, crooked, nimble fingers; behind her magnifying spectacles, for age had impaired her sight, her eyes appeared enormous to me, strangely profound, double.

As far as I can remember from the things which she told me and by which my childish heart was moved, she had the large heart of a poor woman. She told me what had happened in the village, how a cow had escaped from the cowhouse and had been found the next morning in front of Prosper Malet's mill, looking at the sails turning, or about a hen's egg which had been found in the church belfry without anyone being able to understand what creature had been there to lay it, or the queer story of Jean Pila's dog, who had gone ten leagues to bring back his master's breeches which a tramp had stolen while they were hanging up to dry out of doors, after he had been caught in the rain. She told me these simple adventures in such a manner that in my mind they assumed the proportions of never-to-be-forgotten dramas, of grand and mysterious poems; and the ingenious stories invented by the poets, which my mother told me in the evening, had none of the flavor, none of the fullness or of the vigor. of the peasant woman's narratives.

Well, one Thursday when I had spent all the morning in listening to Mother Clochette, I wanted to go upstairs to her again during the day, after picking

hazelnuts with the manservant in the wood behind
the farm. I remember it all as clearly as what happened only yesterday.

On opening the door of the linen-room, I saw the
old seamstress lying on the floor by the side of her
chair, her face turned down and her arms stretched
out, but still holding her needle in one hand and
one of my shirts in the other. One of her legs
in a blue stocking, the longer one no doubt, was
extended under her chair, and her spectacles glistened by the wall, where they had rolled away from
her.

I ran away uttering shrill cries. They all came
running, and in a few minutes I was told that Mother
Clochette was dead.

I cannot describe the profound, poignant, terrible
emotion which stirred my childish heart. I went
slowly down into the drawing-room and hid myself
in a dark corner, in the depths of a great, old armchair, where I knelt and wept. I remained there for
a long time no doubt, for night came on. Suddenly
some one came in with a lamp — without seeing me,
however — and I heard my father and mother talking
with the medical man, whose voice I recognized.

He had been sent for immediately, and he was
explaining the cause of the accident, of which I understood nothing, however. Then he sat down and
had a glass of liqueur and a biscuit.

He went on talking, and what he then said will
remain engraved on my mind until I die! I think
that I can give the exact words which he used.

"Ah!" said he, "the poor woman! she broke her
leg the day of my arrival here. I had not even had

time to wash my hands after getting off the diligence before I was sent for in all haste, for it was a bad case, very bad.

"She was seventeen, and a pretty girl, very pretty! Would anyone believe it? I have never told her story before, in fact no one but myself and one other person, who is no longer living in this part of the country, ever knew it. Now that she is dead, I may be less discreet.

"A young assistant teacher had just come to live in the village; he was good-looking and had the bearing of a soldier. All the girls ran after him, but he was disdainful. Besides that, he was very much afraid of his superior, the schoolmaster, old Grabu, who occasionally got out of bed the wrong foot first.

"Old Grabu already employed pretty Hortense, who has just died here, and who was afterward nicknamed Clochette. The assistant master singled out the pretty young girl, who was no doubt flattered at being chosen by this disdainful conqueror; at any rate, she fell in love with him, and he succeeded in persuading her to give him a first meeting in the hayloft behind the school, at night, after she had done her day's sewing.

"She pretended to go home, but instead of going downstairs when she left the Grabus', she went upstairs and hid among the hay, to wait for her lover. He soon joined her, and he was beginning to say pretty things to her, when the door of the hayloft opened and the schoolmaster appeared, and asked: 'What are you doing up there, Sigisbert?' Feeling sure that he would be caught. the young schoolmaster lost his presence of mind and replied stupidly: 'I came up here to rest a little among the bundles of hay, Monsieur Grabu.'

"The loft was very large and absolutely dark. Sigisbert pushed the frightened girl to the further end and said: 'Go there and hide yourself. I shall lose my situation, so get away and hide yourself.'

"When the schoolmaster heard the whispering, he continued: 'Why, you are not by yourself?'

"'Yes I am, Monsieur Grabu!'

"'But you are not, for you are talking.'

"'I swear I am, Monsieur Grabu.'

"'I will soon find out,' the old man replied, and double-locking the door, he went down to get a light.

"Then the young man, who was a coward such as one sometimes meets, lost his head, and he repeated, having grown furious all of a sudden: 'Hide yourself, so that he may not find you. You will deprive me of my bread for my whole life; you will ruin my whole career! Do hide yourself!'

"They could hear the key turning in the lock again, and Hortense ran to the window which looked out on to the street, opened it quickly, and then in a low and determined voice said: 'You will come and pick me up when he is gone,' and she jumped out.

"Old Grabu found nobody, and went down again in great surprise. A quarter of an hour later, Monsieur Sigisbert came to me and related his adventure. The girl had remained at the foot of the wall unable to get up, as she had fallen from the second story, and I went with him to fetch her. It was raining in torrents, and I brought the unfortunate girl home with me, for the right leg was broken in three places, and the bones had come out through the flesh. She did not complain, and merely said, with admirable resignation: 'I am punished, well punished!'

"I sent for assistance and for the workgirl's friends and told them a made-up story of a runaway carriage which had knocked her down and lamed her, outside my door. They believed me, and the gendarmes for a whole month tried in vain to find the author of this accident.

"That is all! Now I say that this woman was a heroine, and had the fiber of those who accomplish the grandest deeds in history.

"That was her only love affair, and she died a virgin. She was a martyr, a noble soul, a sublimely devoted woman! And if I did not absolutely admire her, I should not have told you this story, which I would never tell anyone during her life: you understand why."

The doctor ceased; mamma cried and papa said some words which I did not catch; then they left the room, and I remained on my knees in the armchair and sobbed, while I heard a strange noise of heavy footsteps and something knocking against the side of the staircase.

They were carrying away Clochette's body.

IN THE WOOD

THE mayor was just going to sit down to breakfast, when he was told that the rural policeman was waiting for him at the *mairie* with two prisoners. He went there immediately, and found old Hochedur standing up and watching a middle-class couple of mature years with stern looks.

The man, a fat old fellow with a red nose and white hair, seemed utterly dejected; while the woman, a little roundabout, stout creature, with shining cheeks, looked at the agent who had arrested them with defiant eyes.

"What is it? What is it, Hochedur?"

The rural policeman made his deposition. He had gone out that morning at his usual time, in order to patrol his beat from the forest of Champioux as far as the boundaries of Argenteuil. He had not noticed anything unusual in the country except that it was a fine day, and that the wheat was doing well, when the son of old Bredel, who was going over his vines a second time, called out to him: "Here, daddy Hochedur, go and have a look into the skirts of the wood, in the first thicket, and you will catch a pair of pigeons there who must be a hundred and thirty years old between them!"

He went in the direction that had been indicated to him, and had gone into the thicket. There he heard words and gasps, which made him suspect a flagrant breach of morality. Advancing, therefore, on his hands and knees as if to surprise a poacher, he had arrested this couple, at the very moment when they were going to abandon themselves to their natural instincts.

The mayor looked at the culprits in astonishment, for the man was certainly sixty, and the woman fifty-five at least. So he began to question them, beginning with the man, who replied in such a weak voice, that he could scarcely be heard.

"What is your name?"

"Nicolas Beaurain."

"Your occupation?"

"Haberdasher, in the Rue des Martyrs, in Paris."

"What were you doing in the wood?"

The haberdasher remained silent, with his eyes on his fat stomach, and his hand resting on his thighs, and the mayor continued:

"Do you deny what the officer of the municipal authorities states?"

"No, Monsieur."

"So you confess it?"

"Yes, Monsieur."

"What have you to say in your defense?"

"Nothing, Monsieur."

"Where did you meet the partner in your misde-
meanor?"

"She is my wife, Monsieur."

"Your wife?"

"Yes, Monsieur."

"Then—then—you do not live together in
Paris?"

"I beg your pardon, Monsieur, but we are living
together!"

"But in that case you must be mad, altogether
mad, my dear sir, to get caught like that in the
country at ten o'clock in the morning."

The haberdasher seemed ready to cry with shame,
and he murmured: "It was she who enticed me! I
told her it was very stupid, but when a woman has
got a thing into her head, you know, you cannot get
it out."

The mayor, who liked open speaking, smiled and
replied:

"In your case, the contrary ought to have happened. You would not be here, if she had had the
idea only in her head."

Then Monsieur Beaurain was seized with rage, and
turning to his wife, he said: "Do you see to what
you have brought us with your poetry? And now
we shall have to go before the Courts, at our age, for
a breach of morals! And we shall have to shut up
the shop, sell our good-will, and go to some other
neighborhood! That's what it has come to!"

Madame Beaurain got up, and without looking at
her husband, explained herself without any embarrassment, without useless modesty, and almost without
hesitation.

"Of course, Monsieur, I know that we have made ourselves ridiculous. Will you allow me to plead my cause like an advocate, or rather like a poor woman; and I hope that you will be kind enough to send us home, and to spare us the disgrace of a prosecution.

"Years ago, when I was young, I made Monsieur Beaurain's acquaintance on Sunday in this neighborhood. He was employed in a draper's shop, and I was a saleswoman in a ready-made clothing establishment. I remember it, as if it were yesterday. I used to come and spend Sundays here occasionally with a friend of mine, Rose Levèque, with whom I lived in the Rue Pigalle, and Rose had a sweetheart, while I had not. He used to bring us here, and one Saturday, he told me laughing, that he should bring a friend with him the next day. I quite understood what he meant, but I replied that it would be no good; for I was virtuous, Monsieur.

"The next day we met Monsieur Beaurain at the railway station. In those days he was good-looking, but I had made up my mind not to yield to him, and I did not yield. Well, we arrived at Bezons. It was a lovely day, the sort of day that tickles your heart. When it is fine even now, just as it used to be formerly, I grow quite foolish, and when I am in the country, I utterly lose my head. The verdure, the swallows flying so swiftly, the smell of the grass, the scarlet poppies, the daisies, all that makes me quite excited! It is like champagne when one is not used to it!

"Well, it was lovely weather, warm and bright, and it seemed to penetrate into your body by your eyes when you looked, and by your mouth when you breathed. Rose and Simon hugged and kissed each other every minute, and that gave me something to look at! Monsieur Beaurain and I walked behind them, without speaking much, for when people do not know each other well, they cannot find much to talk about. He looked timid, and I liked to see his embarrassment. At last we got to the little wood; it was as cool as in a bath there, and we all four sat down. Rose and her lover joked me because I looked rather stern, but you will understand that I could not be otherwise. And then they began to kiss and hug again, without putting any more restraint upon themselves than if we had not been there. Then they whispered together, and got up and went off among the trees without saying a word. You may fancy how I felt, alone with this young fellow whom I saw for the first time. I felt so confused at seeing them go that it gave me courage and I began to talk. I asked him what his business was, and he said he was a linen draper's assistant, as I told you just now. We talked for a few minutes and that made him bold, and he wanted to take liberties with me, but I told him sharply to keep his own place. Is not that true, Monsieur Beaurain?"

Monsieur Beaurain, who was looking at his feet in confusion, did not reply, and she continued: "Then he saw that I was virtuous, and he began to make love to me nicely, like an honorable man, and from that time he came every Sunday, for he was very much in love with me. I was very fond of him also, very fond of him! He was a good-looking fellow, formerly, and in short he married me the next September, and we started business in the Rue des Martyrs.

"It was a hard struggle for some years, Monsieur. Business did not prosper, and we could not afford many country excursions, and then we became unaccustomed to them. One has other things in one's head and thinks more of the cash box than of pretty speeches when one is in business. We were growing old by degrees without perceiving it, like quiet people who do not think much about love. But one does not regret anything as long as one does not notice what one has lost.

"And after that, Monsieur, business went bettei, and we became tranquil as to the future! Then, you see, I do not exactly know what passed within me — no, I really do not know, but I began to dream like a little boarding-school girl. The sight of the little carts full of flowers which are peddled about the streets made me cry; the smell of violets sought me out in my easy-chair, behind my cash box, and made my heart beat! Then I used to get up and go on to the doorstep to look at the blue sky between the roofs. When one looks at the sky from a street, it seems like a river flowing over Paris, winding as it goes, and the swallows pass to and fro in it like fish. These sort of things are very stupid at my age! But what can one do, Monsieur, when one has worked all one's life? A moment comes in which one perceives that one could have done something else, and then, one regrets, oh! yes, one feels great regret! Just think that for twenty years I might have gone and had kisses in the woods, like other women. I used to think how delightful it would be to lie under the trees, loving some one! And I thought of it every day and every night! I dreamed of the moonlight on the water, until I felt inclined to drown myself.

"ʲ did not venture to speak to Monsieur Beaurain about this at first. I knew that he would make fun of me, and send me back to sell my needles and cotton! And then, to speak the truth, Monsieur Beaurain never said much to me, but when I looked in the glass, I also understood quite well that I also no longer appealed to anyone!

"Well, I made up my mind, and I proposed an excursion into the country to him, to the place where we had first become acquainted. He agreed without any distrust, and we arrived here this morning, about nine o'clock.

"I felt quite young again when I got among the corn, for a woman's heart never grows old! And really, I no longer saw my husband as he is at present, but just like he was formerly! That I will swear to you, Monsieur. As true as I am standing here, I was intoxicated. I began to kiss him, and he was more surprised than if I had tried to murder him. He kept saying to me: 'Why, you must be mad this morning! What is the matter with you—' I did not listen to him, I only listened to my own heart, and I made him come into the wood with me. There is the story. I have spoken the truth, Monsieur le Maire, the whole truth."

The mayor was a sensible man. He rose from his chair, smiled, and said: "Go in peace, Madame, and sin no more—under the trees."

THE MARQUIS DE FUMEROL

ROGER DE TOUMEVILLE was sitting astride a chair in the midst of his friends and talking; he held a cigar in his hand, and from time to time took a whiff and blew out a small cloud of smoke.

"We were at dinner when a letter was brought in, and my father opened it. You know my father, who thinks that he is king of France *ad interim*. I call him Don Quixote, because for twelve years he has been running a tilt against the windmill of the Republic, without quite knowing whether it was in the name of Bourbon or of Orléans. At present he is holding the lance in the name of Orléans alone, because there is nobody else left. In any case, he thinks himself the first gentleman in France, the best known, the most influential, the head of the party; and as he is an irremovable senator, he thinks that the neighboring kings' thrones are very insecure.

"As for my mother, she is my father's inspiration, the soul of the kingdom and of religion, the right arm of God on earth, and the scourge of evil-thinkers.

"Well, this letter was brought in while we were at dinner. My father opened and read it, and then he said to my mother: 'Your brother is dying.' She grew very pale. My uncle was scarcely ever mentioned in the house, and I did not know him at all; all I knew from public talk was that he had led, and was still leading, the life of a buffoon. After having spent his fortune with an incalculable number of women, he had only retained two mistresses, with whom he was living in small apartments in the Rue des Martyrs.

"An ex-peer of France and ex-colonel of cavalry, it was said that he believed in neither God nor devil. Having no faith, therefore, in a future life he had abused this present life in every way, and had become a living wound to my mother's heart.

"'Give me that letter, Paul,' she said, and when she had read it, I asked for it in my turn. Here it is:

"'MONSIEUR LE COMTE: I think I ought to let you know that your brother-in-law, Count Fumerol, is going to die. Perhaps you would make preparations and not forget that I told you.

"'Your servant, MÉLANI.'

"'We must think,' my father murmured. 'In my position, I ought to watch over your brother's last moments.'

"My mother continued: 'I will send for Abbé Poivron and ask his advice, and then I will go to my brother's with him and Roger. Stop here, Paul, for you must not compromise yourself; but a woman can, and ought, to do these things. For a politician in your position, it is another matter. It would be a fine thing for one of your opponents to be able to bring one of your most laudable actions up against you.'

"'You are right,' my father said. 'Do as you think best, my dear wife.'

"A quarter of an hour later, the Abbé Poivron came into the drawing-room, and the situation was explained to him, analyzed, and discussed in all its bearings. If the Marquis de Fumerol, one of the greatest names in France, were to die without the succor of religion, it would assuredly be a terrible blow to the nobility in general, to the Count de Tourneville in particular, and the freethinkers would be triumphant. The evilly disposed newspapers would sing songs of victory for six months; my mother's name would be dragged through the mire and brought into the slander of Socialistic journals, and my father's would be bespattered. It was impossible that such a thing should occur.

"A crusade was therefore immediately decided upon, which was to be led by the Abbé Poivron, a little fat, clean, slightly-scented priest, the faithful vicar of a large church in a rich and noble quarter.

"The landau was ordered and we three started, my mother, the curé, and I, to administer the last sacraments to my uncle.

"It had been decided that first of all we should see Madame Mélani who had written the letter, and who was most likely the porter's wife, or my uncle's servant, and I got down as a scout in front of a seven-storied house and went into a dark passage, where I had great difficulty in finding the porter's den. He looked at me distrustfully, and I said: .

"'Madame Mélani, if you please.'

"'Don't know her!'

"'But I have received a letter from her.'

"'That may be, but I don't know her. Are you asking for some kept woman?'

"'No, a servant probably. She wrote me about a place.'

"'A servant—a servant? Perhaps it is the Marquis's. Go and see, the fifth story on the left.'

"As soon as he found I was not asking for a kept woman, he became more friendly and came as far as the passage with me. He was a tall, thin man with white whiskers, the manners of a beadle, and majestic in movement.

"I climbed up a long spiral staircase, whose balusters I did not venture to touch, and I gave three discreet knocks at the left-hand door on the fifth story. It opened immediately, and an enormous dirty woman appeared before me, who barred the entrance with her open arms, which she placed upon the two doorposts, and grumbled out:

"'What do you want?'

"'Are you Madame Mélani?'

"'Yes.'

"'I am the Viscount de Tourneville.'

"'Ah! All right! Come in.'

"'Well, the fact is, my mother is downstairs with a priest.'

"'Oh! All right; go and bring them up; but take care of the porter.'

"I went downstairs and came up again with my mother, who was followed by the abbé, and I fancied that I heard other footsteps behind us. As soon as

we were in the kitchen, Mélani offered us chairs, and
we all four sat down to deliberate.

"'Is he very ill?' my mother asked.

"'Oh! yes, Madame; he will not be here long.'

"'Does he seem disposed to receive a visit from
a priest?'

"'Oh! I do not think so.'

"'Can I see him?'

"'Well—yes—Madame—only—only—those young
ladies are with him.'

"'What young ladies?'

"'Why—why—his lady friends, of course.'

"'Oh!' Mamma had grown scarlet, and the Abbé
Poivron had lowered his eyes.

"The affair began to amuse me, and I said:
'Suppose I go in first? I shall see how he receives
me, and perhaps I shall be able to prepare his heart
for you.'

"My mother, who did not suspect any trick, replied: 'Yes, go my dear.'

"But a woman's voice cried out: 'Mélani!'

"The fat servant ran out and said: 'What do
you want, Mademoiselle Claire?'

"'The omelet, quickly.'

"'In a minute, Mademoiselle.' And coming back
to us, she explained this summons.

"'They ordered a cheese omelet at two o'clock
as a slight collation.' And immediately she began to
break the eggs into a salad bowl, and began to whip
them vigorously, while I went out on to the landing
and pulled the bell, so as to announce my official arrival. Mélani opened the door to me, and made me
sit down in an anteroom, while she went to tell my

uncle that I had come. Then she came back and asked me to go in, while the abbé hid behind the door, so that he might appear at the first sign.

"I was certainly very much surprised at seeing my uncle, for he was very handsome, very solemn, and very elegant—the old rake.

"Sitting, almost lying in a large armchair, his legs wrapped in blankets, with his hands, his long, white hands over the arms of the chair, he was waiting for death with Biblical dignity. His white beard fell on to his chest, and his hair, which was also white, mingled with it on his cheeks.

"Standing behind his armchair, as if to defend him against me, were two young women, two stout young women, who looked at me with the bold eyes of prostitutes. In their petticoats and morning wrappers, with bare arms, with coal-black hair twisted up on to the napes of their necks, with embroidered Oriental slippers which showed their ankles and silk stockings, they looked like the immoral figures of some symbolical painting, by the side of the dying man. Between the easy-chair and the bed, there was a table covered with a white cloth, on which two plates, two glasses, two forks, and two knives, were waiting for the cheese omelet which had been ordered some time before of Mélani.

"My uncle said in a weak, almost breathless, but clear voice: 'Good morning, my child: it is rather late in the day to come and see me; our acquaintanceship will not last long.'

"I stammered out: 'It was not my fault, uncle'; and he replied: 'No; I know that. It is your father's and mother's fault more than yours. How are they;

"'Pretty well, thank you. When they heard that you were ill, they sent me to ask after you.'

"'Ah! Why did they not come themselves?'

"I looked up at the two girls and said gently: 'It is not their fault if they could not come, uncle. But it would be difficult for my father, and impossible for my mother to come in here.' The old man did not reply, but raised his hand toward mine, and I took the pale, cold hand and kept it in my own.

"The door opened, Mélani came in with the omelet and put it on the table, and the two girls immediately sat down in front of their plates and began to eat without taking their eyes off me.

"Then I said: 'Uncle, it would be a great pleasure for my mother to embrace you.'

"'I also—' he murmured, 'should like—' He said no more, and I could think of nothing to propose to him, and nothing more was heard except the noise of the plates and the slight sound of eating mouths.

"Now the abbé, who was listening behind the door, seeing our embarrassment, and thinking we had won the game, thought the time had come to interpose, and showed himself. My uncle was so stupefied at that apparition, that at first he remained motionless; then he opened his mouth as if he meant to swallow up the priest, and cried out in a strong, deep, furious voice: 'What are you doing here?'

"The abbé, who was used to difficult situations, came forward, murmuring: 'I have come in your sister's name, Monsieur le Marquis; she has sent me —she would be so happy, Monsieur—'

"But the Marquis was not listening. Raising one

hand, he pointed to the door with a proud and tragic gesture, and said angrily and gasping for breath: 'Leave this room — go out — robber of souls. Go out from here, you violator of consciences! Go out from here, you picklock of dying men's doors!'

"The abbé went backward, and I too, went to the door, beating a retreat with him; and the two little women, who were avenged, got up, leaving their omelet half eaten, and stood on either side of my uncle's armchair, putting their hands on his arms to calm him, and to protect him against the criminal enterprises of the Family and of Religion.

"The abbé and I rejoined my mother in the kitchen, and Mélani again offered us chairs. 'I knew quite well that you would fail that way; we must try some other means, otherwise he will escape us.' And we began deliberating afresh, my mother being of one opinion and the abbé of another, while I held a third.

"We had been discussing the matter in a low voice for half an hour, perhaps, when a great noise of furniture being moved and of cries uttered by my uncle, more vehement and terrible even than the former had been, made us all jump up.

"Through the doors and walls we could hear him shouting: 'Go out — out — rascals — humbugs; get out, scoundrels — get out — get out!'

"Mélani rushed in, but came back immediately to call me to help her, and I hastened in. Opposite to my uncle who was terribly excited by anger, almost standing up and vociferating, two men, one behind the other, seemed to be waiting till he should be dead with rage.

"By his long, ridiculous coat, his pointed English shoes, by his manners,—like those of a tutor out of a situation,—by his high collar, white necktie and straight hair, by his humble face, I immediately recognized the first as a Protestant minister.

"The second was the porter of the house, who belonged to the Reformed religion and had followed us. Having known of our defeat he had gone to fetch his own pastor, in hope of a better fate. My uncle seemed mad with rage! If the sight of the Catholic priest, of the priest of his ancestors, had irritated the Marquis de Fumerol, who had become a freethinker, the sight of his porter's minister made him altogether beside himself. I therefore took the two men by the arm and threw them out of the room so violently that they fell up against each other twice, between the two doors which led to the staircase; then I disappeared in my turn and returned to the kitchen, which was our headquarters, in order to take counsel with my mother and the abbé.

"But Mélani came back in terror, sobbing out: 'He is dying—he is dying—come immediately—he is dying.'

"My mother rushed out. My uncle had fallen on to the carpet, full length along the floor, and did not move. I fancy he was already dead. My mother was superb at that moment! She went straight up to the two girls who were kneeling by the body and trying to raise it up, and pointing to the door with irresistible authority, dignity, and majesty, she said: 'Now it is for you to go out.'

"And they went out without a protest, and without saying a word. I must add that I was getting

ready to turn them out as unceremoniously as I had
done the parson and the porter.

"Then the Abbé Poivron administered extreme
unction to my uncle with all the customary prayers
and remitted all his sins, while my mother sobbed,
kneeling near her brother. Suddenly, however, she
exclaimed: 'He recognized me; he pressed my hand;
I am sure he recognized me and thanked me! Oh,
God, what happiness!'

"Poor mamma! If she had known or guessed to
whom those thanks ought to have been addressed!

"They laid my uncle on his bed; he was certainly dead that time.

"'Madame,' Mélani said, 'we have no sheets to
bury him in; all the linen belongs to those two young
ladies,' and when I looked at the omelet which
they had not finished, I felt inclined to laugh and to cry
at the same time. There are some strange moments
and some strange sensations in life, occasionally!

"We gave my uncle a magnificent funeral, with
five speeches at the grave. Baron de Croiselles, the
Senator, showed in admirable terms, that God always
returns victorious into well-born souls which have
gone astray for a moment. All the members of the
Royalist and Catholic party followed the funeral procession with triumphant enthusiasm, speaking of that
beautiful death, after a somewhat restless life."

Viscount Roger ceased speaking, and those around
him laughed. Then somebody said: "Bah! That is
the story of all conversions *in extremis*."

SAVED

THE little Marquise de Rennedon came rushing in like a ball through the window. She began to laugh before she spoke, to laugh till she cried, like she had done a month previously, when she had told her friend that she had betrayed the Marquis in order to have her revenge, but only once, just because he was really too stupid and too jealous.

The little Baroness de Grangerie had thrown the book which she was reading on to the sofa, and looked at Annette, curiously. She was already laughing herself, and at last she asked:

"What have you been doing now?"

"Oh! my dear!—my dear! it is too funny—too funny. Just fancy—I am saved!—saved!—saved!"

"How do you mean, saved?"

"Yes, saved!"

"From what?"

(132)

' From my husband, my dear, **saved!** Delivered!
free! free! free!"

"How free? In what?"

"In what? Divorce! yes a divorce! I have my
divorce!"

"You are divorced?"

"No, not yet; how stupid you are! One does
not get divorced in three hours! But I have my
proofs that he has deceived me—caught in the very
act—just think!—in the very act. I have got him
tight."

"Oh! do tell me all about it! So he deceived you?"

"Yes, that is to say no—yes and no—I do not
know. At any rate, I have proofs, and that is the
chief thing."

"How did you manage it?"

"How did I manage it? This is how! I have
been energetic, very energetic. For the last three
months he has been odious, altogether odious, brutal,
coarse, a despot—in one word, vile. So I said to
myself: This cannot last, I must have a divorce!
But how?—for it is not very easy. I tried to make
him beat me, but he would not. He vexed me from
morning till night, made me go out when I did not
wish to, and to remain at home when I wanted to
dine out; he made my life unbearable for me from
one week's end to the other, but he never struck
me.

"Then I tried to find out whether he had a mistress. Yes, he had one, but he took a thousand pre-
cautions in going to see her, and they could never
be caught together. Guess what I did then?"

"I cannot guess."

"Oh! you could never guess. I asked my brother to procure me a photograph of the creature."

"Of your husband's mistress?"

"Yes. It cost Jacques fifteen louis,* the price of an evening, from seven o'clock till midnight, including a dinner, at three louis an hour, and he obtained the photograph into the bargain."

"It appears to me that he might have obtained it anyhow by means of some artifice and without—without—without being obliged to take the original at the same time."

"Oh! she is pretty, and Jacques did not mind the least. And then, I wanted some details about her, physical details about her figure, her breast, her complexion, a thousand things, in fact."

"I do not understand you."

"You shall see. When I had learned all that I wanted to know, I went to a—how shall I put it—to a man of business—you know—one of those men who transact business of all sorts—agents of—of—of publicity and complicity—one of those men—well, you understand what I mean."

"Pretty nearly, I think. And what did you say to him?"

"I said to him, showing the photograph of Clarisse (her name is Clarisse): 'Monsieur, I want a lady's maid who resembles this photograph. I require one who is pretty, elegant, neat, and sharp. I will pay her whatever is necessary, and if it costs me ten thousand francs† so much the worse. I shall not require her for more than three months.'

---

* $60.   † $2000.

"The man looked extremely astonished, and said: 'Do you require a maid of an irreproachable character, Madame?' I blushed, and stammered: 'Yes of course, for honesty.' He continued: 'And—then—as regards morals?' I did not venture to reply, so I only made a sign with my head which signified *No*. Then suddenly, I comprehended that he had a horrible suspicion and losing my presence of mind, I exclaimed: 'Oh! Monsieur,—it is for my husband, in order that I may surprise him.'

"Then the man began to laugh, and from his looks I gathered that I had regained his esteem. He even thought I was brave, and I would willingly have made a bet that at that moment he was longing to shake hands with me. However, he said to me: 'In a week, Madame, I shall have what you require; I will answer for my success, and you shall not pay me until I have succeeded. So this is a photograph of your husband's mistress?'

"'Yes, Monsieur.'

"'A handsome woman, and not too stout. And what scent?'

"I did not understand, and repeated: 'What scent?'

"He smiled: 'Yes, Madame, perfume is essential in tempting a man, for it unconsciously brings to his mind certain reminiscences which dispose him to action; the perfume creates an obscure confusion in his mind, and disturbs and energizes him by recalling his pleasures to him. You must also try to find out what your husband is in the habit of eating when he dines with his lady, and you might give him the same dishes the day you catch him. Oh! we have got him, Madame, we have got him.'

"I went away delighted, for here I had lighted on a very intelligent man.

"Three days later, I saw a tall, dark girl arrive at my house; she was very handsome, and her looks were modest and bold at the same time, the peculiar look of a female rake. She behaved very properly toward me, and as I did not exactly know what she was, I called her Mademoiselle, but she said immediately: 'Oh! pray, Madame, only call me Rose.' And she began to talk.

"'Well, Rose, you know why you have come here?'

"'I can guess it, Madame.'

"'Very good, my girl—and that will not be too much bother for you?'

"'Oh! Madame, this will be the eighth divorce that I shall have caused; I am used to it.'

"'Why, that is capital. Will it take you long to succeed?'

"'Oh? Madame, that depends entirely on Monsieur's temperament. When I have seen Monsieur for five minutes alone, I shall be able to tell you exactly.'

"'You will see him soon, my child, but I must tell you that he is not handsome.'

"'That does not matter to me, Madame. I have already separated some very ugly ones. But I must ask you, Madame, whether you have discovered his favorite perfume?'

"'Yes, Rose—verbena.'

"'So much the better, Madame, for I am also very fond of that scent! Can you also tell me, Madame, whether Monsieur's mistress wears silk underclothing and nightdresses?'

"'No, my child, cambric and lace.'

"'Oh! then she is altogether of superior station, for silk underclothing is getting quite common.'

"'What you say is quite true!'

"'Well, Madame, I will enter your service.' And so as a matter of fact she did immediately, and as if she had done nothing else all her life.

"An hour later my husband came home. Rose did not even raise her eyes to him, but he raised his eyes to her. She already smelled strongly of verbena. In five minutes she left the room, and he immediately asked me: 'Who is that girl?'

"'Why—my new lady's maid.'

"'Where did you pick her up?'

"'Baroness de Grangerie got her for me with the best references.'

"'Ah! she is rather pretty!'

"'Do you think so?'

"'Why, yes—for a lady's maid.'

"I was delighted, for I felt that he was already biting, and that same evening Rose said to me: 'I can now promise you that it will not take more than a fortnight, Monsieur is very easily caught!'

"'Ah! you have tried already?'

"'No, Madame, he only asked what my name was, so that he might hear what my voice was like.'

"'Very well, my dear Rose. Get on as quick as you can.'

"'Do not be alarmed, Madame; I shall only resist long enough not to make myself depreciated.'

"At the end of a week, my husband scarcely ever went out; I saw him roaming about the house the whole afternoon, and what was most significant in the matter was that he no longer prevented me from going out. And I, I was out of doors nearly the whole day long—in order—in order to leave him at liberty.

"On the ninth day, while Rose was undressing me, she said to me with a timid air: 'It happened this morning, Madame.'

"I was rather surprised, or rather overcome even, not at the part itself, but at the way in which she told me, and I stammered out: 'And—and—it went off well?'

"'Oh! yes, very well, Madame. For the last three days he has been pressing me, but I did not wish matters to proceed too quickly. You will tell me when you want us to be caught, Madame.'

"'Yes, certainly. Here! let us say Thursday.'

"'Very well, Madame, I shall grant nothing more till then, so as to keep Monsieur on the alert.'

"'You are sure not to fail?'

"'Oh! quite sure, Madame. I will excite him, so as to make him be there at the very moment which you may appoint.'

"'Let us say five o'clock then.'

"'Very well, Madame, and where?'

"'Well—in my bedroom.'

"'Very good, Madame, in your bedroom.'

"'You will understand what I did then, my dear. I went and fetched mamma and papa first of all, and then my uncle d'Orvelin, the President, and Monsieur Raplet, the Judge, my husband's friend. I had not told them what I was going to show them, but I made them all go on tiptoe as far as the door of my room. I waited till five o'clock exactly, and oh!

how my heart beat! I had made the porter come upstairs as well, so as to have an additional witness!
And then—and then at the moment when the clock
began to strike, I opened the door wide. Ah! ah!
ah! Here he was evidently—it was quite evident, my
dear. Oh! what a head! If you had only seen his
head! And he turned round, the idiot! Oh! how
funny he looked—I laughed, I laughed. And papa
was angry and wanted to give my husband a beating. And the porter, a good servant helped him to
dress himself before us—before us. He buttoned his
braces for him—what a joke it was! As for Rose,
she was perfect, absolutely perfect. She cried—oh!
she cried very well. She is an invaluable girl. If
you ever want her, don't forget!

"And here I am. I came immediately to tell you
of the affair directly. I am free. Long live divorce!"

And she began to dance in the middle of the
drawing-room, while the little Baroness, who was
thoughtful and put out, said:

"Why did you not invite me to see it?"

WHO KNOWS?

MY GOD! My God! I am going to write down at last what has happened to me. But how can I? How dare I? The thing is so bizarre, so inexplicable, so incomprehensible, so silly!

If I were not perfectly sure of what I have seen, sure that there was not in my reasoning any defect, any error in my declarations, any lacuna in the inflexible sequence of my observations, I should believe myself to be the dupe of a simple hallucination, the sport of a singular vision. After all, who knows?

Yesterday I was in a private asylum, but I went there voluntarily, out of prudence and fear. Only one single human being knows my history, and that is the doctor of the said asylum. I am going to write to him. I really do not know why? To disembarrass myself? Yea, I feel as though weighed down by an intolerable nightmare.

Let me explain.

I have always been a recluse, a dreamer, a kind of Isolated philosopher, easy-going, content with but little, harboring ill-feeling against no man, and without even a grudge against heaven. I have constantly lived alone; consequently, a kind of torture takes hold of me when I find myself in the presence of others. How is this to be explained? I do not know. I am not averse to going out into the world, to conversation, to dining with friends, but when they are near me for any length of time, even the most intimate of them, they bore me, fatigue me, enervate me, and I experience an overwhelming, torturing desire to see them get up and go, to take themselves away, and to leave me by myself.

That desire is more than a craving; it is an irresistible necessity. And if the presence of people with whom I find myself were to be continued; if I were compelled, not only to listen, but also to follow, for any length of time, their conversation, a serious accident would assuredly take place. What kind of accident? Ah! who knows? Perhaps a slight paralytic stroke? Probably!

I like solitude so much that I cannot even endure the vicinage of other beings sleeping under the same roof. I cannot live in Paris, because there I suffer the most acute agony. I lead a moral life, and am therefore tortured in body and in nerves by that immense crowd which swarms and lives even when it sleeps. Ah! the sleeping of others is more painful still than their conversation. And I can never find repose when I know and feel that on the other side of a wall several existences are undergoing these regular eclipses of reason.

Why am I thus? Who knows? The cause of it is very simple perhaps. I get tired very soon of everything that does not emanate from me. And there are many people in similar case.

We are, on earth, two distinct races. Those who have need of others, whom others amuse, engage, soothe, whom solitude harasses, pains, stupefies, like the movement of a terrible glacier or the traversing of the desert; and those, on the contrary, whom others weary, tire, bore, silently torture, whom isolation calms and bathes in the repose of independency, and plunges into the humors of their own thoughts. In fine, there is here a normal, physical phenomenon. Some are constituted to live a life outside of themselves, others, to live a life within themselves. As for me, my exterior associations are abruptly and painfully short-lived, and, as they reach their limits, I experience in my whole body and in my whole intelligence an intolerable uneasiness.

As a result of this, I became attached, or rather had become much attached, to inanimate objects, which have for me the importance of beings, and my house has or had become a world in which I lived an active and solitary life, surrounded by all manner of things, furniture, familiar knickknacks, as sympathetic in my eyes as the visages of human beings. I had filled my mansion with them; little by little, I had adorned it with them, and I felt an inward content and satisfaction, was more happy than if I had been in the arms of a beloved girl, whose wonted caresses had become a soothing and delightful necessity.

I had had this house constructed in the center of a beautiful garden, which hid it from the public highways, and which was near the entrance to a city where I could find, on occasion, the resources of society, for which, at moments, I had a longing. All my domestics slept in a separate building, which was situated at some considerable distance from my house, at the far end of the kitchen garden, which in turn was surrounded by a high wall. The obscure envelopment of night, in the silence of my concealed habitation, buried under the leaves of great trees, was so reposeful and so delicious, that before retiring to my couch I lingered every evening for several hours in order to enjoy the solitude a little longer.

One day "Signad" had been played at one of the city theaters. It was the first time that I had listened to that beautiful, musical, and fairy-like drama, and I had derived from it the liveliest pleasures.

I returned home on foot with a light step, my head full of sonorous phrases, and my mind haunted by delightful visions. It was night, the dead of night, and so dark that I could hardly distinguish the broad highway, and consequently I stumbled into the ditch more than once. From the custom-house, at the barriers, to my house, was about a mile, perhaps a little more—a leisurely walk of about twenty minutes. It was one o'clock in the morning, one o'clock or maybe half-past one; the sky had by this time cleared somewhat and the crescent appeared, the gloomy crescent of the last quarter of the moon. The crescent of the first quarter is that which rises about five or six o'clock in the evening and is clear, gay, and fretted with silver; but the one which rises after midnight is reddish, sad, and desolating—it is the true Sabbath crescent. Every prowler by night has made the same observation. The first, though slender as a thread, throws a faint, joyous light which rejoices the heart and lines the ground with distinct shadows; the last sheds hardly a dying glimmer, and is so wan that it occasions hardly any shadows.

In the distance, I perceived the somber mass of my garden, and, I know not why, was seized with a feeling of uneasiness at the idea of going inside. I slackened my pace, and walked very softly, the thick cluster of trees having the appearance of a tomb in which my house was buried.

I opened my outer gate and entered the long avenue of sycamores which ran in the direction of the house, arranged vault-wise like a high tunnel, traversing opaque masses, and winding round the turf lawns, on which baskets of flowers, in the pale darkness, could be indistinctly discerned.

While approaching the house, I was seized by a strange feeling. I could hear nothing, I stood still. Through the trees there was not even a breath of air stirring. "What is the matter with me?" I said to myself. For ten years I had entered and re-entered in the same way, without ever experiencing the least inquietude. I never had any fear at nights. The sight of a man, a marauder, or a thief would have thrown me into a fit of anger, and I would have rushed at him without any hesitation. Moreover, I was armed—I had my revolver. But I did not touch it, for I was anxious to resist that feeling of dread with which I was seized.

What was it? Was it a presentiment—that mysterious presentiment which takes hold of the senses of men who have witnessed something which, to them, is inexplicable? Perhaps? Who knows?

In proportion as I advanced, I felt my skin quiver more and more, and when I was close to the wall, near the outhouses of my large residence, I felt that it would be necessary for me to wait a few minutes before opening the door and going inside. I sat down, then, on a bench, under the windows of my drawing-room. I rested there, a little disturbed, with my head leaning against the wall, my eyes wide open, under the shade of the foliage. For the first few minutes, I did not observe anything unusual around me; I had a humming noise in my ears, but that has happened often to me. Sometimes it seemed to me that I heard trains passing, that I heard clocks striking, that I heard a multitude on the march.

Very soon, those humming noises became more distinct, more concentrated, more determinable, I was deceiving myself. It was not the ordinary tingling of my arteries which transmitted to my ears these rumbling sounds, but it was a very distinct, though confused, noise which came, without any doubt whatever, from the interior of my house. Through the walls I distinguished this continued noise,—I should rather say agitation than noise,—an indistinct moving about of a pile of things, as if people were tossing about, displacing, and carrying away surreptitiously all my furniture.

I doubted, however, for some considerable time yet, the evidence of my ears. But having placed my ear against one of the outhouses, the better to discover what this strange disturbance was, inside my house, I became convinced, certain, that something

2 C. de M.—10

was taking place in my residence which was altogether abnormal and incomprehensible. I had no
fear, but I was — how shall I express it — paralyzed
by astonishment. I did not draw my revolver,
knowing very well that there was no need of my
doing so.

I listened a long time, but could come to no resolution, my mind being quite clear, though in myself
I was naturally anxious. I got up and waited, listening always to the noise, which gradually increased,
and at intervals grew very loud, and which seemed
to become an impatient, angry disturbance, a mysterious commotion.

Then, suddenly, ashamed of my timidity, I seized
my bunch of keys. I selected the one I wanted,
guided it into the lock, turned it twice, and pushing
the door with all my might, sent it banging against
the partition.

The collision sounded like the report of a gun, and
there responded to that explosive noise, from roof to
basement of my residence, a formidable tumult. It
was so sudden, so terrible, so deafening, that I re-
coiled a few steps, and though I knew it to be
wholly useless, I pulled my revolver out of its
case.

I continued to listen for some time longer. I could
distinguish now an extraordinary pattering upon the
steps of my grand staircase, on the waxed floors, on
the carpets, not of boots, or of naked feet, but of
iron and wooden crutches, which resounded like
cymbals. Then I suddenly discerned, on the threshold of my door, an armchair, my large reading
easy-chair, which set off waddling. It went away

through my garden. Others followed it, those of my drawing-room, then my sofas, dragging themselves along like crocodiles on their short paws; then all my chairs, bounding like goats, and the little footstools, hopping like rabbits.

Oh! what a sensation! I slunk back into a clump of bushes where I remained crouched up, watching, meanwhile, my furniture defile past—for everything walked away, the one behind the other, briskly or slowly, according to its weight or size. My piano, my grand piano, bounded past with the gallop of a horse and a murmur of music in its sides; the smaller articles slid along the gravel like snails, my brushes, crystal, cups and saucers, which glistened in the moonlight. I saw my writing desk appear, a rare curiosity of the last century, which contained all the letters I had ever received, all the history of my heart, an old history from which I have suffered so much! Besides, there were inside of it a great many cherished photographs.

Suddenly—I no longer had any fear—I threw myself on it, seized it as one would seize a thief, as one would seize a wife about to run away; but it pursued its irresistible course, and despite my efforts and despite my anger, I could not even retard its pace. As I was resisting in desperation that insuperable force, I was thrown to the ground. It then rolled me over, trailed me along the gravel, and the rest of my furniture, which followed it, began to march over me, tramping on my legs and injuring them. When I loosed my hold, other articles had passed over my body, just as a charge of cavalry does over the body of a dismounted soldier.

Seized at last with terror, I succeeded in dragging myself out of the main avenue, and in concealing myself again among the shrubbery, so as to watch the disappearance of the most cherished objects, the smallest, the least striking, the least unknown which had once belonged to me.

I then heard, in the distance, noises which came from my apartments, which sounded now as if the house were empty, a loud noise of shutting of doors. They were being slammed from top to bottom of my dwelling, even the door which I had just opened myself unconsciously, and which had closed of itself, when the last thing had taken its departure. I took flight also, running toward the city, and only regained my self-composure, on reaching the boulevards, where I met belated people. I rang the bell of a hotel were I was known. I had knocked the dust off my clothes with my hands, and I told the porter that I had lost my bunch of keys, which included also that to the kitchen garden, where my servants slept in a house standing by itself, on the other side of the wall of the inclosure which protected my fruits and vegetables from the raids of marauders.

I covered myself up to the eyes in the bed which was assigned to me, but could not sleep; and I waited for the dawn listening to the throbbing of my heart. I had given orders that my servants were to be summoned to the hotel at daybreak, and my *valet de chambre* knocked at my door at seven o'clock in the morning.

His countenance bore a woeful look.

"A great misfortune has happened during the night, Monsieur," said he.

"What is it?"

"Somebody has stolen the whole of Monsieur's furniture, all, everything, even to the smallest articles."

This news pleased me. Why? Who knows? I was complete master of myself, bent on dissimulating, on telling no one of anything I had seen; determined on concealing and in burying in my heart of hearts a terrible secret. I responded:

"They must then be the same people who have stolen my keys. The police must be informed immediately. I am going to get up, and I will join you in a few moments."

The investigation into the circumstances under which the robbery might have been committed lasted for five months. Nothing was found, not even the smallest of my knickknacks, nor the least trace of the thieves. Good gracious! If I had only told them what I knew— If I had said—I should have been locked up—I, not the thieves—for I was the only person who had seen everything from the first.

Yes! but I knew how to keep silence. I shall never refurnish my house. That were indeed useless. The same thing would happen again. I had no desire even to re-enter the house, and I did not re-enter it; I never visited it again. I moved to Paris, to the hotel, and consulted doctors in regard to the condition of my nerves, which had disquieted me a good deal ever since that awful night.

They advised me to travel, and I followed their counsel.

II.

I began by making an excursion into Italy. The sunshine did me much good. For six months I wandered about from Genoa to Venice, from Venice to Florence, from Florence to Rome, from Rome to Naples. Then I traveled over Sicily, a country celebrated for its scenery and its monuments, relics left by the Greeks and the Normans. Passing over into Africa, I traversed at my ease that immense desert, yellow and tranquil, in which camels, gazelles, and Arab vagabonds roam about—where, in the rare and transparent atmosphere, there hover no vague hauntings, where there is never any night, but always day.

I returned to France by Marseilles, and in spite of all its Provençal gaiety, the diminished clearness of the sky made me sad. I experienced, in returning to the Continent, the peculiar sensation of an illness which I believed had been cured, and a dull pain which predicted that the seeds of the disease had not been eradicated.

I then returned to Paris. At the end of a month I was very dejected. It was in the autumn, and I determined to make, before winter came, an excursion through Normandy, a country with which I was unacquainted.

I began my journey, in the best of spirits, at Rouen, and for eight days I wandered about, passive, ravished, and enthusiastic, in that ancient city, that astonishing museum of extraordinary Gothic monuments.

But one afternoon, about four o'clock, as I was sauntering slowly through a seemingly unattractive street, by which there ran a stream as black as the ink called "Eau de Robec," my attention, fixed for the moment on the quaint, antique appearance of some of the houses, was suddenly attracted by the view of a series of second-hand furniture shops, which followed one another, door after door.

Ah! they had carefully chosen their locality, these sordid traffickers in antiquities, in that quaint little street, overlooking the sinister stream of water, under those tile and slate-pointed roofs on which still grinned the vanes of bygone days.

At the end of these grim storehouses you saw piled up sculptured chests, Rouen, Sévres, and Moustier's pottery, painted statues, others of oak, Christs, Virgins, Saints, church ornaments, chasubles, capes, even sacred vases, and an old gilded wooden tabernacle, where a god had hidden himself away. What singular caverns there are in those lofty houses, crowded with objects of every description, where the existence of things seems to be ended, things which have survived their original possessors, their century, their times, their fashions, in order to be bought as curiosities by new generations.

My affection for antiques was awakened in that city of antiquaries. I went from shop to shop, crossing in two strides, the rotten four plank bridges thrown over the nauseous current of the "Eau de Robec."

Heaven protect me! What a shock! At the end of a vault, which was crowded with articles of every description and which seemed to be the entrance to

the catacombs of a cemetery of ancient furniture, I
suddenly descried one of my most beautiful wardrobes.   I approached it, trembling in every limb,
trembling to such an extent that I dared not touch it.
I put forth my hand, I hesitated.   Nevertheless it
was indeed my wardrobe; a unique wardrobe of the
time of Louis XIII., recognizable by anyone who had
seen it only once.   Casting my eyes suddenly a little
farther, toward the more somber depths of the gallery, I perceived three of my tapestry covered chairs;
and farther on still, my two Henry II. tables, such
rare treasures that people came all the way from
Paris to see them.

Think! only think in what a state of mind I now
was! I advanced, haltingly, quivering with emotion,
but I advanced, for I am brave—I advanced like a
knight of the dark ages.

At every step I found something that belonged to
me; my brushes, my books, my tables, my silks, my
arms, everything, except the bureau full of my letters,
and that I could not discover.

I walked on, descending to the dark galleries, in
order to ascend next to the floors above.   I was
alone; I called out, nobody answered, I was alone;
there was no one in that house—a house as vast
and tortuous as a labyrinth.

Night came on, and I was compelled to sit down
in the darkness on one of my own chairs, for I had
no desire to go away.   From time to time I shouted,
"Hallo, hallo, somebody."

I had sat there, certainly, for more than an hour
when I heard steps, steps soft and slow, I knew not
where.   I was unable to locate them, but bracing

myself up, I called out anew, whereupon I perceived
a glimmer of light in the next chamber.

"Who is there?" said a voice.

"A buyer," I responded.

"It is too late to enter thus into a shop."

"I have been waiting for you for more than an
hour," I answered.

"You can come back to-morrow."

"To-morrow I must quit Rouen."

I dared not advance, and he did not come to me.
I saw always the glimmer of his light, which was
shining on a tapestry on which were two angels flying over the dead on a field of battle. It belonged
to me also. I said:

"Well, come here."

"I am at your service," he answered.

I got up and went toward him.

Standing in the center of a large room, was a
little man, very short, and very fat, phenomenally
fat, a hideous phenomenon.

He had a singular straggling beard, white and
yellow, and not a hair on his head — not a hair!

As he held his candle aloft at arm's length in
order to see me, his cranium appeared to me to resemble a little moon, in that vast chamber encumbered with old furniture. His features were wrinkled
and blown, and his eyes could not be seen.

I bought three chairs which belonged to myself,
and paid at once a large sum for them, giving him
merely the number of my room at the hotel. They
were to be delivered the next day before nine o'clock.

I then started off. He conducted me, with much
politeness, as far as the door.

I immediately repaired to the commissaire's office at the central police depot, and told the commissaire of the robbery which had been perpetrated and of the discovery I had just made. He required time to communicate by telegraph with the authorities who had originally charge of the case, for information, and he begged me to wait in his office until an answer came back. An hour later, an answer came back, which was in accord with my statements.

"I am going to arrest and interrogate this man, at once," he said to me, "for he may have conceived some sort of suspicion, and smuggled away out of sight what belongs to you. Will you go and dine and return in two hours: I shall then have the man here, and I shall subject him to a fresh interrogation in your presence."

"Most gladly, Monsieur. I thank you with my whole heart."

I went to dine at my hotel and I ate better than I could have believed. I was quite happy now, thinking that man was in the hands of the police.

Two hours later I returned to the office of the police functionary, who was waiting for me.

"Well, Monsieur," said he, on perceiving me, "we have not been able to find your man. My agents cannot put their hands on him."

Ah! I felt my heart sinking.

"But you have at least found his house?" I asked.

"Yes, certainly; and what is more, it is now being watched and guarded until his return. As for him, he has disappeared."

"Disappeared?"

"Yes, disappeared. He ordinarily passes his evenings at the house of a female neighbor, who is also a furniture broker, a queer sort of sorceress, the widow Bidoin. She has not seen him this evening and cannot give any information in regard to him. We must wait until to-morrow."

I went away. Ah! how sinister the streets of Rouen seemed to me, now troubled and haunted!

I slept so badly that I had a fit of nightmare every time I went off to sleep.

As I did not wish to appear too restless or eager, I waited till ten o'clock the next day before reporting myself to the police.

The merchant had not reappeared. His shop remained closed.

The commissary said to me:

"I have taken all the necessary steps. The court has been made acquainted with the affair. We shall go together to that shop and have it opened, and you shall point out to me all that belongs to you."

We drove there in a cab. Police agents were stationed round the building; there was a locksmith, too, and the door of the shop was soon opened.

On entering, I could not discover my wardrobes, my chairs, my tables; I saw nothing, nothing of that which had furnished my house, no, nothing, although on the previous evening, I could not take a step without encountering something that belonged to me.

The chief commissary, much astonished, regarded me at first with suspicion.

"My God, Monsieur," said I to him, "the disappearance of these articles of furniture coincides strangely with that of the merchant."

He laughed.

"That is true. You did wrong in buying and paying for the articles which were your own property, yesterday. It was that which gave him the cue."

"What seems to me incomprehensible," I replied, "is that all the places that were occupied by my furniture are now filled by other furniture."

"Oh!" responded the commissary, "he has had all night, and has no doubt been assisted by accomplices. This house must communicate with its neighbors. But have no fear, Monsieur; I will have the affair promptly and thoroughly investigated. The brigand shall not escape us for long, seeing that we are in charge of the den."

*   *   *   *   *   *   *

Ah! My heart, my heart, my poor heart, how it beats!

I remained a fortnight at Rouen. The man did not return. Heavens! good heavens! That man, what was it that could have frightened and surprised him!

But, on the sixteenth day, early in the morning, I received from my gardener, now the keeper of my empty and pillaged house, the following strange letter:

" Monsieur:

"I have the honor to inform Monsieur that something happened, the evening before last, which nobody can understand, and the police no more than the rest of us. The whole of the furniture has been returned, not one piece is missing—everything is in its place, up to the very smallest article. The house is now the same in every respect as it was before the robbery took place. It is enough to make one lose one's head. The thing took place during the night Friday— Saturday. The roads are dug up as though the whole fence had been dragged from its place up to the door. The same thing was observed the day after the disappearance of the furniture.

"We are anxiously expecting Monsieur, whose very humble and obedient servant, I am, PHILLIPE RAUDIN."

"Ah! no, no, ah! never, never, ah! no. I shall never return there!"

I took the letter to the commissary of police.

"It is a very clever restitution," said he. "Let us bury the hatchet. We shall nip the man one of these days."

* * * * * * *

But he has never been nipped. No. They have not nipped him, and I am afraid of him now, as of some ferocious animal that has been let loose behind me.

Inexplicable! It is inexplicable, this chimera of a moon-struck skull! We shall never solve or comprehend it. I shall not return to my former residence. What does it matter to me? I am afraid of encountering that man again, and I shall not run the risk.

And even if he returns, if he takes possession of his shop, who is to prove that my furniture was on his premises? There is only my testimony against him; and I feel that that is not above suspicion.

Ah! no! This kind of existence has become unendurable. I have not been able to guard the secret of what I have seen. I could not continue to live like the rest of the world, with the fear upon me that those scenes might be re-enacted.

So I have come to consult the doctor who directs this lunatic asylum, and I have told him everything.

After questioning me for a long time, he said to me:

"Will you consent, Monsieur, to remain here for some time?"

"Most willingly, Monsieur."

"You have some means?"

"Yes, Monsieur."

"Will you have isolated apartments?"

"Yes, Monsieur."

"Would you care to receive any friends?"

"No, Monsieur, no, nobody. The man from Rouen might take it into his head to pursue me here, to be revenged on me."

 *   *   *   *   *   *   *

I have been alone, alone, all, all alone, for three months. I am growing tranquil by degrees. I have no longer any fears. If the antiquary should become mad . . . and if he should be brought into this asylum! Even prisons themselves are not places of security.

THE SIGNAL

THE little Marchioness de Rennedon was still asleep in her dark and perfumed bedroom.

In her soft, low bed, between sheets of delicate cambric, fine as lace and caressing as a kiss, she was sleeping alone and tranquil, the happy and profound sleep of divorced women. She was awakened by loud voices in the little blue drawing-room, and she recognized her dear friend, the little Baroness de Grangerie, who was disputing with the lady's maid, because the latter would not allow her to go into the Marchioness's room. So the little Marchioness got up, opened the door, drew back the door-hangings and showed her head, nothing but her fair head, hidden under a cloud of hair.

"What is the matter with you, that you have come so early?" she asked. "It is not nine o'clock yet."

The little Baroness, who was very pale, nervous, and feverish, replied: "I must speak to you. Something horrible has happened to me."

"Come in, my dear."

She went in, they kissed each other and the little Marchioness got back into her bed, while the lady's maid opened the windows to let in light and air. Then when she had left the room, Madame de Rennedon went on: "Well, tell me what it is."

Madame de Grangerie began to cry, shedding those pretty bright tears which make women more charming. She sobbed out, without wiping her eyes, so as not to make them red: "Oh! my dear, what has happened to me is abominable, abominable. I have not slept all night, not a minute; do you hear, not a minute. Here, just feel my heart, how it is beating."

And taking her friend's hand, she put it on her breast, on that firm, round covering of women's hearts which often suffices men, and prevents them from seeking beneath. But her heart was really beating violently.

She continued: "It happened to me yesterday during the day, at about four o'clock—or half past four; I cannot say exactly. You know my apartments, and you know that my little drawing-room, where I always sit, looks on to the Rue Saint-Lazare, and that I have a mania for sitting at the window to look at the people passing. The neighborhood of the railway station is very gay; so full of motion and lively—just what I like! So, yesterday, I was sitting in the low chair which I have placed in my window recess; the window was open and I was not thinking of anything, simply breathing the fresh air. You remember how fine it was yesterday!

"Suddenly, I remarked a woman sitting at the window opposite—a woman in red. I was in mauve, you know, my pretty mauve costume. I did not know the woman, a new lodger, who had been there a month, and as it has been raining for a month, I had not yet seen her, but I saw immediately that she was a bad girl. At first I was very much shocked and disgusted that she should be at the window just as I was; and then by degrees, it amused me to watch her. She was resting her elbows on the window ledge, and looking at the men, and the men looked at her also, all or nearly all. One might have said that they knew of her presence by some means as they got near the house, that they scented her, as dogs scent game, for they suddenly raised their heads, and exchanged a swift look with her, a sort of freemason's look. Hers said: 'Will you?' Theirs replied: 'I have no time,' or else: 'Another day'; or else: 'I have not got a sou'; or else: 'Hide yourself, you wretch!'

"You cannot imagine how funny it was to see her carrying on such a piece of work, though after all it is her regular business.

"Occasionally she shut the window suddenly, and I saw a gentleman go in. She had caught him like a fisherman hooks a gudgeon. Then I looked at my watch, and I found that they never stopped longer than from twelve to twenty minutes. In the end she really infatuated me, the spider! And then the creature is so ugly.

"I asked myself: 'How does she manage to make herself understood so quickly, so well and so completely? Does she add a sign of the head or a motion of the hands to her looks?' And I took my opera-glasses to watch her proceedings. Oh! they were very simple: first of all a glance, then a smile,

2 G. de M.—11

then a slight sign with the head which meant: 'Are you coming up?' But it was so slight, so vague, so discreet, that it required a great deal of knack to succeed as she did. And I asked myself: 'I wonder if I could do that little movement, from below up-ward, which was at the same time bold and pretty, as well as she does,' for her gesture was very pretty.

"I went and tried it before the looking-glass, and my dear, I did it better than she, a great deal better! I was enchanted, and resumed my place at the window.

"She caught nobody more then, poor girl, nobody. She certainly had no luck. It must really be very terrible to earn one's bread in that way, terrible and amusing occasionally, for really some of these men one meets in the street are rather nice.

"After that they all came on my side of the road and none on hers; the sun had turned. They came one after the other, young, old, dark, fair, gray, white. I saw some who looked very nice, really very nice, my dear, far better than my husband or than yours—I mean than your late husband, as you have got a divorce. Now you can choose.

"I said to myself: 'If I give them the sign, will they understand me, who am a respectable woman?' And I was seized with a mad longing to make that sign to them. I had a longing, a terrible longing; you know, one of those longings which one cannot resist! I have some like that occasionally. How silly such things are, don't you think so? I believe that we women have the souls of monkeys. I have been told (and it was a physician who told me) that the brain of a monkey is very like ours. Of course we must imitate some one or other. We imitate our husbands when we love them, during the first months after our marriage, and then our lovers, our female friends, our confessors when they are nice. We assume their ways of thought, their manners of speech, their words, their gestures, everything. It is very foolish.

"However, as for me, when I am much tempted to do a thing I always do it, and so I said to myself: 'I will try it once, on one man only, just to see. What can happen to me? Nothing whatever! We shall exchange a smile and that will be all and I shall deny it, most certainly.'

"So I began to make my choice, I wanted some one nice, very nice, and suddenly I saw a tall, fair, very good-looking fellow coming along. I like fair men, as you know. I looked at him, he looked at me; I smiled, he smiled, I made the movement, oh! so faintly; he replied *yes* with his head, and there he was, my dear! He came in at the large door of the house.

"You cannot imagine what passed through my mind then! I thought I should go mad. Oh! how frightened I was. Just think, he will speak to the servants! To Joseph, who is devoted to my husband! Joseph would certainly think that I had known that gentleman for a long time.

"What could I do, just tell me? And he would ring in a moment. What could I do, tell me? I thought I would go and meet him, and tell him he had made a mistake, and beg him to go away. He would have pity on a woman, on a poor woman: So I rushed to the door and opened it, just at the moment when ne was going to ring the bell, and I stammered out, quite stupidly: 'Go away, Monsieur, go away; you have made a mistake, a terrible mistake; I took you for one of my friends whom you are very like. Have pity on me, Monsieur.'

"But he only began to laugh, my dear, and replied: 'Good morning, my dear, I know all about your little story, you may be sure. You are married, and so you want forty francs instead of twenty, and you shall have them, so just show the way.'

"And he pushed me in, closed the door, and as I remained standing before him, horror-struck, he kissed me, put his arm round my waist and made me go back into the drawing-room the door of which had remained open. Then he began to look at everything like an auctioneer, and continued: 'By Jove, it is very nice in your rooms, very nice. You must be very down on your luck just now, to do the window business!'

"Then I began to beg him again: 'Oh! Monsieur, go away, please go away! My husband will be coming in soon, it is just his time. I swear that you have made a mistake!' But he answered quite coolly: 'Come, my beauty, I have had enough of this nonsense, and if your husband comes in, I will give him five francs to go and have a drink at the *café* opposite.' And then seeing Raoul's photograph on the chimney-piece, he asked me: 'Is that your — your husband?'

"'Yes, that is he.'

"'He looks like a nice, disagreeable sort of fellow. And who is this? One of your friends?'

"It was your photograph, my dear, you know, the one in ball dress. I did not know any longer what I was saying and I stammered: 'Yes, it is one of my friends.'

"'She is very nice; you shall introduce me to her.'

"Just then the clock struck five, and Raoul comes home every day at half past! Suppose he were to come home before the other had gone, just fancy what would have happened! Then—then—I completely lost my head—altogether—I thought—I thought—that—that—the best thing would be—to get rid—of—of this man—as quickly as possible—The sooner it was over—you understand."

*   *   *   *   *   *   *

The little Marchioness de Rennedon had begun to laugh, to laugh madly, with her head buried in her pillow, so that the whole bed shook, and when she was a little calmer she asked:

"And—and—was he good-looking?"

"Yes."

"And yet you complain?"

"But—but—don't you see, my dear, he said—he said—he should come again to-morrow—at the same time—and I—I am terribly frightened— You have no idea how tenacious he is and obstinate—What can I do—tell me—what can I do?"

The little Marchioness sat up in bed to reflect, and then she suddenly said: "Have him arrested!"

The little Baroness looked stupefied, and stammered out: "What do you say? What are you thinking of? Have him arrested? Under what pretext?"

"That is very simple. Go to the Commissary of Police and say that a gentleman has been following you about for three months; that he had the insolence to go up to your apartments yesterday; that he has threatened you with another visit to-morrow, and that you demand the protection of the law, and they will give you two police officers who will arrest him."

"But, my dear, suppose he tells—"

"They will not believe him, you silly thing, if you have told your tale cleverly to the commissary, but they will believe you, who are an irreproachable woman, and in society."

"Oh! I shall never dare to do it."

"You must dare, my dear, or you are lost."

"But think that he will—he will insult me if he is arrested."

"Very well, you will have witnesses, and he will be sentenced."

"Sentenced to what?"

"To pay damages. In such cases, one must be pitiless!"

"Ah! speaking of damages—there is one thing that worries me very much—very much indeed. He left me two twenty-franc pieces on the mantelpiece."

"Two twenty-franc pieces?"

"Yes."

"No more?"

"No."

"That is very little. It would have humiliated me. Well?"

"Well! What am I to do with that money?"

The little Marchioness hesitated for a few seconds, and then she replied in a serious voice:

"My dear—you must make—you must make your husband a little present with it. That will be only fair!"

THE DEVIL

THE peasant was standing opposite the doctor, by the bedside of the dying old woman, and she, calmly resigned and quite lucid, looked at them and listened to their talking. She was going to die, and she did not rebel at it, for her life was over—she was ninety-two.

The July sun streamed in at the window and through the open door and cast its hot flames on to the uneven brown clay floor, which had been stamped down by four generations of clodhoppers. The smell of the fields came in also, driven by the brisk wind, and parched by the noontide heat. The grasshoppers chirped themselves hoarse, filling the air with their shrill noise, like that of the wooden crickets which are sold to children at fair time.

The doctor raised his voice and said: "Honoré, you cannot leave your mother in this state; she may die at any moment." And the peasant, in great distress, replied: "But I must get in my wheat, for it has been lying on the ground a long time, and the weather is just right for it; what do you say about it, mother?" And the dying woman, still possessed by her Norman avariciousness, replied *yes* with her eyes and her forehead, and so urged her son to get in his wheat, and to leave her to die alone. But the doctor got angry, and stamping his foot he said: "You are no better than a brute, do you hear, and I will not allow you to do it. Do you understand? And if you must get in your wheat to-day, go and fetch Rapet's wife and make her look after your mother. I *will* have it. And if you do not obey me, I will let you die like a dog, when you are ill in your turn; do you hear me?"

The peasant, a tall, thin fellow with slow movements, who was tormented by indecision, by his fear of the doctor and his keen love of saving, hesitated, calculated, and stammered out: "How much does La Rapet charge for attending sick people?"

"How should I know?" the doctor cried. "That depends upon how long she is wanted for. Settle it with her, by Jove! But I want her to be here within an hour, do you hear."

So the man made up his mind. "I will go for her," he replied; "don't get angry, doctor." And the latter left, calling out as he went: "Take care, you know, for I do not joke when I am angry!" And as soon as they were alone, the peasant turned to his mother, and said in a resigned voice: "I will go and fetch La Rapet, as the man will have it. Don't go off while I am away."

And he went out in his turn.

La Rapet, who was an old washerwoman, watched the dead and the dying of the neighborhood, and then, as soon as she had sewn her customers into that linen cloth from which they would emerge no more, she went and took up her irons to smooth the linen of the living. Wrinkled like a last year's apple, spiteful, envious, avaricious with a phenomenal avarice, bent double, as if she had been broken in half across the loins, by the constant movement of the iron over the linen, one might have said that she had a kind of monstrous and cynical affection for a death struggle. She never spoke of anything but of the people she had seen die, of the various kinds of deaths at which she had been present, and she related, with the greatest minuteness, details which were always the same, just like a sportsman talks of his shots.

When Honoré Bontemps entered her cottage, he found her preparing the starch for the collars of the village women, and he said: "Good evening; I hope you are pretty well, Mother Rapet."

She turned her head round to look at him and said: "Fairly well, fairly well, and you?"

"Oh! as for me, I am as well as I could wish, but my mother is very sick."

"Your mother?"

"Yes, my mother!"

"What's the matter with her?"

"She is going to turn up her toes, that's what's the matter with her!"

The old woman took her hands out of the water and asked with sudden sympathy: "Is she as bad as all that?"

"The doctor says she will not last till morning."

"Then she certainly is very bad!" Honoré hesitated, for he wanted to make a few preliminary remarks before coming to his proposal, but as he could hit upon nothing, he made up his mind suddenly.

"How much are you going to ask to stop with her till the end? You know that I am not rich, and I cannot even afford to keep a servant-girl. It is just that which has brought my poor mother to this state, too much work and fatigue! She used to work for ten, in spite of her ninety-two years. You don't find any made of that stuff nowadays!"

La Rapet answered gravely: "There are two prices. Forty sous by day and three francs by night for the rich, and twenty sous by day, and forty by night for the others. You shall pay me the twenty and forty." But the peasant reflected, for he knew his mother well. He knew how tenacious of life, how vigorous and unyielding she was. He knew, too, that she might last another week, in spite of the doctor's opinion, and so he said resolutely: "No, I would rather you would fix a price until the end. I will take my chance, one way or the other. The doctor says she will die very soon. If that happens, so much the better for you, and so much the worse for me, but if she holds out till to-morrow or longer, so much the better for me and so much the worse for you!"

The nurse looked at the man in astonishment, for she had never treated a death as a speculative job, and she hesitated, tempted by the idea of the possible gain. But almost immediately she suspected that he wanted to juggle her. "I can say nothing until I have seen your mother," she replied.

"Then come with me and see her."

She washed her hands, and went with him immediately. They did not speak on the road; she walked with short, hasty steps, while he strode on with his long legs, as if he were crossing a brook at every step. The cows lying down in the fields, overcome by the heat, raised their heads heavily and lowed feebly at the two passers-by, as if to ask them for some green grass.

When they got near the house, Honoré Bontemps murmured: "Suppose it is all over?" And the unconscious wish that it might be so showed itself in the sound of his voice.

But the old woman was not dead. She was lying on her back, on her wretched bed, her hands covered with a pink cotton counterpane, horribly thin, knotty paws, like some strange animal's, or like crabs' claws, hands closed by rheumatism, fatigue, and the work of nearly a century which she had accomplished.

La Rapet went up to the bed and looked at the dying woman, felt her pulse, tapped her on the chest, listened to her breathing, and asked her questions, so as to hear her speak: then, having looked at her for some time longer, she went out of the room, followed by Honoré. His decided opinion was, that the old woman would not last out the night, and he asked: "Well?" And the sick-nurse replied: "Well, she may last two days, perhaps three. You will have to give me six francs, everything included."

"Six francs! six francs!" he shouted. "Are you out of your mind? I tell you that she cannot last more than five or six hours!" And they disputed angrily for some time, but as the nurse said she would go home, as the time was slipping away, and as his wheat would not come to the farmyard of its own accord, he agreed to her terms at last:

"Very well, then, that is settled; six francs including everything, until the corpse is taken out."

"That is settled, six francs."

And he went away, with long strides, to his wheat, which was lying on the ground under the hot sun which ripens the grain, while the sick-nurse returned to the house.

She had brought some work with her, for she worked without stopping by the side of the dead and dying, sometimes for herself, sometimes for the family, who employed her as seamstress also, paying her rather more in that capacity.   Suddenly she asked:

"Have you received the last sacrament, Mother Bontemps?"

The old peasant woman said "No" with her head, and La Rapet, who was very devout, got up quickly: "Good heavens, is it possible? I will go and fetch the curé"; and she rushed off to the parsonage so quickly, that the urchins in the street thought some accident had happened, when they saw her trotting off like that.

The priest came immediately in his surplice, preceded by a choir-boy, who rang a bell to announce the passage of the Host through the parched and quiet country. Some men, working at a distance, took off their large hats and remained motionless until the white vestment had disappeared behind some farm buildings; the women who were making up the

sheaves stood up to make the sign of the cross; the
frightened black hens ran away along the ditch until
they reached a well-known hole through which they
suddenly disappeared, while a foal, which was tied
up in a meadow, took fright at the sight of the surplice and began to gallop round at the length of its
rope, kicking violently. The choir-boy, in his red
cassock, walked quickly, and the priest, the square
biretta on his bowed head, followed him, muttering
some prayers. Last of all came La Rapet, bent almost double, as if she wished to prostrate herself;
she walked with folded hands, as if she were in
church.

Honoré saw them pass in the distance, and he
asked: "Where is our priest going to?" And his
man, who was more acute, replied: "He is taking
the sacrament to your mother, of course!"

The peasant was not surprised and said: "That is
quite possible," and went on with his work.

Mother Bontemps confessed, received absolution
and extreme unction, and the priest took his departure, leaving the two women alone in the suffocating
cottage. La Rapet began to look at the dying
woman, and to ask herself whether it could last
much longer.

The day was on the wane, and a cooler air came
in stronger puffs, making a view of Epinal, which
was fastened to the wall by two pins, flap up and
down. The scanty window curtains, which had
formerly been white, but were now yellow and covered with fly-specks, looked as if they were going to
fly off, and seemed to struggle to get away, like the
old woman's soul.

Lying motionless, with her eyes open, the old mother seemed to await the death which was so near, and which yet delayed its coming, with perfect indifference. Her short breath whistled in her throat. It would stop altogether soon, and there would be one woman less in the world, one whom nobody would regret.

At nightfall Honoré returned, and when he went up to the bed and saw that his mother was still alive he asked: "How is she?" just as he had done formerly, when she had been sick. Then he sent La Rapet away, saying to her: "To-morrow morning at five o'clock, without fail." And she replied: "To-morrow at five o'clock."

She came at daybreak, and found Honoré eating his soup, which he had made himself, before going to work.

"Well, is your mother dead?" asked the nurse.

"She is rather better, on the contrary," he replied, with a malignant look out of the corner of his eyes. Then he went out.

La Rapet was seized with anxiety, and went up to the dying woman, who was in the same state, lethargic and impassive, her eyes open and her hands clutching the counterpane. The nurse perceived that this might go on thus for two days, four days, eight days, even, and her avaricious mind was seized with fear. She was excited to fury against the cunning fellow who had tricked her, and against the woman who would not die.

Nevertheless, she began to sew and waited with her eyes fixed on the wrinkled face of Mother Bontemps. When Honoré returned to breakfast he seemed quite satisfied, and even in a bantering humor, for he was carrying in his wheat under very favorable circumstances.

La Rapet was getting exasperated; every passing minute now seemed to her so much time and money stolen from her. She felt a mad inclination to choke this old ass, this headstrong old fool, this obstinate old wretch — to stop that short, rapid breath, which was robbing her of her time and money, by squeezing her throat a little. But then she reflected on the danger of doing so, and other thoughts came into her head, so she went up to the bed and said to her: "Have you ever seen the Devil?"

Mother Bontemps whispered: "No."

Then the sick-nurse began to talk and to tell her tales likely to terrify her weak and dying mind. "Some minutes before one dies the Devil appears," she said, "to all. He has a broom in his hand, a saucepan on his head and he utters loud cries. When anybody had seen him, all was over, and that person had only a few moments longer to live"; and she enumerated all those to whom the Devil had appeared that year: Josephine Loisel, Eulalie Ratier, Sophie Padagnau, Séraphine Grospied.

Mother Bontemps, who was at last most disturbed in mind, moved about, wrung her hands, and tried to turn her head to look at the other end of the room. Suddenly La Rapet disappeared at the foot of the bed. She took a sheet out of the cupboard and wrapped herself up in it; then she put the iron pot on to her head, so that its three short bent feet rose up like horns, took a broom in her right hand and a tin pail in her left, which she threw up suddenly, so that it might fall to the ground noisily.

Certainly when it came down, it made a terrible noise. Then, climbing on to a chair, the nurse showed herself, gesticulating and uttering shrill cries into the pot which covered her face, while she menaced the old peasant woman, who was nearly dead, with her broom.

Terrified, with a mad look on her face, the dying woman made a superhuman effort to get up and escape; she even got her shoulders and chest out of bed; then she fell back with a deep sigh. All was over, and La Rapet calmly put everything back into its place; the broom into the corner by the cupboard, the sheet inside it, the pot on to the hearth, the pail on to the floor, and the chair against the wall. Then with a professional air, she closed the dead woman's enormous eyes, put a plate on the bed and poured some holy water into it, dipped the twig of boxwood into it, and kneeling down, she fervently repeated the prayers for the dead, which she knew by heart, as a matter of business.

When Honoré returned in the evening, he found her praying. He calculated immediately that she had made twenty sous out of him, for she had only spent three days and one night there, which made five francs altogether, instead of the six which he owed her.

THE VENUS OF BRANIZA

SOME years ago there lived in Braniza a celebrated Talmudist, renowned no less on account of his beautiful wife, than for his wisdom, his learning, and his fear of God. The Venus of Braniza deserved that name thoroughly; she deserved it for herself, on account of her singular beauty, and even more as the wife of a man deeply versed in the Talmud, for the wives of the Jewish philosophers are, as a rule, ugly or possess some bodily defect.

The Talmud explains this in the following manner: It is well known that marriages are made in heaven, and at the birth of a boy a divine voice calls out the name of his future wife, and *vice versâ*. But just as a good father tries to get rid of his good wares out of doors, and only uses the damaged stuff at home for his children, so God bestows on the Talmudists those women whom other men would not care to have.

Well, God made an exception in the case of our Talmudist, and had bestowed a Venus on him, per-

2 G. de M.—12 (177)

haps only in order to confirm the rule by means of this exception, and to make it appear less hard. This philosopher's wife was a woman who would have done honor to any king's throne, or to a pedestal in any sculpture gallery. Tall, and with a wonderfully voluptuous figure, she carried a strikingly beautiful head, surmounted by thick, black plaits, on her proud shoulders. Two large, dark eyes languished and glowed beneath long lashes, and her beautiful hands looked as if they were carved out of ivory.

This glorious woman, who seemed to have been designed by nature to rule, to see slaves at her feet, to provide occupation for the painter's brush, the sculptor's chisel, and the poet's pen, lived the life of a rare and beautiful flower shut up in a hothouse. She would sit the whole day long wrapped up in her costly furs looking down dreamily into the street.

She had no children; her husband, the philosopher, studied and prayed and studied again from early morning until late at night; his mistress was "the Veiled Beauty," as the Talmudists call the Kabbalah. She paid no attention to her house, for she was rich, and everything went of its own accord like a clock which has only to be wound up once a week; nobody came to see her, and she never went out of the house; she sat and dreamed and brooded and — yawned.

 *   *   *   *   *   *   *

One day when a terrible storm of thunder and lightning had spent its fury over the town, and all windows had been opened in order to let the Messias in, the Jewish Venus was sitting as usual in her comfortable easy-chair, shivering in spite of her furs, and thinking. Suddenly she fixed her glowing eyes on her husband who was sitting before the Talmud, swaying his body backward and forward, and said suddenly:

"Just tell me, when will Messias, the son of David, come?"

"He will come," the philosopher replied, "when all the Jews have become either altogether virtuous or altogether vicious, says the Talmud."

"Do you believe that all the Jews will ever become virtuous?" the Venus continued.

"How am I to believe that?"

"So Messias will come when all the Jews have become vicious?"

The philosopher shrugged his shoulders, and lost himself again in the labyrinth of the Talmud, out of which, so it is said, only one man returned in perfect sanity. The beautiful woman at the window again looked dreamily out into the heavy rain, while her white fingers played unconsciously with the dark furs of her splendid robe.

*   *   *   *   *   *   *

One day the Jewish philosopher had gone to a neighboring town, where an important question of ritual was to be decided. Thanks to his learning, the question was settled sooner than he had expected, and instead of returning the next morning, as he had intended, he came back the same evening with a friend who was no less learned than himself. He got out of the carriage at his friend's house and went home on foot. He was not a little surprised when he saw his windows brilliantly illuminated, and found an officer's servant comfortably smoking his pipe in front of his house.

"What are you doing here?" he asked in a friendly manner, but with some curiosity, nevertheless.

"I am on guard, lest the husband of the beautiful Jewess should come home unexpectedly."

"Indeed? Well, mind and keep a good lookout."

Saying this, the philosopher pretended to go away, but went into the house through the garden entrance at the back. When he got into the first room, he found a table laid for two, which had evidently only been left a short time previously. His wife was sitting as usual at her bedroom window wrapped in her furs, but her cheeks were suspiciously red, and her dark eyes had not their usual languishing look, but now rested on her husband with a gaze which expressed at the same time satisfaction and mockery. At that moment his foot struck against an object on the floor, which gave out a strange sound. He picked it up and examined it in the light. It was a pair of spurs.

"Who has been here with you?" asked the Talmudist.

The Jewish Venus shrugged her shoulders contemptuously, but did not reply.

"Shall I tell you? The Captain of Hussars has been with you."

"And why should he not have been here with me?" she said, smoothing the fur on her jacket with her white hand.

"Woman! are you out of your mind?"

"I am in full possession of my senses," she replied, and a knowing smile hovered round her red voluptuous lips. "But must I not also do my part, in crder that Messias may come and redeem us poor Jews?"

THE RABBIT

O LD Lecacheur appeared at the door of his house at his usual hour, between five and a quarter past five in the morning, to look after his men who were going to work.

With a red face, only half awake, his right eye open and the left nearly closed, he was buttoning his braces over his fat stomach with some difficulty, all the time looking into every corner of the farmyard with a searching glance. The sun was darting his oblique rays through the beech-trees by the side of the ditch and the apple-trees outside, making the cocks crow on the dung-hill, and the pigeons coo on the roof. The smell of the cow stalls came through the open door, mingling in the fresh morning air with the pungent odor of the stable where the horses were neighing, with their heads turned toward the light.

As soon as his trousers were properly fastened, Lecacheur came out, and went first of all toward the hen-house to count the morning's eggs, for he had been suspecting thefts for some time. But the servant girl ran up to him with lifted arms and cried:

"Master! Master! they have stolen a rabbit during the night."

"A rabbit?"

"Yes, Master, the big gray rabbit, from the hutch on the left." Whereupon the farmer quite opened his left eye, and said, simply:

"I must see that."

And off he went to inspect it. The hutch had been broken open and the rabbit was gone. Then he became thoughtful, closed his left eye again, scratched his nose, and after a little consideration, said to the frightened girl, who was standing stupidly before him:

"Go and fetch the gendarmes; say I expect them as soon as possible."

Lecacheur was mayor of the village, Pairgry-le Gras, and ruled it like a tyrant, on account of his money and position. As soon as the servant had disappeared in the direction of the village, which was only about five hundred yards off, he went into the house to have his morning coffee and to discuss the matter with his wife. He found her on her knees in front of the fire, trying to get it to burn up quickly. As soon as he got to the door, he said:

"Somebody has stolen the gray rabbit."

She turned round so quickly that she found herself sitting on the floor, and looking at her husband with distressed eyes, she said:

"What is it, Cacheux! Somebody has stolen a rabbit?"

"The big gray one."

She sighed: "How sad! Who can have done it?"

She was a little, thin, active, neat woman, who knew all about farming. But Lecacheur had his own ideas about the matter.

"It must be that fellow Polyte."

His wife got up suddenly and said in a furious voice:

"He did it! he did it! You need not look for any one else. He did it! You have said it, Cacheux!"

All her peasant's fury, all her avarice, all the rage of a saving woman against the man of whom she had always been suspicious, and against the girl whom she had always suspected, could be seen in the contraction of her mouth, in the wrinkles in her cheeks, and in the forehead of her thin, exasperated face.

"And what have you done?" she asked.

"I have sent for the gendarmes."

This Polyte was a laborer, who had been employed on the farm for a few days, and had been dismissed by Lecacheur for an insolent answer. He was an old soldier, and was supposed to have retained his habits of marauding and debauchery from his campaigns in Africa. He did anything for a livelihood, but whether working as a mason, a navvy, a reaper, whether he broke stones or lopped trees, he was always lazy. So he remained in no position long, and had, at times, to change his neighborhood to obtain work.

From the first day that he came to the farm, Lecacheur's wife had detested him, and now she was sure that he had committed the robbery.

In about half an hour the two gendarmes arrived. Brigadier Sénateur was very tall and thin, and Gendarme Lenient, short and fat. Lecacheur made them sit down and told them the affair, and then they went and saw the scene of the theft, in order to verify the fact that the hutch had been broken open, and to collect all the proofs they could. When they got back to the kitchen, the mistress brought in some wine, filled their glasses and asked with a distrustful look:

"Shall you catch him?"

The brigadier, who had his sword between his legs, appeared thoughtful. Certainly, he was sure of taking him, if he was pointed out to him, but if not, he could not himself answer for being able to discover him. After reflecting for a long time, he put this simple question:

"Do you know the thief?"

And Lecacheur replied, with a look of Normandy slyness in his eyes:

"As for knowing him, I do not, as I did not see him commit the robbery. If I had seen him, I should have made him eat it raw, skin and flesh, without a drop of cider to wash it down. As for saying who it is, I cannot, although I believe it is that good-for-nothing Polyte."

Then he related at length his troubles with Polyte, his leaving his service, his bad reputation, things which had been told him, accumulating insignificant and minute proofs. Then the brigadier, who had been listening very attentively while he emptied his glass and filled it again, turned to his gendarme with an indifferent air, and said:

"We must go and look in the cottage of Severin's wife." At which the gendarme smiled and nodded three times.

Then Madame Lecacheur came to them, and very quietly, with all a peasant's cunning, questioned the brigadier in her turn. The shepherd Severin, a simpleton, a sort of brute who had been brought up from youth among his bleating flocks, and who knew of scarcely anything besides them in the world, had nevertheless preserved the peasant's instinct for saving, at the bottom of his heart. For years and years he had hidden in hollow trees and crevices in the rocks, all that he earned, either as shepherd, or by curing the fractures of animals (for the bonesetter's secret had been handed down to him by the old shepherd whose place he took), by touch or advice, for one day he bought a small property consisting of a cottage and a field, for three thousand francs.

A few months later it became known that he was going to marry a servant notorious for her bad morals, the innkeeper's servant. The young fellows said that the girl, knowing that he was pretty well off, had been to his cottage every night, and had taken him, bewitched him, led him on to matrimony, little by little, night by night.

And then, having been to the mayor's office and to church, she lived in the house which her man had bought, while he continued to tend his flocks, day and night, on the plains.

And the brigadier added:

"Polyte has been sleeping with her for three weeks, for the thief has no place of his own to go to!"

The gendarme made a little joke:

"He takes the shepherd's blankets."

Madame Lecacheur, seized by a fresh access of rage, of rage increased by a married woman's anger against debauchery, exclaimed:

"It is she, I am sure. Go there. Ah! the black guard thieves!"

But the brigadier was quite unmoved.

"A minute," he said. "Let us wait until twelve o'clock; as Polyte goes and dines there every day I shall catch them with it under their noses."

The gendarme smiled, pleased at his chief's idea, and Lecacheur also smiled now, for the affair of the shepherd struck him as very funny: deceived husbands are always amusing.

*　　*　　*　　*　　*　　*　　*

Twelve o'clock has just struck when the brigadier, followed by his man, knocked gently three times at the door of a small lonely house, situated at the corner of a wood, some five hundred yards from the village.

They stood close against the wall, so as not to be seen from within, and waited. As nobody answered, the brigadier knocked again in a minute or two. It was so quiet that the house seemed uninhabited; but Lenient, the gendarme, who had very quick ears, said that he heard somebody moving about inside. Sénateur got angry. He would not allow anyone to resist the authority of the law for a moment, and, knocking at the door with the hilt of his sword, he cried out:

"Open the door, in the name of the law."

As this order had no effect, he roared out:

"If you do not obey, I shall smash the lock. I am the brigadier of the gendarmerie, by G—d! Here, Lenient."

He had not finished speaking when the door opened and Sénateur saw before him a fat girl, with a very red color, blowsy, with pendent breasts, big stomach, and broad hips, a sort of sanguine and sensual female, the wife of the shepherd Severin. He entered the cottage.

"I have come to pay you a visit, as I want to make a little search," he said, and he looked about him. On the table there was a plate, a jug of cider and a glass half full, which proved that a meal had been going on. Two knives were lying side by side, and the shrewd gendarme winked at his superior officer.

"It smells good," the latter said.

"One might swear that it was stewed rabbit," Lenient added, much amused.

"Will you have a glass of brandy?" the peasant woman asked.

"No, thank you; I only want the skin of the rabbit that you are eating."

She pretended not to understand, but she was trembling.

"What rabbit?"

The brigadier had taken a seat, and was calmly wiping his forehead.

"Come, come, you are not going to try and make us believe that you live on couch grass. What were you eating there all by yourself for your dinner?"

"I? Nothing whatever, I swear to you. A mite of butter on my bread."

"You are a novice, my good woman—*a mite of butter on your bread.* You are mistaken; you ought to have said: a mite of butter on the rabbit. By G—d, your butter smells good! It is special butter, extra good butter, butter fit for a wedding; certainly not household butter!"

The gendarme was shaking with laughter, and repeated:

"Not household butter, certainly."

As Brigadier Sénateur was a joker, all the gendarmes had grown facetious, and the officer continued:

"Where is your butter?"

"My butter?"

"Yes, your butter."

"In the jar."

"Then where is the butter jar?"

"Here it is."

She brought out an old cup, at the bottom of which there was a layer of rancid, salt butter. The brigadier smelled it, and said, with a shake of his head:

"It is not the same. I want the butter that smells of the rabbit. Come, Lenient, open your eyes; look under the sideboard, my good fellow, and I will look under the bed."

Having shut the door, he went up to the bed and tried to move it; but it was fixed to the wall, and had not been moved for more than half a century, apparently. Then the brigadier stooped, and made his uniform crack. A button had flown off.

"Lenient," he said.

"Yes, brigadier?"

"Come here, my lad, and look under the bed; I am too tall. I will look after the sideboard."

He got up and waited while his man executed his orders.

Lenient, who was short and stout, took off his kepi, laid himself on his stomach, and putting his face on the floor looked at the black cavity under the bed. Then, suddenly, he exclaimed:

"All right, here we are!"

"What have you got? The rabbit?"

"No, the thief."

"The thief! Pull him out, pull him out!"

The gendarme had put his arms under the bed and laid hold of something. He pulled with all his might, and at last a foot, shod in a thick boot, appeared, which he was holding in his right hand. The brigadier grabbed it, crying:

"Pull! pull!"

And Lenient, who was on his knees by that time, was pulling at the other leg. But it was a hard job, for the prisoner kicked out hard, and arched up his back across the bed.

"Courage! courage! pull! pull!" Sénateur cried, and they pulled with all their strength — so hard that the wooden bar gave way, and the victim came out as far as his head. At last they got that out also, and saw the terrified and furious face of Polyte, whose arms remained stretched out under the bed.

"Pull away!" the brigadier kept on exclaiming. Then they heard a strange noise as the arms followed the shoulders and the hands the arms. In the hands was the handle of a saucepan, and at the end of the handle the pan itself, which contained stewed rabbi

"Good Lord! good Lord!" the brigadier shouted
in his delight, while Lenient took charge of the man.
The rabbit's skin, an overwhelming proof, was discovered under the mattress, and the gendarmes returned in triumph to the village with their prisoner
and their booty.

    *   *   *   *   *   *   *

A week later, as the affair had made much stir,
Lecacheur, on going into the *mairie* to consult the
schoolmaster, was told that the shepherd Severin had
been waiting for him for more than an hour. He
found him sitting on a chair in a corner with his
stick between his legs. When he saw the mayor,
he got up, took off his cap, and said:

"Good morning, Maître Cacheux"; and then he
remained standing, timid and embarrassed.

"What do you want?" the former said.

"This is it, Monsieur. Is it true that somebody
stole one of your rabbits last week?"

"Yes, it is quite true, Severin."

"Who stole the rabbit?"

"Polyte Ancas, the laborer."

"Right! right! And is it also true that it was
found under my bed?"

"What do you mean, the rabbit?"

"The rabbit and then Polyte."

"Yes, my poor Severin, quite true, but who told
you?"

"Pretty well everybody. I understand! And I
suppose you know all about marriages, as you marry *
people?"

---

   * In France, the civil marriage is compulsory.

"What about marriage?"

"With regard to one's rights."

"What rights?"

"The husband's rights and then the wife's rights."

"Of course I do."

"Oh! Then just tell me, M'sieu Cacheux, has my wife the right to go to bed with Polyte?"

"What do you mean by going to bed with Polyte?"

"Yes, has she any right before the law, and seeing that she is my wife, to go to bed with Polyte?"

"Why of course not, of course not."

"If I catch him there again, shall I have the right to thrash him and her also?"

"Why — why — why, yes."

"Very well, then; I will tell you why I want to know. One night last week, as I had my suspicions, I came in suddenly, and they were not behaving properly. I chucked Polyte out, to go and sleep somewhere else; but that was all, as I did not know what my rights were. This time I did not see them; I only heard of it from others. That is over, and we will not say any more about it; but if I catch them again, by G—d! if I catch them again, I will make them lose all taste for such nonsense, Maître Cacheux, as sure as my name is Severin."

A DIVORCE CASE

M. CHASSEL, advocate, rises to speak:

"Mr. President and gentlemen of the jury. The cause that I am charged to plead before you requires medicine rather than justice; and is much more a case of pathology than a case of ordinary law. At first blush the facts seem very simple.

"A young man, very rich, with a noble and cultivated mind, and a generous heart, becomes enamored of a young lady, who is the perfection of beauty, more than beautiful, in fact; she is adorable, besides being as gracious as she is charming, as good and true as she is tender and pretty, and he marries her. For some time, he comports himself toward her not only as a devoted husband, but as a man full of solicitude and tenderness. Then he neglects her, misuses her, seems to entertain for her an insurmountable aversion, an irresistible disgust. One day he even strikes her, not only without any cause, but

(192)

also without the faintest pretext. I am not going, gentlemen, to draw a picture of silly allurements, which no one would comprehend. I shall not paint to you the wretched life of those two beings, and the horrible grief of this young woman. It will be sufficient to convince you, if I read some fragments from a journal written up every day by that poor young man, by that poor fool! For it is in presence of a fool, gentlemen, that we now find ourselves, and the case is all the more curious, all the more interesting, seeing that, in many points, it recalls the insanity of the unfortunate prince who recently died, of the witless king who reigned platonically over Bavaria. I shall hence designate this case — poetic folly.

"You will readily call to mind all that has been told of that most singular prince. He erected veritable fairy castles amid the most magnificent scenery his kingdom afforded. Even the reality of the beauty of the castles themselves, as well as of the sites, did not satisfy him. He invented, he created, in these extraordinary manors factitious horizons, obtained by means of theatrical artifices, changes of view, painted forests, in which the leaves of the trees became precious stones. He had the Alps and their glaciers; steppes, deserts of sand made hot by a blazing sun; and at nights, under the rays of the real moon, lakes which sparkled from below by means of fantastic electric lights. Swans floated on the lakes which glistened with skiffs, while an orchestra, composed of the finest executants in the world, inebriated with poetry the soul of the royal fool. That man was chaste, that man was a virgin. He lived only to

dream his dream divine. One evening he took out
with him in his boat a lady, young and beautiful, a
great artiste, and he begged her to sing. Intoxicated
herself by the magnificent scenery, by the languid
softness of the air, by the perfume of flowers, and by
the ecstasy of that prince, both young and handsome,
she sang, she sang, as women sing who have been
touched by love; then, overcome, trembling, she fell
on the bosom of the king in order to seek out his
lips. But he threw her into the lake, and seizing his
oars, rowed back to the shore, without concerning
himself as to whether anybody saved her or not.

"Gentlemen of the jury, we find ourselves in
presence of a case similar in every way to that. I
shall say no more now, except to read some passages
from the journal which we unexpectedly came upon
in the drawer of an old secretary.

* * * * * * *

"'How sad and weary is everything; always the
same, always hateful. How I dream of a land more
beautiful, more noble, more varied. What a poor
conception they have of their God, if their God exists,
as if he had not created other things, elsewhere. Always woods, little woods, waves which resemble
waves, plains which resemble plains, everything is
sameness and monotony. And Man? Man? What a
horrible animal! wicked, haughty, and repugnant!

* * * * * * *

"'It is essential to love, to love to perdition, without seeing that which one loves. For to see is to
comprehend, and to comprehend is to embrace. It
is necessary to love, to become intoxicated by it,
just as one gets drunk with wine, even to the extent

that one knows no longer what one is drinking.
And to drink, to drink, to drink, without drawing
breath, day and night!

*   *   *   *   *   *   *

"'I have found her, I believe. She has about her
something ideal which does not belong to this world,
and which furnishes wings to my dream. Ah! my
dream! How it reveals to me beings different from
what they really are! She is a blonde, a delicate
blonde, with hair whose delicate shade is inexpres-
sible. Her eyes are blue! Only blue eyes can penetrate my soul. The woman who lives in my heart,
in fact, all women, reveal themselves to me in the
eyes, only in the eyes. Oh! what a mystery, what a
mystery is the eye! The whole universe lives in it,
inasmuch as it sees, inasmuch as it reflects. It contains the universe, both things and beings, forests
and oceans, men and beasts, the settings of the sun,
the stars, the arts—all, all it sees; it collects and
absorbs all. And there is still more in it; the eye of
itself has a soul; it has in it the man who thinks,
the man who loves, the man who laughs, the man
who suffers! Oh! look at the blue eyes of women,
those eyes that are as deep as the sea, as changeful
as the sky, so sweet, so soft—soft as the breezes,
sweet as music, luscious as kisses; so transparent, so
clear that one sees behind them, discerns the soul,
the blue soul which colors them, which animates
them, which electrifies them. Yes, the soul has the
color of the look. The blue soul alone contains in
itself that which dreams; it bears its azure to the
floods and into space. The eye! Think of it, the
eye! It imbibes the visible life in order to nourish

thought. It drinks in the world—color, movement, books, pictures, all that is beautiful, all that is ugly, and weaves ideas out of them. And when it glances at us, it gives us the sensation of a happiness that is not of this earth. It informs us of that of which we have always been ignorant; it makes us comprehend that the realities of our dreams are but noisome things.

> *   *   *   *   *   *   *

"'I love her, too, for her walk. "Even when the bird walks one feels that it has wings," the poet has said. When she passes one feels that she is of a race apart from ordinary women, of a race more delicate and more divine. I shall marry her to-morrow. But I am afraid, I am afraid of so many things!

> *   *   *   *   *   *   *

"'Two beasts, two dogs, two wolves, two foxes, thread their way through the plantation and encounter one another. One of each two is male, the other female. They couple. They couple in consequence of an animal instinct, which forces them to continue the race, their race, the one from which they have sprung, the hairy coat, the form, movements and ways of life. The whole of the animal creation do the same without knowing why.

"'We human beings, also.

"'It is for this that I have married; I have obeyed that insane passion which throws us in the direction of the female.

> *   *   *   *   *   *   *

"'She is my wife. In accordance with my ideal desires, she comes very nearly realizing my unrealizable dream. But in separating from her, even for a second, after I have held her in my arms, she becomes no more than the being whom nature had made use of to disappoint all my hopes.

"'Has she disappointed them? No. And why have I grown weary of her, become loath even to touch her; she cannot graze even the palm of my hand, or the skin of my lips, but my heart throbs with unutterable disgust—not perhaps disgust of her, but a disgust more potent, more widespread, more loathsome; the disgust, in a word, of carnal love so vile in itself that it has become for all refined beings a shameful thing, which it is necessary to conceal, which one never speaks of save in a whisper, nor without blushing.

*　　*　　*　　*　　*　　*　　*

"'I can no longer bear the idea of my wife coming near me, calling me by name, with a smile; I cannot look at her, or touch even her arm—I cannot do it any more. At one time I thought to be kissed by her would be to transport me to Mohammed's seventh heaven. One day, she was suffering from a transient fever, and I smelled in her breath a subtle, slight, almost imperceptible puff of human putridity. I was completely overthrown.

"'Oh! the flesh, with its seductive and eager smell, a putrefaction which walks, which thinks, which speaks, which looks, which laughs, in which nourishment ferments and rots, which, nevertheless, is rose-colored, pretty, tempting, deceitful as the soul itself.

*　　*　　*　　*　　*　　*　　*

"'Why is it that flowers alone, which smell so sweet, those large flowers, glittering or pale, in their tones and shades, make my heart tremble and trouble my eyes? They are so beautiful, their structure is so finished, so varied, and so sensual, semi-open like human organs, more tempting than mouths, with turned-up lips, teeth, flesh, sown with life powders which, in each, give forth a distinct perfume.

"'They reproduce themselves, and they alone in the world, without polluting their inviolable race, shedding around them the divine influence of their love, the odoriferous incense of their caresses, the essence of their incomparable body, adorned with every grace, with every elegance of shape and form, with the coquetry of every hue of color, and the inebriating seductiveness of every variety of perfume.'

*   *   *   *   *   *   *

"FRAGMENTS WHICH WERE SELECTED SIX MONTHS LATER:

"'I love flowers, not as flowers, but as material and delicious beings; I pass my days and my nights in beds of flowers, where they have been concealed from public view like the women of a harem.

"'Who knows, except myself, the sweetness, the infatuation, the quivering, carnal, ideal, superhuman ecstasy of these tendernesses; and those kisses upon the bare flesh of a rose, upon the blushing flesh, upon the white skin, so miraculously different, delicate, rare, subtle, unctuous, of these adorable flowers!

"'I have flower-beds that no one has seen except myself, and which I tend myself.

"'I enter there as one would glide into a place of secret pleasure. In the lofty glass gallery, I pass first through a collection of inclosed corollas, half open or in full bloom, which incline toward the ground, or toward the roof. This is the first kiss they have given me.

"'These flowers I have just mentioned, these flowers which adorn the vestibule of my mysterious passions, are my servants and not my favorites.

"'They salute me by the change of their color and by their first inhalations. They are darlings, coquettes, arranged in eight rows to the right, eight rows to the left, and so laid out that they look like two gardens springing up from under my feet.

"'My heart palpitates, my eyes flash at the sight of them; my blood rushes through my veins, my soul is elated, and my hands tremble from desire as soon as I touch them. I pass on. There are three closed doors at the bottom of that gallery. I can make my choice of them. I have three harems.

"'But I enter most often the habitation of the orchids, my little wheedlers, by preference. Their chamber is low and suffocating. The humid and hot air makes the skin moist, takes away the breath and causes the fingers to quiver. They come, these strange girls, from a country marsh, burning and unhealthy. They draw you toward them as do the sirens, are as deadly as poison, admirably fantastic, enervating, dreadful. The butterflies here would also seem to have enormous wings, tiny feet, and eyes! Yes! they have also eyes! They look at me, they see me, prodigious, incomparable beings, fairies daughters of the sacred earth, of the impalpable air, and of hot sun's rays, that mother bountiful of the universe. Yes, they have wings, they have eyes, and nuances that no painter could imitate, every charm,

every grace, every form that one could dream of.
These wombs are transverse, odoriferous, and transparent, ever open for love and more tempting than
all the flesh of women.   The unimaginable designs of
their little bodies inebriate the soul, and transport it
to a paradise of images and of voluptuous ideals.
They tremble upon their stems as though they would
fly.   When they do fly do they come to me?   No, it
is my heart that hovers o'er them, like a mystic male,
tortured by love.

"'No wing of any animal can keep pace with
them. We are alone, they and I, in the lighted prison
which I have had constructed for them. I worship
them, I contemplate them, I admire them, I adore
them, the one after the other.

"'How healthy, strong, and rosy, a rosiness that
moistens the lips of desire! How I love them! The
border is frizzled, paler than their throat, where the
corolla hides itself away; a mysterious mouth, seductive sugar under the tongue, exhibiting and unveiling
the delicate, admirable, and sacred organs of these
divine little creatures which smell so exquisitely and
do not speak.

"'I sometimes have a passion for some of them
that lasts as long as their existence, which only em-
braces a few days and nights. I then have them
taken away from the common gallery and inclosed
in a pretty glass cabin, in which there murmurs a jet
of water over against a tropical gazon, which has
been brought from one of the Pacific Islands. And I
remain close to it, ardent, feverish, and tormented,
knowing that its death is near, and watch it fading
away, while in thought I possess it, aspire to its love,

drink it in, and then end its short life with an inex
pressible caress.'"

* * * * * * *

When he had finished the reading of these fragments, the advocate continued:

"Decency, gentlemen of the jury, hinders me from
communicating to you the extraordinary avowals of
this shameless, idealistic fool. The fragments that I
have just submitted to you will be sufficient, in my
opinion, to enable you to appreciate this instance of
mental malady, less rare in our epoch of hysterical
insanity and of corrupt decadence than most of us
believe.

"I think, then, that my client is more entitled
than any woman whatever to claim a divorce, in view
of the exceptional circumstances in which the disordered senses of her husband have placed her."

LA MORILLONNE

THEY called her "La Morillonne," * not only on account of her black hair and of a complexion which resembled autumnal leaves, but because of her thick purple lips which were like blackberries, when she curled them.

That she should be as dark as this in a district where everybody was fair, and born of parents who had tow-colored hair and butter-like complexions was one of the mysteries of atavism. A female ancestor must have had intimacy with one of those traveling tinkers who have gone about the country from time immemorial, with faces the color of bister and indigo, crowned by a wisp of light hair.

From that ancestor she derived not only her dark complexion, but also her dark soul and her deceitful eyes, whose depths were at times illuminated by flashes of every vice, the eyes of an obstinate and malicious animal.

---

*A sort of black grape. — EDITOR.

Handsome? Certainly not, nor even pretty. Ugly, with an absolute ugliness! Such a false look! Her nose was flat, having been smashed by a blow, while her unwholesome-looking mouth was always slobbering with greediness, or uttering something vile. Her hair was thick and untidy, a regular nest for vermin, and she had a thin, feverish body, with a limping walk. In short, she was a perfect monster, and yet all the young men of the neighborhood had made love to her, and whoever had been so honored longed for her society again.

From the time that she was twelve, she had been the mistress of every fellow in the village. She had corrupted boys of her own age in every conceivable manner and place.

Young men at the risk of imprisonment, and even steady, old, notable, and venerable men, such as the farmer at Eclausiaux, Monsieur Martin, the ex-mayor, and other highly respectable citizens, had been taken by the manners of that slut. The reason why the rural policeman was not severe upon them, in spite of his love for summoning people before the magistrates, was, so people said, that he would have been obliged to take out a summons against himself.

The consequence was that she had grown up without being interfered with, and was the mistress of every fellow in the village, as said the schoolmaster, who had himself been one of *the fellows*. But the most curious part of the business was that no one was jealous. They handed her on from one to the other, and when some one expressed his astonishment at this to her one day, she said to this unintelligent stranger:

"Is everybody not satisfied?"

And then, how could any one of them, even if he had been jealous, have monopolized her? They had no hold on her. She was not selfish, and though she accepted all gifts, whether in kind or in money, she never asked for anything, and she even appeared to prefer paying herself after her own fashion, by stealing. All she seemed to care about as her reward was pilfering, and a crown put into her hand gave her less pleasure than a half penny which she had stolen. Neither was it any use to dream of ruling her, of being the sole male, or proud master of the hen-roost, for none of them, no matter how broad-shouldered he was, would have been capable of it. Some had tried to vanquish her, but in vain.

How, then, could any of them claim to be her master? It would have been the same as wishing to have the sole right of baking bread in the common oven, in which the whole village baked.

But there was one exception, and that was Bru, the shepherd.

He lived in the fields in a movable hut, feeding on cakes made of unleavened dough, which he kneaded on a stone and baked in the hot ashes, now here, now there, in a hole dug out in the ground, and heated with dead wood. Potatoes, milk, hard cheese, blackberries, and a small cask of old gin distilled by himself, were his daily food. He knew nothing about love, although he was accused of all sorts of horrible things. But nobody dared abuse him to his face; in the first place, because Bru was a spare and sinewy man, who handled his shepherd's crook like a drum-major does his staff; secondly, because of his three sheep dogs, who had teeth like wolves, and obeyed nobody but their master; and lastly, for fear of the evil eye. For Bru, it appeared, knew spells which would blight the corn, give the sheep foot-rot, cattle the rinderpest, make cows die in calving, and set fire to the ricks and stacks.

But as Bru was the only one who did not thirst after La Morillonne, naturally one day she began to think of him, and declared that she, at any rate, was not afraid of his evil eye. So she went after him.

"What do you want?" he said, and she replied boldly:

"What do I want? I want you."

"Very well," he said, "but then you must belong to me alone."

"All right," was her answer, "if you think you can please me."

He smiled and took her into his arms, and she was away from the village for a whole week. She had, in fact, become Bru's exclusive property.

The village grew excited. They were not jealous of one another, but they were of him. What! Could she not resist him? Of course he had charms and spells against every imaginable thing. Then they grew furious; next they grew bold, and watched from behind a tree. She was still as lively as ever, but he, poor fellow, seemed to have suddenly fallen ill, and required nursing at her hands. The villagers, however, felt no compassion for the poor shepherd, and one of them, more courageous than the rest, advanced toward the hut with his gun in his hand:

"Tie up your dogs," he cried out from a distance; "fasten them up, Bru, or I shall shoot them."

"You need not be frightened of the dogs," La Morillonne replied; "I will be answerable for it that they will not hurt you"; and she smiled as the young man with the gun went toward her.

"What do you want?" the shepherd said.

"I can tell you," she replied. "He wants me and I am very willing. There!"

Bru began to cry, and she continued:

"You are a good-for-nothing."

And she went off with the lad. Bru seized his crook, seeing which the young fellow raised his gun.

"Seize him! seize him!" the shepherd shouted, urging on his dogs, while the other had already got his finger on the trigger to fire at them. But La Morillonne pushed down the muzzle and called out:

"Here, dogs! here! *Prr, prr*, my beauties!"

And the three dogs rushed up to her, licked her hands and frisked about as they followed her, while she called to the shepherd from the distance:

"You see, Bru, they are not at all jealous!"

And then, with a short and evil laugh, she added:

"They are my property now."

THE TWENTY-FIVE FRANCS OF THE MOTHER SUPERIOR

HE CERTAINLY looked very droll, did daddy Pavilly, with his great, spider legs and little body, his long arms and pointed head, surrounded by a flame of red hair on the top of the crown.

He was a clown, a peasant clown by nature, born to play tricks, to act parts, simple parts, a peasant's son who could scarcely read. Yes! God had certainly created him to amuse others, the poor country yokels who have neither theaters nor *fêtes*, and he amused them conscientiously. In the *café* people treated him to drink in order to keep him there, and he drank copiously, laughing and joking, hoaxing everybody without vexing anyone, while people laughed heartily around him.

He was so droll that the very girls could not resist him, ugly as he was, because he made them laugh. He would drag them about joking all the

(207)

while, would tickle and squeeze them, saying such
funny things that their sides shook while they pushed
him away.

Toward the end of June he engaged himself for
the harvest to farmer Le Harivan, near Rouville. For
three whole weeks he amused the harvesters, male
and female, with his jokes, by day and night. During the day, when he was in the fields, he wore an
old straw hat which hid his red shock head. You
could see him gathering up the yellow grain and
tying it into bundles with his long, thin arms; and
then suddenly stop to make a funny gesture which
made the laborers, who always kept their eyes on
him, laugh all over the field. At night he would
creep, like some animal, in among the straw in the
barn where the women slept, causing screams and
exciting a disturbance. Driven off by their wooden
clogs, he would escape on all fours, like a grimacing
monkey, amid volleys of laughter from the whole
place.

On the last day, as the wagon, full of reapers
decked with ribbons and playing bagpipes, shouting
and elated with pleasure and drink, went along the
white highroad, slowly drawn by six dapple-gray
horses and driven by a lad in a blouse with a rosette
in his cap, Pavilly, in the midst of the sprawling
women, danced like a drunken satyr, keeping the little dirty-faced boys and astonished peasants staring
at him open-mouthed on the way to the farm.

Suddenly, when they got to the gate of Le Harivan's farmyard, he gave a leap as he was lifting up
his arms. Unfortunately, as he came down, he knocked
against the side of the long wagon, fell over it on to

the wheel, and rebounded into the road. His companions jumped out, but he did not move; one eye was closed, while the other was open, and he was pale with fear. His long limbs were stretched out in the dust, and when they touched his right leg he began to scream, and when they tried to make him stand up, he immediately fell down.

"I think one of his legs is broken," one of the men said.

And so it really was. Harivan, therefore, had him laid on a table and sent off a man on horseback to Rouville to fetch the doctor, who came an hour later.

The farmer generously said that he would pay for the man's treatment in the hospital, so the doctor carried Pavilly off in his carriage to the hospital, and had him put into a whitewashed ward, where the fracture was reduced.

As soon as he knew that it would not kill him, and that he would be taken care of, cuddled, cured, and fed without having anything to do except to lie on his back between the sheets, Pavilly's joy was unbounded, and he began to laugh silently and continuously, so as to show his decayed teeth.

Whenever one of the Sisters of Mercy came near his bed he would make grimaces of satisfaction, winking, twisting his mouth awry and moving his nose, which was very long and mobile. His neighbors in the ward, ill as they were, could not help laughing, and the Mother Superior often came to his bedside, to be amused for a quarter of an hour. He invented all kinds of jokes and stories for her, and as he had the makings of a strolling actor in him, he would be devout in order to please her, speaking of

2 G. de M.—14

religion with the serious air of a man who knows that there are times when jokes are out of place.

One day, he took it into his head to sing to her. She was delighted and came to see him more frequently; then she brought him a hymn-book so as to utilize his voice. Then he might be seen sitting up in bed, for he was beginning to be able to move, singing the praises of the Almighty and of Mary in a falsetto voice, while the kind, stout sister stood by him and beat time with her finger. When he could walk, the Superior offered to keep him for some time longer to sing in chapel, to serve at Mass, and to fulfill the duties of sacristan. He accepted, and for a whole month he might be seen in his surplice, limping and singing the psalms and the responses, with such movements of his head that the number of the faithful increased, and people deserted the parish church to attend vespers at the hospital.

But as everything must come to an end in this world, they were obliged to discharge him when he was quite cured, and the Superior gave him twenty-five francs in return for his services.

As soon as Pavilly found himself in the street with all that money in his pocket, he asked himself what he was going to do. Should he return to the village? Certainly not before having a drink, for he had not had one for a long time, and so he went into a *café*. He had never visited town more than two or three times a year, and had a confused and intoxicating recollection of a particular orgy on one of those visits. So he asked for a glass of the best brandy, which he swallowed at a gulp to grease the passage, and then he had another to see how it tasted.

As soon as the strong and fiery liquor had touched his palate and tongue, awakening more vividly than ever the sensation of which he was so fond, and for which he craved, that feeling which caresses, and stings, and burns the mouth, he knew that he could drink a whole bottle of it. So he asked immediately what it cost, so as to spare himself expense. They charged him three francs, which he paid, and then he began quietly to get drunk.

However, he was methodical in it, as he wished to keep sober enough for other pleasures. So, as soon as he felt that he was on the point of seeing the fireplace bow to him, he got up and went out with unsteady steps, with his bottle under his arm, in search of a house where girls of easy virtue lived.

He found one, with some difficulty, after having asked a carter, who did not know of one; a postman, who directed him wrong; a baker, who began to swear and called him an old pig; and lastly, a soldier, who was obliging enough to take him to it, advised him to choose La Reine.

Although it was barely twelve o'clock, Pavilly went into that palace of delight, where he was received by a servant, who wanted to turn him out again. But he made her laugh by making a grimace, showed her three francs, the usual price of the special luxuries of the place, and followed her with difficulty up a dark staircase, which led to the first floor.

When he had been shown into a room, he asked for La Reine, and had another drink out of the bottle, while waiting. Very shortly the door opened and a girl came in. She was tall, fat, red-faced—enormous. She looked at the drunken fellow who had

fallen into a seat with the eye of a judge of such
matters, and said:

"Are you not ashamed of yourself, at this time of
day?"

"Ashamed of what, Princess?" he stammered.

"Why, of disturbing a lady, before she has even
had time to eat her dinner."

He wanted to have a joke, so he said:

"There is no such thing as time for the brave."

"And there ought to be no time for getting drunk
either, old guzzler."

At this, he got angry:

"I am not a guzzler, and I am not drunk."

"Not drunk?"

"No, I am not."

"Not drunk? Why you cannot even stand
straight"; and she looked at him angrily, thinking
that all this time her companions were having their
dinner.

"I—I could dance a polka," he replied, getting
up, and to prove his stability he got on to the chair,
made a pirouette, and jumped on to the bed, where
his thick, muddy shoes made two great marks.

"Oh! you dirty brute!" the girl cried, and rushing at him, she struck him a blow with her fist in
the stomach, such a blow that Pavilly lost his balance, fell, struck the foot of the bed, and making a
complete somersault tumbled on to the washstand
and then rolled on to the ground, dragging the jug and
basin with him.

The noise was so loud, and his cries so piercing,
that everybody in the house rushed in, master, mistress, servant, and staff.

The master picked him up, but as soon as he had put him on his legs, the peasant lost his balance again, and began to call out that his leg was broken, the other leg, the sound one.

It was true, so they sent for a doctor, who happened to be the same one who had attended him at Le Harivan's.

"What! Is it you again?" said the surgeon.

"Yes, M'sieu."

"What is the matter with you?"

"Somebody has broken my other leg for me, M'sieu."

"Who did it, boy?"

"Why, a female."

Everybody was listening. The girls in their dressing-gowns, with their mouths still greasy from their interrupted dinner, the mistress of the house furious, the master nervous.

"This will be a bad job," the doctor said: "You know that the municipal authorities look upon you with very unfavorable eyes, so we must try and hush the matter up."

"How can it be managed?" the master of the place asked.

"Why the best way would be to send him back to the hospital, out of which he has just come, and to pay for him there."

"I would rather do that," the master of the house replied, "than have any fuss made about the matter."

So half an hour later, Pavilly returned drunk and groaning to the ward which he had left an hour before. The Superior lifted up her hands in sorrow, for she liked him, and with a smile, for she was glad to have him back.

"Well, my good fellow, what is the matter with you now?"

"The other leg is broken, Madame."

"So you have been getting on to another load of straw, you old joker?"

And Pavilly, in great confusion, but still sly, said, with hesitation:

"No—no—not this time, no—not this time. It was not my fault, not my fault. A mattress caused this."

She could get no other explanation out of him, and never knew that his relapse was due to her twenty-five francs.

EPIPHANY

"AH!" SAID Captain the Count de Garens, "I should rather think that I do remember that Epiphany supper, during the war! "At the time I was quartermaster of cavalry, and for a fortnight, I had been lurking about as a scout in front of the German advanced guard. The evening before we had cut down a few Uhlans and had lost three men, one of whom was that poor little Raudeville. You remember Joseph de Raudeville well, of course.

"Well, on that day my captain ordered me to take six troopers and occupy the village of Porterin, where there had been five fights in three weeks, and to hold it all night. There were not twenty houses left standing, nay, not a dozen, in that wasp's nest. So I took ten troopers, and set out at about four o'clock; at five o'clock, while it was still pitch dark, we reached the first houses of Porterin. I halted and ordered Marchas—you know Pierre de Marchas,

who afterward married little Martel-Auvelin, the
daughter of the Marquis de Martel-Auvelin — to go
alone into the village and to report to me what he
saw.

"I had chosen nothing but volunteers, and all of
good family. When on service it is pleasant not to
be forced into intimacy with unpleasant fellows.
This Marchas was as sharp as possible, as cunning
as a fox, and as supple as a serpent. He could scent
the Prussians as well as a dog can scent a hare,
could find victuals where we should have died of
hunger without him, and could obtain information
from everybody — information which was always re-
liable — with incredible cleverness.

"In ten minutes he returned. 'All right,' he said;
'there have been no Prussians here for three days.
It is a sinister place, is this village. I have been
talking to a Sister of Mercy, who is attending to four
or five wounded men in an abandoned convent.'

"I ordered them to ride on, and we penetrated
into the principal street. On the right and left we
could vaguely see roofless walls, hardly visible in the
profound darkness. Here and there a light was burning in a room; some family had remained to keep its
house standing as long as they were able; a family of
brave, or of poor, people. The rain began to fall, a
fine, icy-cold rain, which froze us before it wetted
us through, by merely touching our cloaks. The
horses stumbled against stones, against beams, against
furniture. Marchas guided us, going before us on
foot, and leading his horse by the bridle.

"'Where are you taking us to?' I asked him.
And he replied: 'I have a place for us to lodge

and a rare good one.' And soon we stopped before
a small house, evidently belonging to some person of
the middle class, completely shut up, built on to the
street with a garden in the rear.

"Marchas broke open the lock by means of a big
stone, which he picked up near the garden gate;
then he mounted the steps, smashed in the front door
with his feet and shoulders, lighted a bit of wax candle, which he was never without, and preceded us
into the comfortable apartments of some rich private
individual, guiding us with admirable assurance, just
as if he had lived in this house which he now saw
for the first time.

"Two troopers remained outside to take care of
our horses; then Marchas said to stout Ponderel, who
followed him: 'The stables must be on the left; I
saw that as we came in; go and put the animals up
there, for we do not want them,' and then turning
to me he said: 'Give your orders, confound it all!'

"Marchas always astonished me, and I replied
with a laugh: 'I shall post my sentinels at the country approaches and I will return to you here.'

"'How many men are you going to take?'

"'Five. The others will relieve them at five o'clock
in the evening.'

"'Very well. Leave me four to look after provisions, to do the cooking, and to set the table. I
will go and find out where the wine is hidden away.'

"I went off to reconnoiter the deserted streets,
until they ended in the open country, so as to post
my sentries there.

"Half an hour later I was back, and found Marchas lounging in a great armchair, the covering of

which he had taken off, from love of luxury as he said. He was warming his feet at the fire and smoking an excellent cigar, whose perfume filled the room. He was alone, his elbows resting on the arms of the chair, his cheeks flushed, his eyes bright, and looking delighted.

"I heard the noise of plates and dishes in the next room, and Marchas said to me, smiling in a beatific manner: 'This is famous; I found the champagne under the flight of steps outside, the brandy— fifty bottles of the very finest— in the kitchen garden under a pear-tree, which did not look to me to be quite straight, when I looked at it by the light of my lantern. As for solids, we have two fowls, a goose, a duck, and three pigeons. They are being cooked at this moment. It is a delightful part of the country.'

"I had sat down opposite to him, and the fire in the grate was burning my nose and cheeks.

"'Where did you find this wood?' I asked.

"'Splendid wood,' he replied. 'The owner's carriage. It is the paint which is causing all this flame, an essence of alcohol and varnish. A capital house!'

"I laughed, for I found the creature was funny, and he went on: 'Fancy this being the Epiphany! I have had a bean put into the goose, but there is no queen; it is really very annoying!' And I repeated like an echo: 'It is annoying, but what do you want me to do in the matter?'

"'To find some, of course.'

"'Some women. Women?—you must be mad!'

"'I managed to find the brandy under the pear-tree, and the champagne under the steps; and yet

there was nothing to guide me, while as for you, a
petticoat is a sure sign.   Go and look, old fellow.'

"He looked so grave, so convinced, that I could
not tell whether he was joking or not.   So I replied:
'Look here, Marchas, are you having a joke with
me?'

"'I never joke on duty.'

"'But where the devil do you expect me to find
any women?'

"'Where you like; there must be two or three
remaining in the neighborhood, so ferret them out
and bring them here.'

"I got up, for it was too hot in front of the fire,
and Marchas went on: 'Do you want an idea?'

"'Yes.'

"'Go and see the priest.'

"'The priest?   What for?'

"'Ask him to supper, and beg him to bring a
woman with him.'

"'The priest!   A woman!   Ha! ha! ha!'

"But Marchas continued with extraordinary grav-
ity: 'I am not laughing; go and find the priest and
tell him how we are situated, and, as he must be
horribly dull, he will come.   But tell him that we
want one woman at least, a lady, of course, since we
are all men of the world.   He is sure to have the
names of his female parishioners on the tips of his
fingers, and if there is one to suit us, and you manage it well, he will indicate her to you.'

"'Come, come, Marchas, what are you thinking
of?'

"'My dear Garens, you can do this quite well.   It
will be very funny.   We are well bred, by Jove!

and we will put on our most distinguished manners
and our grandest style. Tell the abbé who we are,
make him laugh, soften him, seduce him, and per-
suade him!'

"'No, it is impossible.'

"He drew his chair close to mine, and as he knew
my weak side, the scamp continued: 'Just think
what a swagger thing it will be to do, and how
amusing to tell about; the whole army will talk about
it, and it will give you a famous reputation.'

"I hesitated, for the adventure rather tempted me.
He persisted: 'Come, my little Garens. You are
in command of this detachment, and you alone can
go and call on the head of the church in this neighborhood. I beg of you to go, and I promise you
that after the war, I will relate the whole affair in
verse in the "Revue des Deux Mondes." You owe
this much to your men, for you have made them
march enough during the last month.'

"I got up at last and asked: 'Where is the parsonage?'

"'Take the second turning at the end of· the
street; you will then see an avenue, and at the end
of the avenue you will find the church. The parsonage is beside it.' As I departed he called out: 'Tell
him the bill of fare, to make him hungry!'

"I discovered the ecclesiastic's little house without any difficulty; it was by the side of a large, ugly,
brick church. As there was neither bell nor knocker,
I knocked at the door with my fist, and a loud voice
from inside asked: 'Who is there?' to which I replied: 'A quartermaster of hussars.'

"I heard the noise of bolts, and of a key being turned. Then I found myself face to face with a tall priest with a large stomach, the chest of a prize-fighter, formidable hands projecting from turned-up sleeves, a red face, and the looks of a kind man. I gave him a military salute and said: 'Good day, Monsieur le Curé.'

"He had feared a surprise, some marauders' ambush, and he smiled as he replied: 'Good day, my friend; come in.' I followed him into a small room, with a red tiled floor, in which a small fire was burning, very different to Marchas's furnace. He gave me a chair and said: 'What can I do for you?'

"'Monsieur, allow me first of all to introduce myself'; and I gave him my card, which he took and read half aloud: 'The Comte de Garens.'

"I continued: 'There are eleven of us here Monsieur l'Abbé, five on grand guard, and six installed at the house of an unknown inhabitant. The names of the six are, Garens (that is I), Pierre de Marchas, Ludovic de Ponderel, Baron d'Etreillis, Karl Massouligny, the painter's son, and Joseph Herbon, a young musician. I have come to ask you, in their name and my own, to do us the honor of supping with us. It is an Epiphany supper, Monsieur le Curé, and we should like to make it a little cheerful.'

"The priest smiled and murmured: 'It seems to me to be hardly a suitable occasion for amusing oneself.'

"I replied: 'We are fighting every day, Monsieur. Fourteen of our comrades have been killed in a month, and three fell as late as yesterday. That is war. We stake our life every moment: have we not,

therefore, the right to amuse ourselves freely? We
are Frenchmen, we like to laugh, and we can laugh
everywhere. Our fathers laughed on the scaffold!
This evening we should like to brighten ourselves
up a little, like gentlemen, and not like soldiers; you
understand me, I hope. Are we wrong?'

"He replied quickly: 'You are quite right, my
friend, and I accept your invitation with great pleasure.' Then he called out: 'Hermance!'

"An old, bent, wrinkled, horrible, peasant woman
appeared and said: 'What do you want?'

"'I shall not dine at home, my daughter.'

"'Where are you going to dine then?'

"'With some gentlemen, hussars.'

"I felt inclined to say: 'Bring your servant with
you,' just to see Marchas's face, but I did not venture
to, and continued: 'Do you know anyone among
your parishioners, male or female, whom I could
invite as well?' He hesitated, reflected, and then said:
'No, I do not know anybody!'

"I persisted: 'Nobody? Come, Monsieur, think;
it would be very nice to have some ladies, I mean to
say, some married couples! I know nothing about
your parishioners. The baker and his wife, the
grocer, the—the—the—watchmaker—the—shoema-
ker—the—the chemist with his wife. We have a
good spread, and plenty of wine, and we should be
enchanted to leave pleasant recollections of ourselves
behind us with the people here.'

"The priest thought again for a long time and
then said resolutely: 'No, there is nobody.'

"I began to laugh. 'By Jove, Monsieur le Curé,
it is very vexing not to have an Epiphany queen, for

we have the bean. Come, think. Is there not a married mayor, or a married deputy-mayor, or a married municipal councilor, or schoolmaster?'

"'No, all the ladies have gone away.'

"'What, is there not in the whole place some good tradesman's wife with her good tradesman, to whom we might give this pleasure, for it would be a pleasure to them, a great pleasure under present circumstances?'

"But suddenly the curé began to laugh, and he laughed so violently that he fairly shook, and exclaimed: 'Ha! ha! ha! I have got what you want, yes. I have got what you want! Ha! ha! ha! We will laugh and enjoy ourselves, my children, we will have some fun. How pleased the ladies will be, I say, how delighted they will be. Ha! ha! Where are you staying?'

"I described the house, and he understood where it was. 'Very good,' he said. 'It belongs to Monsieur Bertin-Lavaille. I will be there in half an hour, with four ladies. Ha! ha! ha! four ladies!'

"He went out with me, still laughing, and left me, repeating: 'That is capital; in half an hour at Bertin-Lavaille's house.'

"I returned quickly, very much astonished and very much puzzled. 'Covers for how many?' Marchas asked, as soon as he saw me.

"'Eleven. There are six of us hussars besides the priest and four ladies.'

"He was thunderstruck, and I triumphant, and he repeated: 'Four ladies! Did you say, four ladies?'

"'I said four women.'

"'Real women?'

" 'Real women.'

" 'Well, accept my compliments!'

" 'I will, for I deserve them.'

"He got out of his armchair, opened the door, and I saw a beautiful, white tablecloth on a long table, round which three hussars in blue aprons were setting out the plates and glasses. 'There are some women coming!' Marchas cried. And the three men began to dance and to cheer with all their might.

"Everything was ready, and we were waiting. We waited for nearly an hour, while a delicious smell of roast poultry pervaded the whole house. At last, however, a knock against the shutters made us all jump up at the same moment. Stout Penderel ran to open the door, and in less than a minute a little Sister of Mercy appeared in the doorway. She was thin, wrinkled, and timid, and successively saluted the four bewildered hussars who saw her enter. Behind her, the noise of sticks sounded on the tiled floor in the vestibule. As soon as she had come into the drawing-room I saw three old heads in white caps, following each other one by one, balancing themselves with different movements, one canting to the right, while the other canted to the left. Then three worthy women showed themselves, limping, dragging their legs behind them, crippled by illness and deformed through old age, three infirm old women, past service, the only three pensioners who were able to walk in the establishment which Sister Saint-Benedict managed.

"She had turned round to her invalids, full of anxiety for them, and then seeing my quartermaster's stripes, she said to me: 'I am much obliged to you for thinking of these poor women. They have very little pleasure in life, and you are at the same time giving them a great treat and doing them a great honor.'

"I saw the priest, who had remained in the obscurity of the passage, and who was laughing heartily, and I began to laugh in my turn, especially when I saw Marchas's face. Then, motioning the nun to the seats, I said: 'Sit down, Sister: we are very proud and very happy that you have accepted our unpretentious invitation.'

"She took three chairs which stood against the wall, set them before the fire, led her three old women to them, settled them on them, took their sticks and shawls which she put into a corner, and then, pointing to the first, a thin woman with an enormous stomach, who was evidently suffering from the dropsy, she said: 'This is Mother Paumelle, whose husband was killed by falling from a roof, and whose son died in Africa; she is sixty years old.' Then she pointed to another, a tall woman, whose head shook unceasingly: 'This is Mother Jean-Jean, who is sixty-seven. She is nearly blind, for her face was terribly singed in a fire, and her right leg was half burned off.'

"Then she pointed to the third, a sort of dwarf, with protruding, round, stupid eyes, which she rolled incessantly in all directions. 'This is La Putois, an idiot. She is only forty-four.'

"I bowed to the three women as if I were being presented to some Royal Highness, and turning to the priest I said: 'You are an excellent man, Monsieur l'Abbé, and we all owe you a debt of gratitude.'

"Everybody was laughing, in fact, except Marchas, who seemed furious, and just then Karl Massouligny cried: 'Sister Saint-Benedict, supper is on the table!'

"I made her go first with the priest, then I helped up Mother Paumelle, whose arm I took and dragged her into the next room, which was no easy task, for her swollen stomach seemed heavier than a lump of iron.

"Stout Ponderel gave his arm to Mother Jean-Jean, who bemoaned her crutch, and little Joseph Herbon took the idiot, La Putois, to the dining-room, which was filled with the odor of the viands.

"As soon as we were opposite our plates, the Sister clapped her hands three times, and, with the precision of soldiers presenting arms, the women made a rapid sign of the cross, and then the priest slowly repeated the 'Benedictus' in Latin. Then we sat down, and the two fowls appeared, brought in by Marchas, who chose to wait rather than to sit down as a guest at this ridiculous repast.

"But I cried: 'Bring the champagne at once!' and a cork flew out with the noise of a pistol, and in spite of the resistance of the priest and the kind Sister, the three hussars sitting by the side of the three invalids, emptied their three full glasses down their throats by force.

"Massouligny, who possessed the faculty of making himself at home, and of being on good terms with everyone, wherever he was, made love to Mother Paumelle, in the drollest manner. The dropsical woman, who had retained her cheerfulness in spite of her misfortunes, answered him banteringly in a high falsetto voice which seemed to be assumed,

and she laughed so heartily at her neighbor's jokes
that her large stomach looked as if it were going to
rise up and get on to the table. Little Herbon had
seriously undertaken the task of making the idiot
drunk, and Baron d'Etreillis whose wits were not always particularly sharp, was questioning old Jean-
Jean about the life, the habits, and the rules in the
hospital.

"The nun said to Massouligny in consternation:
'Oh! oh! you will make her ill; pray do not make
her laugh like that, Monsieur. Oh! Monsieur.' Then
she got up and rushed at Herbon to take a full glass
out of his hands which he was hastily emptying
down La Putois's throat, while the priest shook with
laughter, and said to the Sister: 'Never mind, just
this once, it will not hurt her. Do leave them alone.'

"After the two fowls they ate the duck, which
was flanked by the three pigeons and a blackbird,
and then the goose appeared, smoking, golden-
colored, and diffusing a warm odor of hot, browned
fat meat. La Paumelle who was getting lively, clapped
her hands; La Jean-Jean left off answering the Baron's
numerous questions, and La Putois uttered grunts of
pleasure, half cries and half sighs, like little children
do when one shows them sweets. 'Allow me to
carve this bird,' the curé said. 'I understand these
sort of operations better than most people.'

"'Certainly, Monsieur l'Abbé,' and the Sister said:
'How would it be to open the window a little; they
are too warm, and I am afraid they will be ill.'

"I turned to Marchas: 'Open the window for a
minute.' He did so; the cold outer air as it came in
made the candles flare, and the smoke from the

goose—which the curé was scientifically carving, with a table napkin round his neck—whirl about. We watched him doing it, without speaking now, for we were interested in his attractive handiwork, and also seized with renewed appetite at the sight of that enormous golden-colored bird, whose limbs fell one after another into the brown gravy at the bottom of the dish. At that moment, in the midst of greedy silence which kept us all attentive, the distant report of a shot came in at the open window.

"I started to my feet so quickly that my chair fell down behind me, and I shouted: 'Mount, all of you! You, Marchas, will take two men and go and see what it is. I shall expect you back here in five minutes.' And while the three riders went off at full gallop through the night, I got into the saddle with my three remaining hussars, in front of the steps of the villa, while the curé, the Sister, and the three old women showed their frightened faces at the window.

"We heard nothing more, except the barking of a dog in the distance. The rain had ceased, and it was cold, very cold. Soon I heard the gallop of a horse, of a single horse, coming back. It was Marchas, and I called out to him: 'Well?'

"'It is nothing; François has wounded an old peasant who refused to answer his challenge and who continued to advance in spite of the order to keep off. They are bringing him here, and we shall see what is the matter.'

"I gave orders for the horses to be put back into the stable, and I sent my two soldiers to meet the others, and returned to the house. Then the curé,

Marchas and I took a mattress into the room to put the wounded man on; the Sister tore up a table napkin in order to make lint, while the three frightened women remained huddled up in a corner.

"Soon I heard the rattle of sabers on the road, and I took a candle to show a light to the men who were returning. They soon appeared, carrying that inert, soft, long, and sinister object which a human body becomes when life no longer sustains it.

"They put the wounded man on the mattress that had been prepared for him, and I saw at the first glance that he was dying. He had the death rattle, and was spitting up blood which ran out of the corners of his mouth, forced out of his lungs by his gasps. The man was covered with it! His cheeks, his beard, his hair, his neck, and his clothes seemed to have been rubbed, to have been dipped in a red tub; the blood had congealed on him, and had become a dull color which was horrible to look at.

"The old man, wrapped up in a large shepherd's cloak, occasionally opened his dull, vacant eyes. They seemed stupid with astonishment, like the eyes of hunted animals which fall at the sportsman's feet, half dead before the shot, stupefied with fear and surprise.

"The curé exclaimed: 'Ah! there is old Placide, the shepherd from Les Marlins. He is deaf, poor man, and heard nothing. Ah! Oh, God! they have killed the unhappy man!' The Sister had opened his blouse and shirt, and was looking at a little blue hole in the middle of his chest, which was not bleeding any more. 'There is nothing to be done,' she said.

"The shepherd was gasping terribly and bringing up blood with every breath. In his throat to the very depth of his lungs, they could hear an ominous and continued gurgling. The curé, standing in front of him, raised his right hand, made the sign of the cross, and in a slow and solemn voice pronounced the Latin words which purify men's souls. But before they were finished, the old man was shaken by a rapid shudder, as if something had broken inside him; he no longer breathed. He was dead.

"When I turned round I saw a sight which was even more horrible than the death struggle of this unfortunate man. The three old women were standing up huddled close together, hideous, and grimacing with fear and horror. I went up to them, and they began to utter shrill screams, while La Jean-Jean, whose leg had been burned and could not longer support her, fell to the ground at full length.

"Sister Saint-Benedict left the dead man, ran up to her infirm old women, and without a word or a look for me wrapped their shawls round them, gave them their crutches, pushed them to the door, made them go out, and disappeared with them into the dark night.

"I saw that I could not even let a hussar accompany them, for the mere rattle of a sword would have sent them mad with fear.

"The curé was still looking at the dead man; but at last he turned to me and said:

"'Oh! What a horrible thing!'"

SIMON'S PAPA

NOON had just struck. The school-door opened and the youngsters streamed out tumbling over one another in their haste to get out quickly. But instead of promptly dispersing and going home to dinner as was their daily wont, they stopped a few paces off, broke up into knots and set to whispering.

The fact was that that morning Simon, the son of La Blanchotte, had, for the first time, attended school.

They had all of them in their families heard of La Blanchotte; and although in public she was welcome enough, the mothers among themselves treated her with compassion of a some-what disdainful kind, which the children had caught without in the least knowing why.

As for Simon himself, they did not know him, for he never went abroad, and did not play around with them through the streets of the village or along the banks of the river. So they loved him but little; and it was with a certain delight, mingled with astonishment, that they gathered in groups this morning, repeating to each other this sentence, concocted by a lad of fourteen or fifteen who appeared to know all about it, so sagaciously did he wink: "You know Simon —well, he has no papa."

La Blanchotte's son appeared in his turn upon the threshold of the school.

He was seven or eight years old, rather pale, very neat, with a timid and almost awkward manner.

He was making his way back to his mother's house when the various groups of his schoolfellows, perpetually whispering, and watching him with the mischievous and heartless eyes of children bent upon playing a nasty trick, gradually surrounded him and ended by inclosing him altogether. There he stood amid them, surprised and embarrassed, not under-standing what they were going to do with him. But the lad who had brought the news, puffed up with the success he had met with, demanded:

"What do you call yourself?"

He answered: "Simon."

"Simon what?" retorted the other.

The child, altogether bewildered, repeated: "Simon."

The lad shouted at him: "You must be named Simon something! That is not a name—Simon in-deed!"

And he, on the brink of tears, replied for the third time:

"I am named Simon."

The urchins began laughing. The lad triumphantly lifted up his voice: "You can see plainly that he has no papa."

A deep silence ensued. The children were dumfounded by this extraordinary, impossibly monstrous thing—a boy who had not a papa; they looked upon him as a phenomenon, an unnatural being, and they felt rising in them the hitherto inexplicable pity of their mothers for La Blanchotte. As for Simon, he had propped himself against a tree to avoid falling, and he stood there as if paralyzed by an irreparable disaster. He sought to explain, but he could think of no answer for them, no way to deny this horrible charge that he had no papa. At last he shouted at them quite recklessly: "Yes, I have one."

"Where is he?" demanded the boy.

Simon was silent, he did not know. The children shrieked, tremendously excited. These sons of toil, nearly related to animals, experienced the cruel craving which makes the fowls of a farmyard destroy one of their own kind as soon as it is wounded. Simon suddenly spied a little neighbor, the son of a widow, whom he had always seen, as he himself was to be seen, quite alone with his mother.

"And no more have you," he said, "no more have you a papa."

"Yes," replied the other, "I have one."

"Where is he?" rejoined Simon.

"He is dead," declared the brat with superb dignity, "he is in the cemetery, is my papa."

A murmur of approval rose amid the scapegraces, as if the fact of possessing a papa dead in a cemetery made their comrade big enough to crush the other one who had no papa at all. And these rogues, whose fathers were for the most part evildoers, drunkards, thieves, and ill-treaters of their wives hustled each other as they pressed closer and closer to Simon as though they, the legitimate ones, would stifle in their pressure one who was beyond the law.

The lad next Simon suddenly put his tongue out at him with a waggish air and shouted at him:

"No papa! No papa!"

Simon seized him by the hair with both hands and set to work to demolish his legs with kicks, while he bit his cheek ferociously. A tremendous struggle ensued between the two boys, and Simon found himself beaten, torn, bruised, rolled on the ground in the middle of the ring of applauding little vagabonds. As he arose, mechanically brushing his little blouse all covered with dust with his hand, some one shouted at him:

"Go and tell your papa."

He then felt a great sinking in his heart. They were stronger than he, they had beaten him and he had no answer to give them, for he knew it was true that he had no papa. Full of pride he tried for some moments to struggle against the tears which were suffocating him. He had a choking fit, and then without cries he began to weep with great sobs which shook him incessantly. Then a ferocious joy broke out among his enemies, and, just like savages in fearful festivals, they took one another by the hand and danced in a circle about him as they repeated in refrain:

"No papa! No papa!"

But suddenly Simon ceased sobbing. Frenzy overtook him. There were stones under his feet; he picked them up and with all his strength hurled

them at his tormentors. Two or three were struck
and ran away yelling, and so formidable did he appear that the rest became panic-stricken. Cowards,
like a jeering crowd in the presence of an exasperated man, they broke up and fled. Left alone, the
little thing without a father set off running toward
the fields, for a recollection had been awakened which
nerved his soul to a great determination. He made
up his mind to drown himself in the river.

He remembered, in fact, that eight days ago a poor
devil who begged for his livelihood had thrown himself into the water because he had no more money.
Simon had been there when they fished him out again;
and the sight of the fellow, who had seemed to him
so miserable and ugly, had then impressed him—his
pale cheeks, his long drenched beard, and his open
eyes being full of calm. The bystanders had said:

"He is dead."

And some one had added:

"He is quite happy now."

So Simon wished to drown himself also because
he had no father, just as the wretched being did who
had no money.

He reached the water and watched it flowing.
Some fishes were rising briskly in the clear stream
and occasionally made little leaps and caught the flies
on the surface. He stopped crying in order to watch
them, for their feeding interested him vastly. But, at
intervals, as in the lulls of a tempest, when tremendous gusts of wind snap off trees and then die away,
this thought would return to him with intense pain:

"I am about to drown myself because I have no
papa."

It was very warm and fine weather. The pleasant sunshine warmed the grass; the water shone like a mirror; and Simon enjoyed for some minutes the happiness of that languor which follows weeping, desirous even of falling asleep there upon the grass in the warmth of noon.

A little green frog leaped from under his feet. He endeavored to catch it. It escaped him. He pursued it and lost it three times following. At last he caught it by one of its hind legs and began to laugh as he saw the efforts the creature made to escape. It gathered itself up on its large legs and then with a violent spring suddenly stretched them out as stiff as two bars.

Its eyes stared wide open in their round, golden circle, and it beat the air with its front limbs, using them as though they were hands. It reminded him of a toy made with straight slips of wood nailed zigzag one on the other, which by a similar movement regulated the exercise of the little soldiers fastened thereon. Then he thought of his home and of his mother, and overcome by great sorrow he again began to weep. His limbs trembled; and he placed himself on his knees and said his prayers as before going to bed. But he was unable to finish them, for such hurried and violent sobs overtook him that he was completely overwhelmed. He thought no more, he no longer heeded anything around him but was wholly given up to tears.

Suddenly a heavy hand was placed upon his shoulder, and a rough voice asked him:

"What is it that causes you so much grief, my fine fellow?"

Simon turned round. A tall workman, with a black beard and hair all curled, was staring at him good-naturedly. He answered with his eyes and throat full of tears:

"They have beaten me because—I—I have no papa—no papa."

"What!" said the man smiling, "why, everybody has one."

The child answered painfully amid his spasms of grief:

"But I—I—I have none."

Then the workman became serious. He had recognized La Blanchotte's son, and although a recent arrival to the neighborhood he had a vague idea of her history.

"Well," said he, "console yourself, my boy, and come with me home to your mother. She will give you a papa."

And so they started on the way, the big one holding the little one by the hand. The man smiled afresh, for he was not sorry to see this Blanchotte, who by popular report was one of the prettiest girls in the country-side—and, perhaps, he said to himself, at the bottom of his heart, that a lass who had erred once might very well err again.

They arrived in front of a very neat little white house.

"There it is," exclaimed the child, and he cried: 'Mamma.'

A woman appeared, and the workman instantly left off smiling, for he at once perceived that there was no more fooling to be done with the tall pale girl, who stood austerely at her door as though to defend from one man the threshold of that house where she had already been betrayed by another. Intimidated, his cap in his hand, he stammered out:

"See, Madame, I have brought you back your little boy, who had lost himself near the river."

But Simon flung his arms about his mother's neck and told her, as he again began to cry:

"No, mamma, I wished to drown myself, because the others had beaten me—had beaten me—because I have no papa."

A burning redness covered the young woman's cheeks, and, hurt to the quick, she embraced her child passionately, while the tears coursed down her face. The man, much moved, stood there, not knowing how to get away. But Simon suddenly ran to him and said:

"Will you be my papa?"

A deep silence ensued. La Blanchotte, dumb and tortured with shame, leaned against the wall, her hands upon her heart. The child, seeing that no answer was made him, replied:

"If you do not wish it, I shall return to drown myself."

The workman took the matter as a jest and answered laughing:

"Why, yes, I wish it certainly."

"What is your name, then," went on the child, "so that I may tell the others when they wish to know your name?"

"Philip," answered the man.

Simon was silent a moment so that he might get the name well into his memory; then he stretched out his arms, quite consoled, and said:

"Well, then, Philip, you are my papa."

The workman, lifting him from the ground, kissed him hastily on both cheeks, and then strode away quickly.

When the child returned to school next day he was received with a spiteful laugh, and at the end of school, when the lads were on the point of recommencing, Simon threw these words at their heads as he would have done a stone: "He is named Philip, my papa."

Yells of delight burst out from all sides.

"Philip who? Philip what? What on earth is Philip? Where did you pick up your Philip?"

Simon answered nothing; and immovable in faith he defied them with his eye, ready to be martyred rather than fly before them. The schoolmaster came to his rescue and he returned home to his mother.

For a space of three months, the tall workman, Philip, frequently passed by La Blanchotte's house, and sometimes made bold to speak to her when he saw her sewing near the window. She answered him civilly, always sedately, never joking with him, nor permitting him to enter her house. Notwithstanding this, being, like all men, a bit of a coxcomb, he imagined that she was often rosier than usual when she chatted with him.

But a fallen reputation is so difficult to recover, and always remains so fragile that, in spite of the shy reserve La Blanchotte maintained, they already gossiped in the neighborhood.

As for Simon, he loved his new papa much, and walked with him nearly every evening when the day's work was done. He went regularly to school and mixed in a dignified way with his schoolfellows without ever answering them back.

One day, however, the lad who had first attacked him said to him:

"You have lied. You have not a papa named Philip."

"Why do you say that?" demanded Simon, much disturbed.

The youth rubbed his hands. He replied:

"Because if you had one he would be your mamma's husband."

Simon was confused by the truth of this reasoning; nevertheless he retorted:

"He is my papa all the same."

"That can very well be," exclaimed the urchin with a sneer, "but that is not being your papa altogether."

La Blanchotte's little one bowed his head and went off dreaming in the direction of the forge belonging to old Loizon, where Philip worked.

This forge was entombed in trees. It was very dark there, the red glare of a formidable furnace alone lit up with great flashes five blacksmiths, who hammered upon their anvils with a terrible din. Standing enveloped in flame, they worked like demons, their eyes fixed on the red-hot iron they were pounding; and their dull ideas rising and falling with their hammers.

Simon entered without being noticed and quietly plucked his friend by the sleeve. Philip turned round. All at once the work came to a standstill and the men looked on very attentively. Then, in the midst of this unaccustomed silence, rose the little slender pipe of Simon:

"Philip, explain to me what the lad at La Michande has just told me, that you are not altogether my papa."

"And why that?" asked the smith.

The child replied in all innocence:

"Because you are not my mamma's husband."

No one laughed. Philip remained standing, leaning his forehead upon the back of his great hands, which held the handle of his hammer upright upon the anvil. He mused. His four companions watched him, and, like a tiny mite among these giants, Simon anxiously waited. Suddenly, one of the smiths, voicing the sentiment of all, said to Philip:

"All the same La Blanchotte is a good and honest girl, stalwart and steady in spite of her misfortune, and one who would make a worthy wife for an honest man."

"That is true," remarked the three others.

The smith continued:

"Is it the girl's fault if she has fallen? She had been promised marriage, and I know more than one who is much respected to-day and has sinned every bit as much."

"That is true," responded the three men in chorus.

He resumed:

"How hard she has toiled, poor thing, to educate her lad all alone, and how much she has wept since she no longer goes out, save to church, God only knows."

"That also is true," said the others.

Then no more was heard save the roar of the bellows which fanned the fire of the furnace. Philip hastily bent himself down to Simon:

2 G. de M.—16

"Go and tell your mamma that I shall come to speak to her."

Then he pushed the child out by the shoulders. He returned to his work and in unison the five hammers again fell upon their anvils. Thus they wrought the iron until nightfall, strong, powerful, happy, like Vulcans satisfied. But as the great bell of a cathedral. resounds upon feast days above the jingling of the other bells, so Philip's hammer, dominating the noise of the others, clanged second after second with a deafening uproar. His eye on the fire, he plied his trade vigorously, erect amid the sparks.

The sky was full of stars as he knocked at La Blanchotte's door. He had his Sunday blouse on, a fresh shirt, and his beard was trimmed. The young woman showed herself upon the threshold and said in a grieved tone:

"It is ill to come thus when night has fallen, Mr. Philip."

He wished to answer, but stammered and stood confused before her.

She resumed:

"And you understand quite well that it will not do that I should be talked about any more."

Then he said all at once:

"What does that matter to me, if you will be my wife!"

No voice replied to him, but he believed that he heard in the shadow of the room the sound of a body falling. He entered very quickly; and Simon, who had gone to his bed, distinguished the sound of a kiss and some words that his mother said very softly. Then he suddenly found himself lifted up by the

hands of his friend, who, holding him at the length
of his herculean arms, exclaimed to him:

"You will tell your school-fellows that your papa
is Philip Remy, the blacksmith, and that he will pull
the ears of all who do you any harm."

On the morrow, when the school was full and
lessons were about to begin, little Simon stood up
quite pale with trembling lips:

"My papa," said he in a clear voice, "is Philip
Remy, the blacksmith, and he has promised to box
the ears of all who do me any harm."

This time no one laughed any longer, for he was
very well known, was Philip Remy, the blacksmith,
and he was a papa of whom anyone in the world
would be proud.

WAITER, A "BOCK"*

WHY on this particular evening, did I enter a certain beer shop? I cannot explain it. It was bitterly cold. A fine rain, a watery mist floated about, veiling the gas jets in a transparent fog, making the pavements under the shadow of the shop fronts glitter, which revealed the soft slush and the soiled feet of the passers-by.

I was going nowhere in particular; was simply having a short walk after dinner. I had passed the Credit Lyonnais, the Rue Vivienne, and several other streets. Suddenly I descried a large *café*, which was more than half full. I walked inside, with no object in mind. I was not the least thirsty.

By a searching glance I detected a place where I would not be too much crowded. So I went and sat down by the side of a man who seemed to me to be old, and who smoked a half-penny clay pipe, which

* Bavarian beer.

(244)

had become as black as coal. From six to eight beer
saucers were piled up on the table in front of him,
indicating the number of "bocks" he had already
absorbed. With that same glance I had recognized
in him a "regular toper," one of those frequenters of
beer-houses, who come in the morning as soon as
the place is open, and only go away in the evening
when it is about to close. He was dirty, bald to
about the middle of the cranium, while his long
gray hair fell over the neck of his frock coat. His
clothes, much too large for him, appeared to have
been made for him at a time when he was very stout.
One could guess that his pantaloons were not held
up by braces, and that this man could not take ten
paces without having to pull them up and readjust
them. Did he wear a vest? The mere thought of
his boots and the feet they enveloped filled me with
horror. The frayed cuffs were as black at the edges
as were his nails.

As soon as I had sat down near him, this queer
creature said to me in a tranquil tone of voice:

"How goes it with you?"

I turned sharply round to him and closely scanned
his features, whereupon he continued:

"I see you do not recognize me."

"No, I do not."

"Des Barrets."

I was stupefied. It was Count Jean des Barrets,
my old college chum.

I seized him by the hand, so dumfounded that I
could find nothing to say. I, at length, managed to
stammer out:

"And you, how goes it with you?"

He responded placidly:

"With me? Just as I like."

He became silent. I wanted to be friendly, and I selected this phrase:

"What are you doing now?"

"You see what I am doing," he answered, quite resignedly.

I felt my face getting red. I insisted:

"But every day?"

"Every day is alike to me," was his response, accompanied with a thick puff of tobacco smoke.

He then tapped on the top of the marble table with a sou, to attract the attention of the waiter, and called out:

"Waiter, two 'bocks.'"

A voice in the distance repeated:

"Two 'bocks,' instead of four."

Another voice, more distant still, shouted out:

"Here they are, sir, here they are."

Immediately there appeared a man with a white apron, carrying two "bocks," which he set down foaming on the table, the foam running over the edge, on to the sandy floor.

Des Barrets emptied his glass at a single draught and replaced it on the table, sucking in the drops of beer that had been left on his mustache. He next asked:

"What is there new?"

"I know of nothing new, worth mentioning, really," I stammered: "But nothing has grown old for me; I am a commercial man."

In an equable tone of voice, he said:

"Indeed — does that amuse you?"

"No, but what do you mean by that? Surely you must do something!"

"What do you mean by that?"

"I only mean, how do you pass your time!"

"What's the use of occupying myself with any-thing. For my part, I do nothing at all, as you see, never anything. When one has not got a sou one can understand why one has to go to work. What is the good of working? Do you work for your-self, or for others? If you work for yourself you do it for your own amusement, which is all right; if you work for others, you reap nothing but ingrati-tude."

Then sticking his pipe into his mouth, he called out anew:

"Waiter, a 'bock.' It makes me thirsty to keep calling so. I am not accustomed to that sort of thing. Yes, I do nothing; I let things slide, and I am grow-ing old. In dying I shall have nothing to regret. If so, I should remember nothing, outside this public-house. I have no wife, no children, no cares, no sorrows, nothing. That is the very best thing that could hap-pen to one."

He then emptied the glass which had been brought him, passed his tongue over his lips, and resumed his pipe.

I looked at him stupefied and asked him:

"But you have not always been like that?"

"Pardon me, sir; ever since I left college."

"It is not a proper life to lead, my dear sir; it is simply horrible. Come, you must indeed have done something, you must have loved something, you must have friends."

"No; I get up at noon, I come here, I have my breakfast, I drink my 'bock'; I remain until the evening, I have my dinner, I drink 'bock.' Then about one in the morning, I return to my couch, because the place closes up. And it is this latter that embitters me more than anything. For the last ten years, I have passed six-tenths of my time on this bench, in my corner; and the other four-tenths in my bed, never changing. I talk sometimes with the *habitués.*"

"But on arriving in Paris what did you do at first?"

"I paid my *devoirs* to the Café de Medicis."

"What next?"

"Next? I crossed the water and came here."

"Why did you take even that trouble?"

"What do you mean? One cannot remain all one's life in the Latin Quarter. The students make too much noise. But I do not move about any longer. Waiter, a 'bock.'"

I now began to think that he was making fun of me, and I continued:

"Come now, be frank. You have been the victim of some great sorrow; despair in love, no doubt! It is easy to see that you are a man whom misfortune has hit hard. What age are you?"

"I am thirty years of age, but I look to be forty-five at least."

I looked him straight in the face. His shrunken figure, badly cared for, gave one the impression that he was an old man. On the summit of his cranium, a few long hairs shot straight up from a skin of doubtful cleanness. He had enormous eyelashes, a large mustache, and a thick beard. Suddenly I had

a kind of vision, I know not why—the vision of a
basin filled with noisome water, the water which
should have been applied to that poll. I said to him:

"Verily, you look to be more than that age. Of
a certainty you must have experienced some great
disappointment."

He replied:

"I tell you that I have not. I am old because I
never take air. There is nothing that vitiates the life
of a man more than the atmosphere of a *café*."

I could not believe him.

"You must surely have been married as well?
One could not get as baldheaded as you are without
having been much in love."

He shook his head, sending down his back little
hairs from the scalp:

"No, I have always been virtuous."

And raising his eyes toward the luster, which beat
down on our heads, he said:

"If I am baldheaded, it is the fault of the gas.
It is the enemy of hair. Waiter, a 'bock.' You
must be thirsty also?"

"No, thank you. But you certainly interest me.
When did you have your first discouragement?
Your life is not normal, is not natural. There is
something under it all."

"Yes, and it dates from my infancy. I received
a heavy blow when I was very young. It turned
my life into darkness, which will last to the end."

"How did it come about?"

"You wish to know about it? Well, then, listen. You recall, of course, the castle in which I was
brought up, seeing that you used to visit it for five

or six months during the vacations? You remember
that large, gray building in the middle of a great
park, and the long avenues of oaks, which opened
toward the four cardinal points! You remember my
father and my mother, both of whom were ceremonious, solemn, and severe.

"I worshiped my mother; I was suspicious of
my father; but I respected both, accustomed always
as I was to see everyone bow before them. In the
country, they were Monsieur le Comte and Madame
la Comtesse; and our neighbors, the Tannemares, the
Ravelets, the Brennevilles, showed the utmost consideration for them.

"I was then thirteen years old, happy, satisfied
with everything, as one is at that age, and full of
joy and vivacity.

"Now toward the end of September, a few days
before entering the Lycée, while I was enjoying myself in the mazes of the park, climbing the trees
and swinging on the branches, I saw crossing an
avenue my father and mother, who were walking together.

"I recall the thing as though it were yesterday.
It was a very windy day. The whole line of trees
bent under the pressure of the wind, moaned and
seemed to utter cries—cries dull, yet deep—so that
the whole forest groaned under the gale.

"Evening had come on, and it was dark in the
thickets. The agitation of the wind and the branches
excited me, made me skip about like an idiot, and
howl in imitation of the wolves.

"As soon as I perceived my parents, I crept fur-
tively toward them, under the branches, in order to

surprise them, as though I had been a veritable wolf. But suddenly seized with fear, I stopped a few paces from them. My father, a prey to the most violent passion, cried:

"'Your mother is a fool; moreover, it is not your mother that is the question, it is you. I tell you that I want money, and I will make you sign this.'

"My mother responded in a firm voice:

"'I will not sign it. It is Jean's fortune, I shall guard it for him and I will not allow you to devour it with strange women, as you have your own heritage.'

"Then my father, full of rage, wheeled round and seized his wife by the throat, and began to slap her full in the face with the disengaged hand.

"My mother's hat fell off, her hair became disheveled and fell down her back: she essayed to parry the blows, but could not escape from them. And my father, like a madman, banged and banged at her. My mother rolled over on the ground, covering her face in both her hands. Then he turned her over on her back in order to batter her still more, pulling away the hands which were covering her face.

"As for me, my friend, it seemed as though the world had come to an end, that the eternal laws had changed. I experienced the overwhelming dread that one has in presence of things supernatural, in presence of irreparable disaster. My boyish head whirled round and soared. I began to cry with all my might, without knowing why, a prey to terror, to grief, to a dreadful bewilderment. My father heard me, turned round, and, on seeing me, made as though he would rush at me. I believed that he wanted to kill me, and I fled like a hunted animal, running straight in front of me through the woods.

"I ran perhaps for an hour, perhaps for two, I know not. Darkness had set in, I tumbled over some thick herbs, exhausted, and I lay there lost, devoured by terror, eaten up by a sorrow capable of breaking forever the heart of a child. I became cold, I became hungry. At length day broke. I dared neither get up, walk, return home, nor save myself, fearing to encounter my father whom I did not wish to see again.

"I should probably have died of misery and of hunger at the foot of a tree if the guard had not discovered me and led me away by force.

"I found my parents wearing their ordinary aspect. My mother alone spoke to me:

"'How you have frightened me, you naughty boy; I have been the whole night sleepless.'

"I did not answer, but began to weep. My father did not utter a single word.

"Eight days later I entered the Lycée.

"Well, my friend, it was all over with me. I had witnessed the other side of things, the bad side; I have not been able to perceive the good side since that day. What things have passed in my mind, what strange phenomena have warped my ideas, I do not know. But I no longer have a taste for anything, a wish for anything, a love for anybody, a desire for anything whatever, no ambition, no hope. And I can always see my poor mother lying on the ground, in the avenue, while my father was maltreating her. My mother died a few years after; my father lives still. I have not seen him since. Waiter, a 'bock.'"

A waiter brought him his "bock," which he swallowed at a gulp. But, in taking up his pipe again,
trembling as he was, he broke it. Then he made a
violent gesture:

"Zounds! This is indeed a grief, a real grief. I
have had it for a month, and it was coloring so
beautifully!"

Then he went off through the vast saloon, which
was now full of smoke and of people drinking, calling out:

"Waiter, a 'bock'—and a new pipe."

PAUL'S MISTRESS

THE Restaurant Grillon, a small commonwealth of boatmen, was slowly emptying. In front of the door all was tumult—cries and calls—and jolly rowers in white flannels gesticulated with oars on their shoulders.

The ladies in bright spring toilettes stepped aboard the skiffs with care, and seating themselves astern, arranged their dresses, while the landlord of the establishment, a mighty, red-bearded, self-possessed individual of renowned strength, offered his hand to the pretty creatures, and kept the frail crafts steady.

The rowers, bare-armed, with bulging chests, took their places in their turn, posing for their gallery as they did so—a gallery consisting of middle-class people dressed in their Sunday clothes, of workmen and soldiers leaning upon their elbows on the parapet of the bridge, all taking a great interest in the sight.

One by one the boats cast off from the landing stage. The oarsmen bent forward and then threw

themselves backward with even swing, and under
the impetus of the long curved oars, the swift skiffs
glided along the river, grew smaller in the distance,
and finally disappeared under the railway bridge, as
they descended the stream toward La Grenouillère.
One couple only remained behind. The young man,
still almost beardless, slender, with a pale countenance,
held his mistress, a thin little brunette with the gait
of a grasshopper, by the waist; and occasionally they
gazed into each other's eyes. The landlord shouted:
"Come, Mr. Paul, make haste," and they drew
near.

Of all the guests of the house, Mr. Paul was the
most liked and most respected. He paid well and
punctually, while the others hung back for a long
time if indeed they did not vanish without paying.
Besides which he was a sort of walking advertise-
ment for the establishment, inasmuch as his father
was a senator. When a stranger would inquire:
"Who on earth is that little chap who thinks so
much of himself because of his girl?" some *habitué*
would reply, half-aloud, with a mysterious and important air: "Don't you know? That is Paul Baron,
a senator's son."

And invariably the other would exclaim:
"Poor devil! He is not half-grown."

Mother Grillon, a good and worthy business woman,
described the young man and his companion as
"her two turtledoves," and appeared quite touched
by this passion, which was profitable for her house.

The couple advanced at a slow pace. The skiff
"Madeleine" was ready, and at the moment of em-
barking they kissed each other, which caused the

public collected on the bridge to laugh. Mr. Paul
took the oars, and rowed away for La Grenouillère.

When they arrived it was just upon three o'clock
and the large floating *café* overflowed with people.

The immense raft, sheltered by a tarpaulin roof,
is joined to the charming island of Croissy by two
narrow footbridges, one of which leads into the
center of the aquatic establishment, while the other
unites with a tiny islet, planted with a tree and
called "The Flower Pot," and thence leads to land
near the bath office.

Mr. Paul made fast his boat alongside the establishment, climbed over the railing of the *café*, and
then, grasping his mistress's hands, assisted her out
of the boat. They both seated themselves at the end
of a table opposite each other.

On the opposite side of the river along the
market road, a long string of vehicles was drawn
up. Cabs alternated with the fine carriages of the
swells; the first, clumsy, with enormous bodies crushing the springs, drawn by broken-down hacks with
hanging heads and broken knees; the second, slightly
built on light wheels, with horses slender and
straight, their heads well up, their bits snowy with
foam, and with coachmen solemn in livery, heads
erect in high collars, waiting bolt upright, with whips
resting on their knees.

The bank was covered with people who came off
in families, or in parties, or in couples, or alone. They
plucked at the blades of grass, went down to the
water, ascended the path, and having reached the
spot, stood still awaiting the ferryman. The clumsy
punt plied incessantly from bank to bank, discharg-

ing its passengers upon the island. The arm of the river (called the Dead Arm) upon which this refresh-ment wharf lay, seemed asleep, so feeble was the current. Fleets of yawls, of skiffs, of canoes, of pod-oscaphs (a light boat propelled by wheels set in motion by a treadle), of gigs, of craft of all forms and of all kinds, crept about upon the motionless stream, crossing each other, intermingling, running foul of one another, stopping abruptly under a jerk of the arms only to shoot off afresh under a sudden strain of the muscles and gliding swiftly along like great yellow or red fishes.

Others arrived continually; some from Chaton up the stream; others from Bougival down it; laughter crossed the water from one boat to another, calls, admonitions, or imprecations. The boatmen exposed the bronzed and knotted muscles of their biceps to the heat of the day; and like strange floating flowers, the silk parasols, red, green, blue, or yellow, of the ladies bloomed in the sterns of the boats.

A July sun flamed high in the heavens; the at-mosphere seemed full of burning merriment; not a breath of air stirred the leaves of the willows or pop-lars.

Down there Mont-Valérien reared its fortified ram-parts, tier above tier, in the intense light; while on the right the divine slopes of Louviennes, following the bend of the river, disposed themselves in a semi-circle, displaying in turn across the rich and shady lawns of large gardens the white walls of country seats.

Upon the outskirts of La Grenouillère a crowd of promenaders moved about beneath the giant trees

2 G. de M.—17

which make this corner of the island one of the most
delig ·tiul parks in the world.

Women and girls with breasts developed beyond
all measurement, with exaggerated bustles, their complexions plastered with rouge, their eyes daubed with
charcoal, their lips blood-red, laced up, rigged out in
outrageous dresses, trailed the crying bad taste of
their toilettes over the fresh green sward; while beside them young men posed in their fashion-plate
garments with light gloves, varnished boots, canes
the size of a thread, and single eyeglasses emphasi-
zing the insipidity of their smiles.

Opposite La Grenouillère the island is narrow, and
on its other side, where also a ferryboat plies, bringing people unceasingly across from Croissy, the rapid
branch of the river, full of whirlpools and eddies and
foam, rushes along with the strength of a torrent.

A detachment of pontoon-builders, in the uniform
of artillerymen, was encamped upon this bank, and
the soldiers seated in a row on a long beam watched
the water flowing.

In the floating establishment there was a boisterous
and uproarious crowd. The wooden tables upon which
the spilt refreshments made little sticky streams were
covered with half-empty glasses and surrounded by
half-tipsy individuals. The crowd shouted, sang, and
brawled. The men, their hats at the backs of their
heads, their faces red, with the shining eyes of
drunkards, moved about vociferating and evidently
looking for the quarrels natural to brutes. The
women, seeking their prey for the night, sought for
free liquor in the meantime; and in the unoccupied
space between the tables, the ordinary local public

outnumbered a whole regiment of boatmen, *Row-kickers-up*, with their companions in short flannel petticoats.

One of them performed on the piano and appeared to play with his feet as well as his hands; four couples glided through a quadrille, and some young men watched them, polished and correct, men who would have looked demure even if vice itself had appeared.

For there you see in full the pomp and vanity of the world, all its well-bred debauchery, all the seamy side of Parisian society—a mixture of counter-jumpers, of strolling players, of low journalists, of gentlemen in tutelage, of rotten stock-jobbers, of ill-famed debauchees, of old, used-up fast men; a doubtful crowd of suspicious characters, half-known, half-sunk, half-recognized, half-criminal, pickpockets, rogues, procurers of women, sharpers with dignified manners, and a bragging air which seems to say: "I shall kill the first who treats me as a scoundrel."

The place reeks of folly, and stinks of the scum and the gallantry of the shops. Male and female there give themselves airs. There dwells an odor of so-called love, and there one fights for a yes, or for a no, in order to sustain a worm-eaten reputation, which a thrust of the sword or a pistol bullet would destroy further.

Some of the neighboring inhabitants looked in out of curiosity every Sunday; some young men, very young, appeared there every year to learn how to live, some promenaders lounging about showed themselves there; some greenhorns wandered thither. With good reason is it named La Grenouillère. At the side

of the covered wharf where they drank, and quite
close to the Flower Pot, people bathed. Those among
the women who possessed the requisite roundness of
form came there to display their wares and to make
clients. The rest, scornful, although well filled out
with wadding, shored up with springs, corrected here
and altered there, watched their dabbling sisters with
disdain.

The swimmers crowded on to a little platform to
dive thence headforemost. Straight like vine poles,
or round like pumpkins, gnarled like olive branches,
bowed over in front, or thrown backward by the size
of their stomachs, and invariably ugly, they leaped into
the water splashing it almost over the drinkers in the
café.

Notwithstanding the great trees which overhang
the floating-house, and notwithstanding the vicinity
of the water a suffocating heat filled the place. The
fumes of the spilt liquors mingled with the effluvia of
the bodies and with the strong perfumes with which
the skin of the trader in love is saturated and which
evaporate in this furnace. But beneath all these di-
verse scents a slight aroma of rice-powder lingered, disappearing and reappearing, and perpetually encountered
as though some concealed hand had shaken an invisible powder-puff in the air. The show was upon the
river, whither the perpetual coming and going of the
boats attracted the eyes. The boatwomen sprawled
upon their seats opposite their strong-wristed males,
and scornfully contemplated the dinner hunters prowling about the island.

Sometimes when a succession of boats, just started,
passed at full speed, the friends who stayed ashore

gave vent to shouts, and all the people as if suddenly seized with madness set to work yelling.

At the bend of the river toward Chaton fresh boats continually appeared. They came nearer and grew larger, and if only faces were recognized, the vociferations broke out anew.

A canoe covered with an awning and manned by four women came slowly down the current. She who rowed was petite, thin, faded, in a cabin-boy's costume, her hair drawn up under an oilskin cap. Opposite her, a lusty blonde, dressed as a man, with a white flannel jacket, lay upon her back at the bottom of the boat, her legs in the air, resting on the seat at each side of the rower. She smoked a cigarette, while at each stroke of the oars, her chest and her stomach quivered, shaken by the stroke. At the back, under the awning, two handsome girls, tall and slender, one dark and the other fair, held each other by the waist as they watched their companions.

A cry arose from La Grenouillère, "There is Lesbos," and all at once a furious clamor, a terrifying scramble, took place; the glasses were knocked down; people clambered on to the tables; all in a frenzy of noise bawled: " Lesbos! Lesbos! Lesbos! " The shout rolled along, became indistinct, was no longer more than a kind of deafening howl, and then suddenly it seemed to start anew, to rise into space, to cover the plain, to fill the foliage of the great trees, to extend to the distant slopes, and reach even to the sun.

The rower, in the face of this ovation, had quietly stopped. The handsome blonde, stretched out upon the bottom of the boat, turned her head with a careless air, as she raised herself upon her elbows; and the two girls at the back commenced laughing as they saluted the crowd.

Then the hullabaloo was doubled, making the floating establishment tremble. The men took off their hats, the women waved their handkerchiefs, and all voices, shrill or deep, together cried:

"Lesbos."

It was as if these people, this collection of the corrupt, saluted their chiefs like the war-ships which fire guns when an admiral passes along the line.

The numerous fleet of boats also saluted the women's boat, which pushed along more quickly to land farther off.

Mr. Paul, contrary to the others, had drawn a key from his pocket and whistled with all his might. His nervous mistress grew paler, caught him by the arm to make him be quiet, and upon this occasion she looked at him with fury in her eyes. But he appeared exasperated, as though borne away by jealousy of some man or by deep anger, instinctive and ungovernable. He stammered, his lips quivering with indignation:

"It is shameful! They ought to be drowned like puppies with a stone about the neck."

But Madeleine instantly flew into a rage; her small and shrill voice became a hiss, and she spoke volubly, as though pleading her own cause:

"And what has it to do with you — you indeed? Are they not at liberty to do what they wish since they owe nobody anything? A truce to your airs, and mind your own business."

But he cut her speech short:

"It is the police whom it concerns, and I will h.ive them marched off to St. Lazare; indeed I will."

She gave a start:

"You?"

"Yes, I! And in the meantime I forbid you to speak to them — you understand, I forbid you to do so."

Then she shrugged her shoulders and grew calm in a moment:

"My friend, I shall do as I please; if you are not satisfied, be off, and instantly. I am not your wife, am I? Very well then, hold your tongue."

He made no reply and they stood face to face, their lips tigh'ly closed and their breathing rapid.

At the other end of the great wooden *café* the four women made their entry. The two in men's costumes marched in front: the one thin like an oldish tomboy, with yellow lines on her temples; the other filling out her white flannel garments with her fat, swelling out her big trousers with her buttocks and swaying about like a fat goose with enormous legs and yielding knees. Their two friends followed them, and the crowd of boatmen thronged about to shake their hands.

The four had hired a small cottage close to the water's edge, and lived there as two households would have lived.

Their vice was public, recognized, patent to all. People talked of it as a natural thing, which almost excited their sympathy, and whispered in very low tones strange stories of dramas begotten of furious feminine jealousies, of the stealthy visit of well-known women and of actresses to the little house close to the water's edge.

A neighbor, horrified by these scandalous rumors, apprised the police, and the inspector, accompanied by a man, had come to make inquiry. The mission was a delicate one; it was impossible, in short, to accuse these women, who did not abandon themselves to prostitution, of any tangible crime. The inspector, very much puzzled, and, indeed, ignorant of the nature of the offenses suspected, had asked questions at random, and made a lofty report conclusive of their innocence.

They laughed about it all the way to St. Germain. They walked about the Grenouillère establishment with stately steps like queens; and seemed to glory in their fame, rejoicing in the gaze that was fixed on them, so superior to this crowd, to this mob, to these plebeians.

Madeleine and her lover watched them approach, and the girl's eyes lightened.

When the first two had reached the end of the table, Madeleine cried:

"Pauline!"

The large woman turned and stopped, continuing all the time to hold the arm of her feminine cabin-boy:

"Good gracious, Madeleine! Do come and talk to me, my dear."

Paul squeezed his fingers upon his mistress's wrist, but she said to him, with such an air: "You know, my fine fellow, you can be off," that he said nothing and remained alone.

Then they chatted in low voices, all three of them standing. Many pleasant jests passed their lips, they spoke quickly; and Pauline now and then looked at Paul, by stealth, with a shrewd and malicious smile.

At last, putting up with it no longer, he suddenly rose and in a single bound was at their side, trembling in every limb. He seized Madeleine by the shoulders.

"Come, I wish it," said he; "I have forbidden you to speak to these scoundrels."

Whereupon Pauline raised her voice and set to work blackguarding him with her Billingsgate vocabulary. All the bystanders laughed; they drew near him; they raised themselves on tiptoe in order the better to see him. He remained dumb under this downpour of filthy abuse. It appeared to him that the words which came from that mouth and fell upon him defiled him like dirt, and, in presence of the row which was beginning, he fell back, retraced his steps, and rested his elbows on the railing toward the river, turning his back upon the victorious women.

There he stayed watching the water, and sometimes with rapid gesture as though he could pluck it out, he removed with his sinewy fingers the tear formed in his eye.

The fact was that he was hopelessly in love, without knowing why, notwithstanding his refined instincts, in spite of his reason, in spite, indeed, of his will. He had fallen into this love as one falls into a sloughy hole. Of a tender and delicate disposition, he had dreamed of liaisons, exquisite, ideal, and impassioned, and there that little bit of a woman, stupid, like all girls, with an exasperating stupidity, not even pretty, but thin and a spitfire, had taken him prisoner, possessing him from head to foot, body and soul. He had submitted to this feminine witchery, mysterious and all powerful, this unknown power, this prodigious domination—arising no one knows whence, but from the demon of the flesh—which casts the most sensible man at the feet of some girl or other without there being anything in her to explain her fatal and sovereign power.

And there at his back he felt that some infamous thing was brewing. Shouts of laughter cut him to the heart. What should he do? He knew well, but he could not do it.

He steadily watched an angler upon the bank opposite him, and his motionless line.

Suddenly, the worthy man jerked a little silver fish, which wriggled at the end of his line, out of the river. Then he endeavored to extract his hook, pulled and turned it, but in vain. At last, losing patience, he commenced to tear it out, and all the bleeding gullet of the fish, with a portion of its intestines came out. Paul shuddered, rent to his heartstrings. It seemed to him that the hook was his love, and that if he should pluck it out, all that he had in his breast would come out in the same way at the end of a curved iron, fixed in the depths of his being, to which Madeleine held the line.

A hand was placed upon his shoulder; he started and turned; his mistress was at his side. They did not speak to each other; and like him she rested her elbows upon the railing, and fixed her eyes upon the river.

He sought for what he ought to say to her and could find nothing. He could not even disentangle his own emotions; all that he was sensible of was joy at feeling her there close to him, come back again, as well as shameful cowardice, a craving to pardon everything, to permit everything, provided she never left him.

At last, at the end of some minutes, he asked her in a very gentle voice:

"Do you wish that we should leave? It will be nicer in the boat."

She answered: "Yes, my dear."

And he assisted her into the skiff, pressing her hands, all softened, with some tears still in his eyes. Then she looked at him with a smile and they kissed each other anew.

They reascended the river very slowly, skirting the willow-bordered, grass-covered bank, bathed and still in the afternoon warmth. When they had returned to the Restaurant Grillon, it was barely six o'clock. Then leaving their boat they set off on foot toward Bezons, across the fields and along the high poplars which bordered the river. The long grass ready to be mowed was full of flowers. The sinking sun glowed from beneath a sheet of red light, and in the tempered heat of the closing day the floating exhalations from the grass, mingled with the damp scents from the river, filled the air with a soft languor, with a happy light, with an atmosphere of blessing.

A soft weakness overtook his heart, a species of communion with this splendid calm of evening, with this vague and mysterious chilliness of unhidden life, with the keen and melancholy poetry which seems to arise from flowers and things, and reveals itself to the senses at this sweet and pensive time.

Paul felt all that; but for her part she did not understand anything of it. They walked side by side;

and, suddenly, tired of being silent, she sang. She
sang in her shrill and false voice some street song,
some catchy air, which jarred upon the profound
and serene harmony of the evening.

Then he looked at her and felt an impassable
abyss between them. She beat the grass with her
parasol, her head slightly inclined, admiring her feet
and singing, spinning out the notes, attempting
trills, and venturing on shakes. Her smooth little
brow, of which he was so fond, was at that time
absolutely empty! empty! There was nothing therein
but this music of a bird-organ; and the ideas which
formed there by chance were like this music. She
did not understand anything of him; they were now
as separated as if they did not live together. Did his
kisses never go any further than her lips?

Then she raised her eyes to him and laughed again.
He was moved to the quick and, extending his arms
in a paroxysm of love, he embraced her passionately.

As he was rumpling her dress she ended by dis-
engaging herself, murmuring by way of compensation
as she did so:

"That's enough. You know I love you!"

But he clasped her round the waist and seized by
madness, carried her rapidly away. He kissed her on
the cheek, on the temple, on the neck, all the while
dancing with joy. They threw themselves down
panting at the edge of a thicket, lit up by the rays
of the setting sun, and before they had recovered
breath they were friends again without her under-
standing his transport.

They returned, holding each other by the hand,
when, suddenly, through the trees, they perceived on

the river the skiff manned by the four women. Fat
Pauline also saw them, for she drew herself up and
blew kisses to Madeleine. And then she cried:

"Until to-night!"

Madeleine replied: "Until to-night!"

Paul felt as if his heart had suddenly been frozen.

They re-entered the house for dinner and installed
themselves in one of the arbors, close to the water.
They set about eating in silence. When night arrived, the waiter brought a candle inclosed in a glass
globe, which gave a feeble and glimmering light; and
they heard every moment the bursting out of the
shouts of the boatmen in the great saloon on the
first floor.

Toward dessert, Paul, taking Madeleine's hand,
tenderly said to her:

"I feel very tired, my darling; unless you have
any objection, we will go to bed early."

She, however, understood the ruse, and shot an
enigmatical glance at him—that glance of treachery
which so readily appears in the depth of a woman's
eyes. Having reflected she answered:

"You can go to bed if you wish, but I have
promised to go to the ball at La Grenouillère."

He smiled in a piteous manner, one of those
smiles with which one veils the most horrible suffering, and replied in a coaxing but agonized tone:

"If you were very kind, we should remain here,
both of us."

She indicated no with her head, without opening
her mouth.

He insisted:

"I beg of you, my darling."

Then she roughly broke out:

"You know what I said to you. If you are not satisfied, the door is open. No one wishes to keep you. As for myself, I have promised; I shall go."

He placed his two elbows upon the table, covered his face with his hands and remained there pondering sorrowfully.

The boat people came down again, shouting as usual, and set off in their vessels for the ball at La Grenouillère.

Madeleine said to Paul:

"If you are not coming, say so, and I will ask one of these gentlemen to take me."

Paul rose:

"Let us go!" murmured he.

And they left.

The night was black, the sky full of stars, but the air was heat-laden by oppressive breaths of wind, burdened with emanations, and with living germs, which destroyed the freshness of the night. It offered a heated caress, made one breathe more quickly, gasp a little, so thick and heavy did it seem. The boats started on their way, bearing Venetian lanterns at the prow. It was not possible to distinguish the craft, but only the little colored lights, swift and dancing up and down like glowworms in a fit, while voices sounded from all sides in the shade. The young people's skiff glided gently along. Now and then, when a fast boat passed near them, they could, for a moment, see the white back of the rower, lit up by his lantern.

When they turned the elbow of the river, La Grenouillère appeared to them in the distance. The establishment, *en fête*, was decorated with sconces and with colored garlands draped with clusters of lights. On the Seine some great barges moved about slowly, representing domes, pyramids, and elaborate erections in fires of all colors. Illuminated festoons hung right down to the water, and sometimes a red or blue lantern, at the end of an immense invisible fishing-rod, seemed like a great swinging star.

All this illumination spread a light around the *café*, lit up the great trees on the bank, from top to bottom, the trunks standing out in pale gray and the leaves in milky green upon the deep black of the fields and the heavens. The orchestra, composed of five suburban artists, flung far its public-house dance-music, poor of its kind and jerky, inciting Madeleine to sing anew.

She desired to enter at once. Paul desired first to take a stroll on the island, but he was obliged to give way. The attendance was now more select. The boatmen, always alone, remained, with here and there some citizens, and some young men escorted by girls. The director and organizer of this majestic *cancan*, in a jaded black suit, walked about in every direction, baldheaded and worn by his old trade of purveyor of cheap public amusements.

Fat Pauline and her companions were not there; and Paul breathed again.

. They danced; couples opposite each other capered in the maddest fashion, throwing their legs in the air, until they were upon a level with the noses of their partners.

The women, whose thighs seemed disjointed, kicked their feet up above their heads with astounding facility, balanced their bodies, wagged their backs and shook their sides, shedding around them the enticing scent of womanhood.

The men squatted like toads, some making signs; some twisted and distorted themselves, grimacing and hideous; some turned cart-wheels on their hands, or, perhaps, trying to make themselves funny, sketched the manners of the day with exaggerated gracefulness.

A fat servant-maid and two waiters served refreshments.

The *café* boat being only covered with a roof and having no wall. whatever to shut it in, this hare-brained dance was open to the face of the peaceful night and of the firmament powdered with stars.

Suddenly, Mont-Valérien, opposite, appeared, illumined, as if some conflagration had arisen behind it. The radiance spread itself and deepened upon the sky, describing a large luminous circle of white, wan light. Then something or other red appeared, grew greater, shining with a burning crimson, like that of hot metal upon the anvil. It gradually developed into a round body rising from the earth; and the moon, freeing herself from the horizon, rose slowly into space. As she ascended, the purple tint faded and became yellow, a shining bright yellow, and the satellite grew smaller in proportion as her distance increased.

Paul watched the moon for some time, lost in contemplation, forgetting his mistress; when he returned to himself the latter had vanished.

He sought for her, but could not find her. He threw his anxious eye over table after table, going to and fro unceasingly, inquiring after her from this one and that one. No one had seen her. He was tormented with disquietude, when one of the waiters said to him:

"You are looking for Madame Madeleine, are you not? She left but a few moments ago, in company with Madame Pauline." And at the same instant, Paul perceived the cabin-boy and the two pretty girls standing at the other end of the *café*, all three holding each others' waists and lying in wait for him, whispering to one another. He understood, and, like a madman, dashed off into the island.

He first ran toward Chaton, but having reached the plain, retraced his steps. Then he began to search the dense coppices, occasionally roaming about distractedly, or halting to listen.

The toads all about him poured out their short metallic notes.

From the direction of Bougival, some unknown bird warbled a song which reached him from the distance.

Over the large lawns the moon shed a soft light, resembling powdered wool; it penetrated the foliage, silvered the bark of the poplars, and riddled with its brilliant rays the waving tops of the great trees. The entrancing poetry of this summer night had, in spite of himself, entered into Paul, athwart his infatuated anguish, stirring his heart with a ferocious irony, and increasing even to madness his craving for an ideal tenderness, for passionate outpourings on the bosom of an adored and faithful woman. He was compelled to stop, choked by hurried and rending sobs.

The convulsion over, he started anew.

2 G. de M.—18

Suddenly, he received what resembled the stab of a poniard. There, behind that bush, some people were kissing. He ran thither; and found an amorous couple whose faces were united in an endless kiss.

He dared not call, knowing well that she would not respond, and he had a frightful dread of discovering them all at once.

The flourishes of the quadrilles, with the ear-splitting solos of the cornet, the false shriek of the flute, the shrill squeaking of the violin, irritated his feelings, and increased his suffering. Wild and limping music was floating under the trees, now feeble, now stronger, wafted hither and thither by the breeze.

Suddenly he thought that possibly she had returned. Yes, she had returned! Why not? He had stupidly lost his head, without cause, carried away by his fears, by the inordinate suspicions which had for some time overwhelmed him. Seized by one of those singular calms which will sometimes occur in cases of the greatest despair, he returned toward the ball-room.

With a single glance of the eye, he took in the whole room. He made the round of the tables, and abruptly again found himself face to face with the three women. He must have had a doleful and queer expression of countenance, for all three burst into laughter.

He made off, returned to the island, and threw himself into the coppice panting. He listened again, listened a long time, for his ears were singing. At last, however, he believed he heard farther off a little, sharp laugh, which he recognized at once; and he advanced very quietly, on his knees, removing the branches from his path, his heart beating so rapidly, that he could no longer breathe.

Two voices murmured some words, the meaning of which he did not understand, and then they were silent.

Next, he was possessed by a frightful longing to fly, to save himself, forever, from this furious passion which threatened his existence. He was about to return to Chaton and take the train, resolved never to come back again, never again to see her. But her likeness suddenly rushed in upon him, and he mentally pictured the moment in the morning when she would awake in their warm bed, and would press coaxingly against him, throwing her arms around his neck, her hair disheveled, and a little entangled on the forehead, her eyes still shut and her lips apart ready to receive the first kiss. The sudden recollection of this morning caress filled him with frantic recollections and the maddest desire.

The couple began to speak again; and he approached, stooping low. Then a faint cry rose from under the branches quite close to him. He advanced again, always in spite of himself, invincibly attracted, without being conscious of anything—and he saw them.

He stood there astounded and speechless, as if he had suddenly stumbled upon a corpse, dead and mutilated. Then, in an involuntary flash of thought, he remembered the little fish whose entrails he had felt being torn out! But Madeleine spoke to her companion in the same tone in which she had often called him by name, and he was seized by such a fit of anguish that he turned and fled.

He struck against two trees, fell over a root, set off again, and suddenly found himself near the rapid branch of the river, which was lit up by the moon. The torrent-like current made great eddies where the light played upon it. The high bank dominated the stream like a cliff, leaving a wide obscure zone at its foot where the eddies could be heard swirling in the darkness.

On the other bank, the country seats of Croissy could be plainly seen.

Paul saw all this as though in a dream; he thought of nothing, understood nothing, and all things, even his very existence, appeared vague, far-off, forgotten, done with.

The river was there. Did he know what he was doing? Did he wish to die? He was mad. He turned, however, toward the island, toward her, and in the still air of the night, in which the faint and persistent burden of the music was borne up and down, he uttered, in a voice frantic with despair, bitter beyond measure, and superhumanly low, a frightful cry:

"Madeleine!"

His heartrending call shot across the great silence of the sky, and sped around the horizon. Then with a tremendous leap, with the bound of a wild animal, he jumped into the river. The water rushed on, closed over him, and from the place where he had disappeared a series of great circles started, enlarging their brilliant undulations, until they finally reached the other bank. The two women had heard the noise of the plunge. Madeleine drew herself up and exclaimed:

"It is Paul,"—a suspicion having arisen in her soul,—"he has drowned himself"; and she rushed toward the bank, where Pauline rejoined her.

A clumsy punt, propelled by two men, turned and returned on the spot. One of the men rowed, the other plunged into the water a great pole and appeared to be looking for something. Pauline cried:

"What are you doing? What is the matter?"

An unknown voice answered:

"It is a man who has just drowned himself."

The two ghastly women, squeezing each other tightly, followed the maneuvers of the boat. The music of La Grenouillère continued to sound in the distance, seeming with its cadences to accompany the movements of the somber fishermen; and the river which now concealed a corpse, whirled round and round, illuminated. The search was prolonged. The horrible suspense made Madeleine shiver all over. At last, after at least half an hour, one of the men announced:

"I have got it."

And he pulled up his long pole very gently, very gently. Then something large appeared upon the surface.

The other mariner left his oars, and by uniting their strength and hauling upon the inert weight, they succeeded in getting it into their boat.

Then they made for land, seeking a place well lighted and low. At the moment they landed, the women also arrived. The moment she saw him, Madeleine fell back with horror. In the moonlight he already appeared green, with his mouth, his eyes, his nose, his clothes full of slime. His fingers, closed and stiff, were hideous. A kind of black and liquid plaster covered his whole body. The face appeared swollen, and from his hair, glued up by the ooze, there ran a stream of dirty water.

"Do you know him?" asked one.

The other, the Croissy ferryman, hesitated:

"Yes, it certainly seems to me that I have seen that head; but you know when a body is in that state one cannot recognize it easily." And then, suddenly:

"Why, it's Mr. Paul!"

"Who is Mr. Paul?" inquired his comrade.

The first answered:

"Why, Mr. Paul Baron, the son of the senator, the little chap who was so amorous."

The other added, philosophically:

"Well, his fun is ended now; it is a pity, all the same, when one is rich!"

Madeleine sobbed and fell fainting. Pauline approached the body and asked:

"Is he indeed quite dead?"

The men shrugged their shoulders.

"Oh! after that length of time, certainly."

Then one of them asked:

"Was it not at the Grillon that he lodged?"

"Yes," answered the other; "we had better take him back there, there will be something to be made of it."

They embarked again in their boat and set out, moving off slowly on account of the rapid current. For a long time after they were out of sight of the place where the women remained, the regular splash of the oars in the water could be heard.

Then Pauline took the poor weeping Madeleine in her arms, petted her, embraced her for a long while, and consoled her.

"What would you have; it is not your fault, is It? It is impossible to prevent men committing folly. He wished it; so much the worse for him, after all!"

And then lifting her up:

"Come, my dear, come and sleep at the house; It is impossible for you to go back to the Grillon to-night."

And she embraced her again, saying: "Come, we will cure you."

Madeleine arose, and weeping all the while but with fainter sobs, laid her head upon Pauline's shoulder, as though it had found a refuge in a closer and more certain affection, more familiar and more confiding, and set off with very slow steps.

THE
SEQUEL TO A DIVORCE

CERTAINLY, although he had been engaged in the most extraordinary, most unlikely, most extravagant, and funniest cases, and had won legal games without a trump in his hand—although he had worked out the obscure law of divorce, as if it had been a Californian gold mine, Maître* Garrulier, the celebrated, the only Garrulier, could not check a movement of surprise, nor a disheartening shake of the head, nor a smile, when the Countess de Baudémont explained her affairs to him for the first time.

He had just opened his correspondence, and his slender hands, on which he bestowed the greatest attention, buried themselves in a heap of female letters, and one might have thought oneself in the confessional of a fashionable preacher, so impregnated was the atmosphere with delicate perfumes.

---

* Title given to advocates in France.

Immediately—even before she had said a word—
with the sharp glance of a practised man of the
world, that look which made beautiful Madame de
Serpenoise say: "He strips your heart bare!" the
lawyer had classed her in the third category. Those
who suffer came into his first category, those who
love, into the second, and those who are bored, into
the third—and she belonged to the latter.

She was a pretty windmill, whose sails turned and
flew round, and fretted the blue sky with a delicious
shiver of joy, as it were, and had the brain of a bird,
in which four correct and healthy ideas cannot exist
side by side, and in which all dreams and every kind
of folly are engulfed, like a great kaleidoscope.

Incapable of hurting a fly, emotional, charitable,
with a feeling of tenderness for the street girl who
sells bunches of violets for a penny, for a cab horse
which a driver is ill-using, for a melancholy pauper's
funeral, when the body, without friends or relations
to follow it, is being conveyed to the common grave,
doing anything that might afford five minutes'
amusement, not caring if she made men miserable for
the rest of their days, and taking pleasure in kindling
passions which consumed men's whole being, looking upon life as too short to be anything else than
one uninterrupted round of gaiety and enjoyment, she
thought that people might find plenty of time for
being serious and reasonable in the evening of life,
when they are at the bottom of the hill, and their
looking-glasses reveal a wrinkled face, surrounded
with white hair.

A thorough-bred Parisian, whom one would follow
to the end of the world, like a poodle; a woman

whom one adores with the head, the heart, and the senses until one is nearly driven mad, as soon as one has inhaled the delicate perfume that emanates from her dress and hair, or touched her skin, and heard her laugh; a woman for whom one would fight a duel and risk one's life without a thought; for whom a man would remove mountains, and sell his soul to the devil several times over, if the devil were still in the habit of frequenting the places of bad repute on this earth.

She had perhaps come to see this Garrulier, whom she had so often heard mentioned at five o'clock teas, so as to be able to describe him to her female friends subsequently in droll phrases, imitating his gestures and the unctuous inflections of his voice, in order, perhaps, to experience some new sensation, or, perhaps, for the sake of dressing like a woman who was going to try for a divorce; and, certainly, the whole effect was perfect. She wore a splendid cloak embroidered with jet—which gave an almost serious effect to her golden hair, to her small slightly turned-up nose, with its quivering nostrils, and to her large eyes, full of enigma and fun—over a dark stuff dress, which was fastened at the neck by a sapphire and a diamond pin.

The barrister did not interrupt her, but allowed her to get excited and to chatter, to enumerate her causes for complaint against poor Count de Baudé-mont, who certainly had no suspicion of his wife's escapade, and who would have been very much surprised if anyone had told him of it at that moment, when he was taking his fencing lesson at the club.

When she had quite finished, he said coolly, as if he were throwing a pail of water on some burning straw:

"But, Madame, there is not the slightest pretext for a divorce in anything that you have told me here. The judges would ask me whether I took the Law Courts for a theater, and intended to make fun of them."

And seeing how disheartened she was,—that she looked like a child whose favorite toy had been broken, that she was so pretty that he would have liked to kiss her hands in his devotion, and as she seemed to be witty, and very amusing, and as, moreover, he had no objection to such visits being prolonged, when papers had to be looked over, while sitting close together,—Maître Garrulier appeared to be considering. Taking his chin in his hand, he said:

"However, I will think it over; there is sure to be some dark spot that can be made out worse. Write to me, and come and see me again."

In the course of her visits, that black spot had increased so much, and Madame de Baudémont had followed her lawyer's advice so punctually, and had played on the various strings so skillfully that a few months later, after a lawsuit, which is still spoken of in the Courts of Justice, and during the course of which the President had to take off his spectacles, and to use his pocket-handkerchief noisily, the divorce was pronounced in favor of the Countess Marie Anne Nicole Bournet de Baudémont, *née* de Tanchart de Peothus.

The Count, who was nonplussed at such an adventure turning out so seriously, first of all flew into a terrible rage, rushed off to the lawyer's office and threatened to cut off his knavish ears for him. But when his access of fury was over, and he thought of it, he shrugged his shoulders and said:

"All 'the better for her, if it amuses her!"

Then he bought Baron Silberstein's yacht, and with some friends, got up a cruise to Ceylon and India.

Marie Anne began by triumphing, and felt as happy as a schoolgirl going home for the holidays; she committed every possible folly, and soon, tired, satiated, and disgusted, began to yawn, cried, and found out that she had sacrificed her happiness, like a millionaire who has gone mad and has cast his banknotes and shares into the river, and that she was nothing more than a disabled waif and stray. Consequently, she now married again, as the solitude of her home made her morose from morning till night; and then, besides, she found a woman requires a mansion when she goes into society, to race meetings, or to the theater.

And so, while she became a marchioness, and pronounced her second "Yes," before a very few friends, at the office of the mayor of the English urban district, malicious people in the Faubourg were making fun of the whole affair, and affirming this and that, whether rightly or wrongly, and comparing the present husband to the former one, even declaring that he had partially been the cause of the former divorce. Meanwhile Monsieur de Baudémont was wandering over the four quarters of the globe trying to overcome his homesickness, and to deaden his longing for love, which had taken possession of his heart and of his body, like a slow poison.

He traveled through the most out-of-the-way places,
and the most lovely countries, and spent months and
months at sea, and plunged into every kind of dis-
sipation and debauchery. But neither the supple
forms nor the luxurious gestures of the bayaderes,
nor the large passive eyes of the Creoles, nor flirta-
tions with English girls with hair the color of new
cider, nor nights of waking dreams, when he saw
new constellations in the sky, nor dangers during
which a man thinks it is all over with him, and mut-
ters a few words of prayer in spite of himself, when
the waves are high, and the sky black, nothing was
able to make him forget that little Parisian woman
who smelled so sweet that she might have been taken
for a bouquet of rare flowers; who was so coaxing,
so curious, so funny; who never had the same ca-
price, the same smile, or the same look twice, and
who, at bottom, was worth more than many others,
either saints or sinners.

He thought of her constantly, during long hours
of sleeplessness. He carried her portrait about with
him in the breast pocket of his pea-jacket — a charming portrait in which she was smiling, and showing
her white teeth between her half-open lips. Her
gentle eyes with their magnetic look had a happy,
frank expression, and from the mere arrangement of
her hair, one could see that she was fair among the
fair.

He used to kiss that portrait of the woman who
had been his wife as if he wished to efface it,
would look at it for hours, and then throw himself
down on the netting and sob like a child as he
looked at the infinite expanse before him, seeming to

see their lost happiness, the joys of their perished affections, and the divine remembrance of their love, in the monotonous waste of green waters. And he tried to accuse himself for all that had occurred, and not to be angry with her, to think that his grievances were imaginary, and to adore her in spite of everything and always.

And so he roamed about the world, tossed to and fro, suffering and hoping he knew not what. He ventured into the greatest dangers, and sought for death just as a man seeks for his mistress, and death passed close to him without touching him, perhaps amused at his grief and misery.

For he was as wretched as a stone-breaker, as one of those poor devils who work and nearly break their backs over the hard flints the whole day long, under the scorching sun or the cold rain; and Marie Anne herself was not happy, for she was pining for the past and remembered their former love.

At last, however, he returned to France, changed, tanned by exposure, sun, and rain, and transformed as if by some witch's philter.

Nobody would have recognized the elegant and effeminate clubman, in this corsair with broad shoulders, a skin the color of tan, with very red lips, who rolled a little in his walk; who seemed to be stifled in his black dress-coat, but who still retained the distinguished manners and bearing of a nobleman of the last century, one of those who, when he was ruined, fitted out a privateer, and fell upon the English wherever he met them, from St. Malo to Calcutta. And wherever he showed himself his friends exclaimed:

"Why! Is that you? I should never have known you again!"

He was very nearly starting off again immediately; he even telegraphed orders to Havre to get the steam-yacht ready for sea directly, when he heard that Marie Anne had married again.

He saw her in the distance, at the Théâtre Français one Tuesday, and when he noticed how pretty, how fair, how desirable she was,—looking so melancholy, with all the appearance of an unhappy soul that regrets something,—his determination grew weaker, and he delayed his departure from week to week, and waited, without knowing why, until, at last, worn out with the struggle, watching her wherever she went, more in love with her than he had ever been before, he wrote her long, mad, ardent letters in which his passion overflowed like a stream of lava.

He altered his handwriting, as he remembered her restless brain, and her many whims. He sent her the flowers which he knew she liked best, and told her that she was his life, that he was dying of waiting for her, of longing for her, for her his idol.

At last, very much puzzled and surprised, guessing—who knows?—from the instinctive beating of her heart, and her general emotion, that it must be he this time, he whose soul she had tortured with such cold cruelty, and knowing that she could make amends for the past and bring back their former love, she replied to him, and granted him the meeting that he asked for. She fell into his arms, and they both sobbed with joy and ecstasy. Their kisses were those which lips give only when they have lost each other and found each other again at last, when they meet and exhaust themselves in each other's looks, thirsting for tenderness, love, and enjoyment.

*	*	*	*	*	*	*

Last week Count de Baudémont carried off Marie Anne quietly and coolly, just like one resumes possession of one's house on returning from a journey, and drives out the intruders. And when Maître Garrulier was told of this unheard of scandal, he rubbed his hands—the long, delicate hands of a sensual prelate—and exclaimed:

"That is absolutely logical, and I should like to be in their place."

THE CLOWN

THE hawkers' cottage stood at the end of the Esplanade, on the little promontory where the jetty is, and where all the winds, all the rain, and all the spray met. The hut, both walls and roof, was built of old planks, more or less covered with tar; its chinks were stopped with oakum, and dry wreckage was heaped up against it. In the middle of the room an iron pot stood on two bricks, and served as a stove, when they had any coal, but as there was no chimney, it filled the room, which was ventilated only by a low door, with acrid smoke, and there the whole crew lived, eighteen men and one woman. Some had undergone various terms of imprisonment, and nobody knew what the others had done, but though they were all, more or less, suffering from some physical defect and were virtually old men, they were still all strong enough for hauling. For the "Chamber of Commerce" tolerated them there, and allowed them that hovel to live in, on condition that they should be ready to haul, by day and by night.

For every vessel they hauled, each got a penny by day, and twopence by night. It was not certain, however, on account of the competition of retired sailors, fishermen's wives, laborers who had nothing to do, people who were all stronger than those half-starved wretches in the hut.

And yet they lived there, those eighteen men and one woman. Were they happy? Certainly not. Hopeless? Not that, either; for they occasionally got a little besides their scanty pay, and then they stole occasionally, fish, lumps of coal, things without any value to those who lost them, but of great value to the poor, beggarly thieves.

The eighteen supported the woman, and there was no jealousy on her account ! She had no special favorite among them.

She was a fat woman of about forty, chubby-faced and puffy, of whom daddy La Bretagne, who was one of the eighteen, used to say: "She does us honor."

If she had had a favorite among them, daddy La Bretagne would certainly have had the greatest right to that privilege, for although he was one of the most crippled among them, being partially paralyzed in his legs, he showed himself as skillful and strong-armed as any of them, and in spite of his infirmities, he always managed to secure a good place in the row of haulers. None of them knew as well as he how to inspire visitors with pity during the season, and to make them put their hands into their pockets.

ne was a past master at cadging, so that among
those empty stomachs and penniless rascals he had
wind-falls of victuals and coppers more frequently
than fell rightly to his share. But he did not make
use of them in order to monopolize their common
mistress.

"I am just," he used to say. "Let each of us
have his spoonful in turn, and no more, when we
are all eating out of the same dish."

With the coal he picked up, he used to make a
good fire for the whole band in the iron pot, over
which he cooked whatever he brought home with
him, without anyone complaining about it, for he
used to say:

"It gives you a good fire at which to warm your-
selves, for nothing, and the smell of my stew into
the bargain."

As for his money, he spent it in drink with the
trollop, and afterward, what was left of it, with the
others.

"You see," he used to say, "I am just, and more
than just. I give her up to you, because it is your
right."

The consequence was, that they all liked daddy
La Bretagne, so that he gloried in it, and said
proudly:

"What a pity that we are living under the Republic! These fellows would think nothing of making me king."

And one day, when he said this, his trollop replied: "The king is here, old fellow!" And at the
same time she presented a new comrade to them,

who was no less ragged or wretched looking than the eighteen, but quite young by the side of him. He was a tall, thin fellow of about forty, and with-out a gray streak in his long hair. He was dressed only in a pair of trousers and a shirt, which he wore outside them, like a blouse, and the trollop said:

"Here, daddy La Bretagne, you have two knitted vests on, so just give him one."

"Why should I?" the hauler asked.

"Because I choose you to," the woman replied. "I have been living with you set of old men for a long time, so now I want to have a young one; there he is, so you must give him a vest, and keep him here, or I shall throw you up. You may take it or leave it, as you like; do you understand me?"

The eighteen looked at each other open-mouthed, and good daddy La Bretagne scratched his head, and then said:

"What she asks is quite right, and we must give way," he replied.

Then they explained themselves, and came to an understanding. The poor devil did not come like a conqueror, for he was a wretched clown who had just been released from prison, where he had undergone three years' hard labor for an attempted outrage on a girl, but with one exception, the best fellow in the world, so people declared.

"And something nice for me," the trollop added, "for I can assure you that I mean him to reward me for anything I may do for him."

From that time, the household of eighteen persons was increased to nineteen, and at first all went well.

The clown was very humble, and tried not to be burdensome to them. Fed, clothed, and supplied with tobacco, he tried not to be too exacting in the other matter, and if needful, he would have hauled like the others, but the woman would not allow it.

"You shall not fatigue yourself, my little man," she said. "You must reserve yourself entirely for home."

And he did as she wished.

And soon the eighteen, who had never been jealous of each other, grew jealous of the favored lover. Some tried to pick a quarrel with him. He resisted. The best fellow in the world, no doubt, but he was not going to be taken for a mussel shut up in its shell, for all that. Let them call him as lazy as a priest if they liked; he did not mind that, but when they put hairs into his coffee, armfuls of rushes among his wreckage, and filth into his soup, they had better look out!

"None of that, all the lot of you, or you will see what I can do," he used to say.

They repeated their practical jokes, however, and he thrashed them. He did not try to find out who the culprits were, but attacked the first one he met, so much the worse for him. With a kick from his wooden clog (it was his speciality) he smashed their noses into a pulp, and having thus acquired the knowledge of his strength, and urged on by his trollop, he soon became a tyrant. The eighteen felt that they were slaves, and their former paradise, where concord and perfect equality had reigned, became a hell, and that state of things could not last.

"Ah !" daddy La Bretagne growled, "if only I were twenty years younger, I would nearly kill him ! I have my Breton's hot head still, but my confounded legs are no good any longer."

And he boldly challenged the clown to a duel, in which the latter was to have his legs tied, and then both of them were to sit on the ground and hack at each other with knives.

"Such a duel," he said, "would be perfectly fair!" he replied, kicking him in the side with one of his clogs, and the woman burst out laughing, and said:

"At any rate you cannot compete with him on equal terms as regards myself, so do not worry yourself about it."

Daddy La Bretagne was lying in his corner and spitting blood, and none of the rest spoke. What could the others do, when he, the blusterer of them all, had been served so? The jade had been right when she had brought in the intruder, and said:

"The king is here, old fellow."

Only, she ought to have remembered that, after all, she alone kept his subjects in check, and as daddy La Bretagne said, by a right object. With her to console them, they would no doubt have borne anything, but she was foolish enough to cut down their food, and not to fill their common dish as full as it used to be. She wanted to keep everything for her lover, and that raised the exasperation of the eighteen to its height. So one night when she and the clown were asleep, among all these fasting men, the eighteen threw themselves on them. They wrapped the despot's arms and legs up in tarpaulin, and in the presence of the woman who was firmly bound, they flogged him till he was black and blue.

"Yes," old Bretagne said to me himself. "Yes, Monsieur, that was our revenge. The king was guillotined in 1793, and so we guillotined our king also."

And he concluded with a sneer, saying: "But we wished to be just, and as it was not his head that had made him our king, by Jove, we settled him."

THE MAD WOMAN

"I CAN tell you a terrible story about the Franco-Prussian war," Monsieur d'Endolin said to some friends assembled in the smoking-room of Baron de Ravot's château. "You know my house in the Faubourg de Cormeil. I was living there when the Prussians came, and I had for a neighbor a kind of mad woman, who had lost her senses in consequence of a series of misfortunes. At the age of seven and twenty she had lost her father, her husband, and her newly born child, all in the space of a month.

"When death has once entered into a house, it almost invariably returns immediately, as if it knew the way, and the young woman, overwhelmed with grief, took to her bed and was delirious for six weeks. Then a species of calm lassitude succeeded that violent crisis, and she remained motionless, eating next to nothing, and only moving her eyes. Every time they tried to make her get up, she screamed as if they were

(296)

about to kill her, and so they ended by leaving her continually in bed, and only taking her out to wash her, to change her linen, and to turn her mattress.

"An old servant remained with her, to give her something to drink, or a little cold meat, from time to time. What passed in that despairing mind? No one ever knew, for she did not speak at all now. Was she thinking of the dead? Was she dreaming sadly, without any precise recollection of anything that had happened? Or was her memory as stagnant as water without any current? But however this may have been, for fifteen years she remained thus inert and secluded.

"The war broke out, and in the beginning of December the Germans came to Cormeil. I can remember it as if it were but yesterday. It was freezing hard enough to split the stones, and I myself was lying back in an armchair, being unable to move on account of the gout, when I heard their heavy and regular tread, and could see them pass from my window.

"They defiled past interminably, with that peculiar motion of a puppet on wires, which belongs to them. Then the officers billeted their men on the inhabitants, and I had seventeen of them. My neighbor, the crazy woman, had a dozen, one of whom was the Commandant, a regular violent, surly swash-buckler.

"During the first few days, everything went on as usual. The officers next door had been told that the lady was ill, and they did not trouble themselves about that in the least, but soon that woman whom they never saw irritated them. They asked what her illness was, and were told that she had been in bed for fifteen years, in consequence of terrible grief. No doubt they did not believe it, and thought that the poor mad creature would not leave her bed out of pride, so that she might not come near the Prussians, or speak to them or even see them.

"The Commandant insisted upon her receiving him. He was shown into the room and said to her roughly: 'I must beg you to get up, Madame, and to come downstairs so that we may all see you.' But she merely turned her vague eyes on him, without replying, and so he continued: 'I do not intend to tolerate any insolence, and if you do not get up of your own accord, I can easily find means to make you walk without any assistance.'

"But she did not give any signs of having heard him, and remained quite motionless. Then he got furious, taking that calm silence for a mark of supreme contempt; so he added: 'If you do not come downstairs to-morrow—' And then he left the room.

"The next day the terrified old servant wished to dress her, but the mad woman began to scream violently, and resisted with all her might. The officer ran upstairs quickly, and the servant threw herself at his feet and cried: 'She will not come down, Monsieur, she will not. Forgive her, for she is so unhappy.'

"The soldier was embarrassed, as in spite of his anger, he did not venture to order his soldiers to drag her out. But suddenly he began to laugh, and gave some orders in German, and soon a party of soldiers was seen coming out supporting a mattress as if they were carrying a wounded man. On that bed, which had not been unmade, the mad woman, who was still silent, was lying quite quietly, for she was quite indifferent to anything that went on, as long as they let her lie. Behind her, a soldier was carrying a parcel of feminine attire, and the officer said, rubbing his hands: 'We will just see whether you cannot dress yourself alone, and take a little walk.'

"And then the procession went off in the direction of the forest of Imauville; in two hours the soldiers came back alone, and nothing more was seen of the mad woman. What had they done with her? Where had they taken her to? No one knew.

"The snow was falling day and night, and enveloped the plain and the woods in a shroud of frozen foam, and the wolves came and howled at our very doors.

"The thought of that poor lost woman haunted me, and I made several applications to the Prussian authorities in order to obtain some information, and was nearly shot for doing so. When spring returned, the army of occupation withdrew, but my neighbor's house remained closed, and the grass grew thick in the garden walks. The old servant had died during the winter, and nobody troubled any longer about the occurrence; I alone thought about it constantly. What had they done with the woman? Had she escaped through the forest? Had somebody found her, and taken her to a hospital, without being able to obtain any information from her? Nothing happened to relieve my doubts; but by degrees, time assuaged my fears.

"Well, in the following autumn the woodcock were very plentiful, and as my gout had left me for a time, I dragged myself as far as the forest. I had already killed four or five of the long-billed birds, when I knocked over one which fell into a ditch full of branches, and I was obliged to get into it, in order to pick it up, and I found that it had fallen close to a dead, human body. Immediately the recollection of the mad woman struck me like a blow in the chest. Many other people had perhaps died in the wood during that disastrous year, but though I do not know why, I was sure, sure, I tell you, that I should see the head of that wretched maniac.

"And suddenly I understood, I guessed everything. They had abandoned her on that mattress in the cold, deserted wood; and, faithful to her fixed idea, she had allowed herself to perish under that thick and light counterpane of snow, without moving either arms or legs.

"Then the wolves had devoured her, and the birds had built their nests with the wool from her torn bed, and I took charge of her bones. I only pray that our sons may never see any wars again."

MADEMOISELLE

H E HAD been registered under the names of Jean Marie Mathieu Valot, but he was never called anything but "Mademoiselle." He was the idiot of the district, but not one of those wretched, ragged idiots who live on public charity. He lived comfortably on a small income which his mother had left him, and which his guardian paid him regularly, and so he was rather envied than pitied. And then, he was not one of those idiots with wild looks and the manners of an animal, for he was by no means an unpleasing object, with his half-open lips and smiling eyes, and especially in his constant make-up in female dress. For he dressed like a girl, and showed by that how little he objected to being called Mademoiselle.

And why should he not like the nickname which his mother had given him affectionately, when he was a mere child, so delicate and weak, and with a

fair complexion—a poor little diminutive lad not as
tall as many girls of the same age? It was in pure
love that, in his earlier years, his mother whispered
that tender Mademoiselle to him, while his old grand-
mother used to say jokingly:

"The fact is, that as for the male element in him
it is really not worth mentioning in a Christian—no
offense to God in saying so." And his grandfather,
who was equally fond of a joke, used to add: "I
only hope it will not disappear as he grows up."

And they treated him as if he had really been a
girl and coddled him, the more so as they were very
prosperous and did not require to toil to keep things
together.

When his mother and grandparents were dead,
Mademoiselle was almost as happy with his paterna'
uncle, an unmarried man, who had carefully attended
the idiot, and who had grown more and more at--
tached to him by dint of looking after him; and the
worthy man continued to call Jean Marie Mathieu
Valot, Mademoiselle.

He was called so in all the country round as well,
not with the slightest intention of hurting his feelings, but, on the contrary, because all thought they
would please the poor gentle creature who harmed
nobody in doing so.

The very street boys meant no harm by it, accustomed as they were to call the tall idiot in a frock
and cap by the nickname; but it would have struck
them as very extraordinary, and would have led them
to rude fun, if they had seen him dressed like a boy.

Mademoiselle, however, took care of that, for his
dress was as dear to him as his nickname. He

delighted in wearing it, and, in fact, cared for nothing else, and what gave it a particular zest was that he knew that he was not a girl, and that he was living in disguise. And this was evident by the exaggerated feminine bearing and walk he put on, as if to show that it was not natural to him. His enormous, carefully filled cap was adorned with large variegated ribbons. His petticoat, with numerous flounces, was distended behind by many hoops. He walked with short steps, and with exaggerated swaying of the hips, while his folded arms and crossed hands were distorted into pretensions of comical coquetry.

On such occasions, if anybody wished to make friends with him, it was necessary to say:

"Ah! Mademoiselle, what a nice girl you make."

That put him into a good humor, and he used to reply, much pleased:

"Don't I? But people can see I only do it for a joke."

But, nevertheless, when they were dancing at village festivals in the neighborhood, he would always be invited to dance as Mademoiselle, and would never ask any of the girls to dance with him; and one evening when somebody asked him the reason for this, he opened his eyes wide, laughed as if the man had said something very stupid, and replied:

"I cannot ask the girls, because I am not dressed like a lad. Just look at my dress, you fool!"

As his interrogator was a judicious man, he said to him:

"Then dress like one, Mademoiselle."

He thought for a moment, and then said with a cunning look:

"But if I dress like a lad, I shall no longer be a girl; and then, I am a girl"; and he shrugged his shoulders as he said it.

But the remark seemed to make him think.

For some time afterward, when he met the same person, he would ask him abruptly:

"If I dress like a lad, will you still call me Mademoiselle?"

"Of course, I shall," the other replied. "You will always be called so."

The idiot appeared delighted, for there was no doubt that he thought more of his nickname than he did of his dress, and the next day he made his appearance in the village square, without his petticoats and dressed as a man. He had taken a pair of trousers, a coat, and a hat from his guardian's clothespress. This created quite a revolution in the neighborhood, for the people who had been in the habit of smiling at him kindly when he was dressed as a woman, looked at him in astonishment and almost in fear, while the indulgent could not help laughing, and visibly making fun of him.

The involuntary hostility of some, and the too evident ridicule of others, the disagreeable surprise of all, were too palpable for him not to see it, and to be hurt by it, and it was still worse when a street urchin said to him in a jeering voice, as he danced round him:

"Oh! oh! Mademoiselle, you wear trousers! Oh! oh! Mademoiselle!"

And it grew worse and worse, when a whole band of these vagabonds were on his heels, hooting and yelling after him, as if he had been somebody in a masquerading dress during the Carnival.

It was quite certain that the unfortunate creature
looked more in disguise now than he had formerly.
By dint of living like a girl, and by even exag-
gerating the feminine walk and manners, he had
totally lost all masculine looks and ways. His smooth
face, his long flax-like hair, required a cap with ribbons, and became a caricature under the high
chimney-pot hat of the old doctor, his grandfather.

Mademoiselle's shoulders, and especially her swelling stern, danced about wildly in this old-fashioned
coat and wide trousers. And nothing was as funny
as the contrast between his quiet dress and slow
trotting pace, the winning way he used his head, and
the conceited movements of his hands, with which
he fanned himself like a girl.

Soon the older lads and the girls, the old women,
men of ripe age and even the Judicial Councilor,
joined the little brats, and hooted Mademoiselle, while
the astonished idiot ran away, and rushed into the
house with terror. There he took his poor head between both hands, and tried to comprehend the matter. Why were they angry with him? For it was
quite evident that they were angry with him. What
wrong had he done, and whom had he injured, by
dressing as a boy? Was he not a boy, after all?
For the first time in his life, he felt a horror for
his nickname, for had he not been insulted through
it? But immediately he was seized with a horrible
doubt.

"Suppose that, after all, I am a girl?"

He would have liked to ask his guardian about it
but he did not like to, for he somehow felt, although
only obscurely, that he, worthy man, might not tell

him the truth, out of kindness. And, besides, he
preferred to find out for himself, without asking anyone.

All his idiot's cunning, which had been lying
latent up till then, because he never had any occasion
to make use of it, now came out and urged him to
a solitary and dark action.

The next day he dressed himself as a girl again,
and made his appearance as if he had perfectly forgotten his escapade of the day before, but the people,
especially the street boys, had not forgotten it. They
looked at him sideways, and, even the best of them,
could not help smiling, while the little blackguards
ran after him and said:

"Oh! oh! Mademoiselle, you had on a pair of
breeches!"

But he pretended not to hear, or even to guess to
what they were alluding. He seemed as happy and
glad to look about him as he usually did, with half-
open lips and smiling eyes. As usual, he wore an
enormous cap with variegated ribbons, and the same
large petticoats; he walked with short, mincing steps,
swaying and wriggling his hips and gesticulating like
a coquette, and licked his lips when they called him
Mademoiselle, while really he would have liked to
have jumped at the throat of those who called him so.

Days and months passed, and by degrees those
about him forgot all about his strange escapade. But
he had never left off thinking about it, or trying to
find out—for which he was ever on the alert—how
he could ascertain his qualities as a boy, and how to
assert them victoriously. Really innocent, he had
reached the age of twenty without knowing anything

or without ever having any natural impulse, but being tenacious of purpose, curious and dissembling, he asked no questions, but observed all that was said and done.

Often at their village dances, he had heard young fellows boasting about girls whom they had seduced, and girls praising such and such a young fellow, and often, also, after a dance, he saw the couples go away together, with their arms round each other's waists. They had no suspicions of him, and he listened and watched, until, at last, he discovered what was going on.

And then, one night, when dancing was over, and the couples were going away with their arms round each other's waists, a terrible screaming was heard at the corner of the woods through which those going to the next village had to pass. It was Josephine, pretty Josephine, and when her screams were heard, they ran to her assistance, and arrived only just in time to rescue her, half strangled, from Mademoiselle's clutches.

The idiot had watched her and had thrown himself upon her in order to treat her as the other young fellows did the girls, but she resisted him so stoutly that he took her by the throat and squeezed it with all his might until she could not breathe, and was nearly dead.

In rescuing Josephine from him, they had thrown him on the ground, but he jumped up again immediately, foaming at the mouth and slobbering, and exclaimed:

"I am not a girl any longer, I am a young man, I am a young man, I tell you."

THE MAN WITH THE DOGS

His wife, even when talking to him, always called him Monsieur Bistaud, but in all the country round, within a radius of ten leagues, in France and Belgium, he was known as *Cet homme aux chiens.** It was not a very valuable reputation, however, and "That man with the dogs," became a sort of pariah.

In Thierache they are not very fond of the custom-house officers, for everybody, high or low, profits by smuggling; thanks to which many articles, and especially coffee, gunpowder, and tobacco, are to be had cheap. It may here be stated that on that wooded, broken country, where the meadows are surrounded by brushwood, and the lanes are dark and narrow, smuggling is carried on chiefly by means of sporting dogs, who are broken in to become smuggling dogs. Scarcely an evening passes without some of them being seen.

---

*That man with the dogs.

loaded with contraband, trotting silently along, pushing their nose through a hole in a hedge, with furtive
and uneasy looks, and sniffing the air to scent the
custom-house officers and their dogs. These dogs also
are specially trained, and are very ferocious, and can
easily kill their unfortunate congeners, who become
the game instead of hunting for it.

Now, nobody was capable of imparting this unnatural education to them so well as the man with
the dogs, whose business consisted in breaking in
dogs for the custom-house authorities. Everybody
looked upon it as a dirty business, a business which
could only be performed by a man without any
proper feeling.

"He is a men's robber," the women said, "to
take honest dogs in to nurse, and to make a lot of
traitors out of them."

While the boys shouted insulting verses behind
his back, and the men and the women abused him,
no one ventured to do it to his face, for he was not
very patient, and was always accompanied by one of
his huge dogs, and that served to make him respected.

Certainly without that bodyguard, he would have
had a bad time of it, especially at the hands of the
smugglers, who had a deadly hatred for him. By
himself, and in spite of his quarrelsome looks, he did
not appear very formidable. He was short and thin,
his back was round, his legs were bandy, and his
arms were as long and as thin as spiders' legs, and
he could easily have been knocked down by a back-
handed blow or a kick. But then, he had those
confounded dogs, which intimidated even the bravest

smugglers. How could they risk even a blow when he had those huge brutes, with their fierce and bloodshot eyes, and their square heads, with jaws like a vise, and enormous white teeth, sharp as daggers, and with huge molars which crunched up beef-bones to a pulp? They were wonderfully broken in, were always by him, obeyed him by signs, and were taught not only to worry the smugglers' dogs, but also to fly at the throats of the smugglers themselves.

The consequence was that both he and his dogs were left alone, and people were satisfied with calling them names and sending them all to Coventry. No peasant ever set foot in his cottage, although Bistaud's wife kept a small shop and was a handsome woman, and the only persons who went there were the custom-house officers. The others took their revenge on them all by saying that the man with the dogs sold his wife to the custom-house officers, like he did his dogs.

"He keeps her for them, as well as his dogs," they said jeeringly. "You can see that he is a born cuckold with his yellow beard and eyebrows, which stick up like a pair of horns."

His hair was certainly red or rather yellow, his thick eyebrows were turned up in two points on his temples, and he used to twirl them mechanically as if they had been a pair of mustaches. And certainly, with hair like that, and with his long beard and shaggy eyebrows, with his sallow face, blinking eyes, and dull looks, with his dogged mouth, thin lips, and his miserable, deformed body, he was not a pleasing object.

But he assuredly was not a complaisant cuckold,
and those who said that of him had never seen him
at home. On the contrary, he was always jealous,
and kept as sharp a lookout on his wife as he did
on his dogs, and if he had broken her in at all, it
was to be as faithful to him as they were.

She was a handsome and, what they call in the
country, a fine body of a woman; tall, well-built,
with a full bust and broad hips, and she certainly
made more than one exciseman squint at her. But
it was no use for them to come and sniff round her
too closely, or else there would have been blows. At
least, that is what the custom-house officers said,
when anybody joked with them and said to them:
"That does not matter; no doubt, you and she have
hunted for your fleas together."

It was no use for them to defend Madame Bistaud's fierce virtue; nobody believed them, and the
only answer they got, was: "You are hiding your
game, and are ashamed of going to seduce a woman
who belongs to such a wretched creature."

And, certainly, nobody would have believed that
such a buxom woman, who must have liked to be
well attended to, could be satisfied with such a puny
husband, with such an ugly, weak, red-headed fellow,
who smelled of his dogs, and of the mustiness of
the carrion which he gave to his hounds.

But they did not know that the man with the
dogs had some years before given her, once for all,
a lesson in fidelity, and that for a mere trifle, a venial
sin! He had surprised her for allowing herself to be
kissed by some gallant, that was all! He had not
taken any notice, but when the man was gone,

he brought two of his hounds into the room, and said:

"If you do not want them to tear your inside out as they would a rabbit's, go down on your knees so that I may thrash you!"

She obeyed in terror, and the man with the dogs had beaten her with a whip until his arm dropped with fatigue. And she did not venture to scream, although she was bleeding under the blows of the thong, which tore her dress, and cut into the flesh; all she dared to do was to utter low, hoarse groans; for while beating her, he kept on saying:

"Don't make a noise, by——; don't make a noise, or I will let the dogs fly at you."

From that time she had been faithful to Bistaud, though she had naturally not told anyone the reason for it, or for her hatred either, not even Bistaud himself, who thought that she was subdued for all time, and always found her very submissive and respectful. But for six years she had nourished her hatred in her heart, feeding it on silent hopes and promises of revenge. And it was that flame of hope and that longing for revenge, which made her so coquettish with the custom-house officers, for she hoped to find a possible avenger among her inflammable admirers.

At last she came across the right man. He was a splendid sub-officer of the customs, built like a Hercules, with fists like a butcher's, and had long leased four of his ferocious dogs from her husband.

As soon as they had grown accustomed to their new master, and especially after they had tasted the flesh of the smugglers' dogs, they had, by degrees become detached from their former master, who had reared them. No doubt they still recognized him a little, and would not have sprung at his throat, as if he were a perfect stranger, but still, they did not hesitate between his voice and that of their new master, and they obeyed the latter only.

Although the woman had often noticed this, she had not hitherto been able to make much use of the circumstance. A custom-house officer, as a rule, only keeps one dog, and Bistaud always had half-a-dozen, at least, in training, without reckoning a personal guard which he kept for himself, which was the fiercest of all. Consequently, any duel between some lover assisted by only one dog, and the dog-breaker defended by his pack, was impossible.

But on that occasion, the chances were more equal. Just then he had only five dogs in the kennel, and two of them were quite young, though certainly old Bourreau* counted for several. After all they could risk a battle against him and the other three, with the two couples of the custom-house officer, and they must profit by the occasion.

So one fine evening, as the brigadier of the custom-house officers was alone in the shop with Bistaud's wife and was squeezing her waist, she said to him abruptly:

"Do you really want to have something to do with me, Môssieu† Fernand?"

He kissed her on the lips as he replied: "Do I really want to? I would give my stripes for it; so you see."

---

*Executioner, hangman.

†Vulgar for Monsieur.

"Very well!" she replied, "do as I tell you, and upon my word, as an honest woman, I will be your commodity to do what you like with."

And laying a stress on that word *commodity,* which in that part of the country means strumpet, she whispered hotly into his ear:

"A commodity who knows her business, I can tell you, for my beast of a husband has trained me up in such a way that I am now absolutely disgusted with him."

Fernand, who was much excited, promised her everything that she wished, and feverishly, malignantly she told him how shamefully her husband had treated her a short time before, how her fair skin had been cut, and of her hatred and thirst for revenge. The brigadier acquiesced, and that same evening came to the cottage accompanied by his four hounds, with their spiked collars on.

"What are you going to do with them?" the man with the dogs asked.

"I have come to see whether you did not rob me, when you leased them to me," the brigadier replied.

"What do you mean by 'robbed you?'"

"Well, robbed! I have been told that they could not tackle a dog like your Bourreau, and that many smugglers have dogs who are as good as he is."

"Impossible."

"Well, in case any of them should have one, I should like to see how the dogs that you sold me could tackle them."

The woman laughed an evil laugh, and her husband grew suspicious, when he saw that the brigadier replied to it by a wink. But his suspicions came too late. The breaker had no time to go to the kennel to let out his pack, for Bourreau had been seized by the custom-house officer's four dogs. At the same time, the woman locked the door; already her husband was lying motionless on the floor, while Bourreau could not go to his assistance, as he had enough to do to defend himself against the furious attack of the other dogs, who were almost tearing him to pieces, in spite of his strength and courage. Five minutes later two of the attacking hounds were totally disabled, with their bowels protruding, but Bourreau himself was dying, with his throat gaping.

Then the woman and the custom-house officer kissed each other before the breaker, whom they bound firmly. The two dogs of the custom-house officer that were still on their legs were panting for breath, and the other three were wallowing in their blood. And now the amorous couple were carrying on all sorts of capers, still further excited by the rage of the dog-breaker, who was forced to look at them, and who shouted in his despair:

"You wretches! you shall pay for this!" And the woman's only reply was, to say: "Cuckold! cuckold! cuckold!"

When she was tired of larking, her hatred was not yet satisfied, and she said to the brigadier:

"Fernand, go to the kennels and shoot the five other brutes, otherwise he will make them kill me to-morrow. Off you go, old fellow!"

The brigadier obeyed, and immediately five shots were heard in the darkness; it did not take long, but that short time had been enough for the man

with the dogs to show what he could do. While
he was tied, the two dogs of the custom-house officer had gradually recognized him, and came and
fondled him, and as soon as he was alone with his
wife, as she was insulting him, he said in his usual
voice of command to the dogs:

"At her, Flanbard! at her, Garou!" The two
dogs sprang at the wretched woman, and one seized
her by the throat, while the other caught her by the
side.

When the brigadier came back, she was dying on
the ground in a pool of blood, and the man with
the dogs said with a laugh: "There you see, that
is the way I break in my dogs!"

The custom-house officer rushed out in horror,
followed by his hounds, who licked his hands as
they ran, and made them quite red.

The next morning the man with the dogs was
found still bound, but chuckling, in his hovel that
was turned into a slaughter-house.

They were both arrested and tried; the man with
the dogs was acquitted, and the brigadier sentenced to a term of imprisonment. The matter gave
much food for talk in the district, and is indeed still
talked about, for the man with the dogs returned there,
and is more celebrated than ever under his nickname.
But his celebrity is not of a bad kind, for he is now
just as much respected and liked as he was despised
and hated formerly. He is still, as a matter of fact,
the man with the dogs, as he is rightly called, for
he has not his equal as a dog-breaker, for leagues
round. But now he no longer breaks in mastiffs, as
he has given up teaching honest dogs to "act the

part of Judas," as he says, for those dirty custom-house officers. He only devotes himself to dogs to be used for smuggling, and he is worth listening to, when he says:

"You may depend upon it, that I know how to punish such commodities as she, when they have sinned! I was glad to see my dogs tearing that strumpet's skin and her lying mouth."

LaVergne, TN USA
29 May 2010
184435LV00002B/94/A